THE ALCHEMIST OF RIDDLE AND RUIN

AN ACCIDENTAL ALCHEMIST MYSTERY

BOOK SIX

◈

GIGI PANDIAN

GARGOYLE GIRL PRODUCTIONS

The Alchemist of Riddle and Ruin: An Accidental Alchemist Mystery © 2022 by Gigi Pandian.

Gargoyle Girl Productions

All rights reserved. No part of this book may be used or reproduced in any manner whatsoever, including Internet usage, without permission from Gargoyle Girl Productions, except for brief quotations in articles and reviews.

First edition

Cover design by Gargoyle Girl Productions

Cover gargoyle illustration by Hugh D'Andrade/Jennifer Vaughn Artist Agent

Poems *Hansel* and *An Almanac of Flowers* by Sue Parman. Used with permission of the author.

This is a work of fiction. Names, characters, places, and incidents are either the product of the author's imagination or are used fictitiously, and any resemblance to actual persons, living or dead, business establishments, events, or locales is entirely coincidental.

Print ISBN: 978-1-938213-20-5

eBook ISBN: 978-1-938213-19-9

ACKNOWLEDGMENTS

There are always so many people to thank when thinking back on how a book came to be. I'm so fortunate to have a wonderful circle of author friends and a fantastic publishing team. Thank you to Diane Vallere, Ellen Byron, and Lisa Mathews for your weekly inspiration. Thank you to Nancy Adams, Amy Glaser, and Carmen King for your editorial feedback and eagle eyes. Thank you to Amanda Crooke of Locust Light Farm for your herbalist tips. Thank you to Mia P. Manansala and Sujata Massey for your springtime walks that helped me figure out the heart of this story. Thank you to Julie and Eric for making sure I got Dorian's French right. Thank you to my mom for contributing her wonderful poetry to this book! Thank you to James… for *everything*. And last, but far from least, thank you to my readers! You're the reason this series is going strong. I love hearing from you. You can connect via my website www.gigipandian.com.

CHAPTER 1

I was already uneasy before the door opened and my real troubles began.

The wind swept my white hair around my face as a woman in a cheerful yellow dress held open the door of Blue Sky Teas for her sullen teenage daughter. The gust carried in a faint scent of pinecones and charred wood.

The summer solstice would be here within a week, which the temperature reflected, but I'd woken up at dawn this morning to the howls of a fierce wind wreaking havoc on my backyard garden. It looked as if a giant from a fairy tale had trampled the summer squash, strangled the Persian Cucumber vines, and kicked the Blue Jay Blueberry bushes to see how far the unripe berries would scatter. Still, my anguish wasn't from the damage. It was because of how much I cherished my garden sanctuary, Portland, and the people I'd come to love here. Yet with every passing season, it grew closer to the time I knew I'd have to leave.

The harsh breeze from the open door followed the pair inside and disturbed the leaves of the weeping fig tree rooted in the center of the café. The owner, Blue, had saved the tree when she opened the café. I couldn't imagine Blue Sky Teas without its living tree centerpiece. I hoped the wind wouldn't last long. All varieties of Ficus detest being disturbed.

I tucked the largest offending lock of hair behind my ear as Heather set a pot of tea on our tree ring table nestled next to one of the front windows. The two braids of her blond hair were pinned into a loose bun. I'd become friends with her teenage son Brixton a year and a half ago when he'd broken into my house on a dare and worked off the expense of the broken window by tending to my garden.

"Blue says to let this steep for three more minutes before pouring." Heather grinned at me. "It's an herbal blend that's supposed to cheer you up."

"I'm sure it will." I grinned back at her. She'd sensed my growing melancholy as the season shifted from spring to summer.

"Should we set a timer? You know I'm *the worst* at keeping time. Did I tell you I painted until after midnight last night? I thought it was nine o'clock at the latest."

I didn't see whether Heather set a timer on her phone or not. Something else had drawn my attention away from our cozy table.

The sulky teenage girl didn't get in line with the older woman. I no longer thought the woman in the yellow dress was her mother. Not because of a lack of resemblance, which wouldn't have told me anything about their relationship regardless, but because there was no familiarity. Not even a sign of recognition. They'd parted ways as soon as they stepped through the door. The older woman had simply extended a small kindness by holding open the door for a stranger.

I didn't worry about a teenager being at the café unaccompanied. I'd left home at sixteen, along with my fourteen-year-old brother. No, that wasn't my worry or what had drawn my curiosity. There was something *off* about the girl. What I'd initially observed as sullenness wasn't exactly that. She wasn't simply a petulant teenager.

She was *afraid*.

And her movements... As she'd walked through the door, she'd swept in gracefully, almost floating, like the steps of a dancer. But as soon as she crossed the threshold, her gait transformed. Her steps became halting. It wasn't that she'd tripped. Nothing hindered her path. It was almost like I was watching a movie that had thrown a glitch.

Dressed in leggings and an oversize flannel shirt I remembered so many young people wearing a couple of decades ago when grunge was at its peak, she took another two halting steps before stopping in front of the weeping fig tree. Its branches stretched up to the faux sky ceiling. Now that she was closer to me, I realized where the scent of charred pine had come from. Rosemary. A sprig of flowering rosemary was tucked into the pocket of the flannel shirt. Long bangs of light brown hair covered much of her face, so I still couldn't see her clearly. But as she tilted her head upward toward the top of the tree, her bangs parted, revealing more of her face. Her lips didn't smile, but her eyes did. That's when I saw it.

Her eyes were gold.

Not a natural hazel that sparkled with flecks of gold, like the distinctive eyes of my dear friend Tobias. But truly gold.

"Earth to Zoe?" Heather's voice startled me. "I think you didn't get a good night's sleep last night either. Let me guess. Is Max back?"

I turned my attention to Heather as she lifted the teapot over our mismatched handcrafted ceramic mugs.

"Max *isn't* back." I missed him terribly, even though he was only a couple of hours' drive away from Portland in Astoria, gathering a few more items for the opening of his shop, The Alchemy of Tea. I planned to see him later that day. The thought excited me, but also filled me with a sense of trepidation. It frightened me to think about how much I'd come to love Max, as well as so many dear friends here —when I knew, deep down, that no matter what choices I made, I could never stay and grow old here.

"Then you have no excuse," Heather giggled.

"I slept fine until I discovered this wind's destruction to my garden. That's not why I wasn't paying attention. I was distracted by the teenage girl who's standing in front of the tree." The café was bustling enough that I only had to lower my voice a little to be certain we wouldn't be overheard.

Heather turned her head. She froze. A pained expression washed over her face. The teapot slipped from her fingers. The pot clattered as it crashed into her mug, sending shards of earthenware across the table. Hot tea splashed over the side.

Several heads turned our way—including the girl's.

Only... it wasn't a natural motion. The other customers had reacted quickly, as soon as the crash sounded. One of them rushed forward with a handful of napkins as Blue stepped out from behind the counter with a larger towel and assured Heather it was nothing to worry about and she'd fix us another pot of tea.

As the scene unfolded, the girl who had unknowingly caused it stood still. Her entire body remained rigid, standing at that awkward angle—except for her head, which turned in excruciatingly slow motion to look at us. Her gaze only reached us when Blue did.

"Riddle?" Heather whispered.

The girl couldn't have heard her, but as soon as Heather spoke, the strange young woman swept gracefully toward the exit, following two men out the door. Three leaves from the weeping fig tree fluttered to the floor. One of them was so dry it looked like a brittle scrap of paper. I'd examine the tree's health later. For now, Heather needed my full attention.

"Are you all right?" I asked.

"I know her." Heather's voice shook.

"One of Brixton's school friends?" Blue wiped up the last of the spilled liquid and stood. Her mom jeans were wet at the knees with cinnamon ginger tea, but she wore a smile on her face as usual. "I didn't recognize her. Don't think she's been in here before. *Damn.* You think she couldn't afford to buy anything? I should go after her—"

"You won't find her." Heather's eyes were wide. *Frightened.* More frightened than the look I'd seen on the girl's face.

"What's going on?" I asked. I was missing something. Something big.

Heather gripped a shard of her broken mug so tightly that a spot of blood appeared on her hand. She didn't seem to notice.

"Do you believe in ghosts?" she whispered.

"You don't really think—?"

"There's no such thing as ghosts." Blue spoke the words forcefully enough to cut me off. Her voice was friendly, yet with the authority in each word, there was no question who was in charge. I imagined her in a courtroom in her previous life before she began anew here in Portland. Gray curls framed her friendly face, which still wore a smile.

Though I agreed with Blue, I knew why Heather had asked. The young woman's awkward movements had struck me like I was watching a film with a glitch in the recording. The other-worldly eyes. And something else I couldn't quite place...

"You're wrong." Heather's voice shook. "She's—"

"I'm putting an end to this." Blue was already at the door. "I'll find her. Back in a minute."

"Blue's right." I put my hand on Heather's to assure her. "That girl is the right age to be in high school with Brixton. You can't place her even though you're sure you know her, which is always a jarring feeling."

Heather yanked her hand away. "She's not one of Brix's friends. I know exactly who she is. I'm the one who went to high school with her. Ridley Price. She was my best friend—until she was murdered sixteen years ago."

CHAPTER 2

"Murder?" Dorian drummed his clawed fingertips together. The morning was shaping up to be *très intéressant*, indeed. As much as he did not wish to admit it to his friend and roommate Zoe, or even to himself, he had been feeling homesick of late. He welcomed distraction, however macabre it might be.

"Attempted murder," his young friend Brixton clarified. "A strange girl appeared in the middle of a road last night and ran someone off the road. The guy was hurt, but survived."

"*Bof.* This sounds more like an accident."

"But wait until you hear this," said Brixton. The boy paused for effect, looking from Dorian to his best friend Veronica and back again. "The girl vanished."

"Cowardly," said Dorian, disappointed, "yet not unusual."

"Don't you see?" The boy's eyes were wide and his voice agitated. "She didn't run away. She was just *gone*."

"Ah, so. You speak of a ghost?" Perhaps this was not so mundane after all.

"Ghosts," said Veronica, "don't exist." Her expression reflected her skepticism.

"One should have an open mind," Dorian pointed out. "Most people would not believe a gargoyle could exist." He wriggled his horns.

THE ALCHEMIST OF RIDDLE AND RUIN

"That's different," Veronica insisted. "You found alchemy. You're not a ghost. You're nothing supernatural. You're just extra-living."

"Extra-living," Dorian repeated the words. He did not dislike the sound of it.

Dorian Robert-Houdin was entertaining his two young friends in his attic. The 150-year-old gargoyle had been born in France—*carved* was the more accurate word for his birth—and had lived there all his life until he stowed away in Zoe Faust's crates being shipped to Portland a year and a half before. He spoke English with a thick French accent.

Brixton had known of Dorian's existence from the day the gargoyle arrived in Portland, but he had been sworn to secrecy and later became a staunch ally. When Brixton's friends had accidentally seen Dorian a year later, he had to keep their friendship a secret at first, lest Zoe accuse him of not being careful enough. One could only maintain a certain level of caution if one wished to live fully! Like Brixton, the boy's friends were trustworthy individuals. Dorian had been uncertain about Ethan at first, because of the boy's initial reaction. Yet just as Brixton had been won over by Dorian's charms, eventually so was Ethan.

Veronica Chen-Mendoza was the only one of the teenage friends who had not been distressed when she first gazed upon Dorian's true form. They had already spoken to each other on the telephone many times, when Dorian had enlisted her assistance with his investigations. She had initially believed him to be a deformed man who did not wish to be seen, and it pained her to think he did not trust her to not judge him by his appearance. When she saw with her own eyes that he was actually a gargoyle, she was no longer offended. Even she could imagine the leap of faith required to trust someone with such a secret.

When their friendship was kept secret from Zoe, the teenagers could not visit Dorian at the house when Zoe was home and awake. This was no longer a problem, so Brixton and Veronica had stopped by after they had eaten breakfast—which was quite late, since they were on summer vacation. Children of this age, Dorian had learned, slept a generous number of hours when not required to rise early for schooling. Their friend Ethan was not with them, as his feuding parents had sent him to visit his grandparents that summer.

"Have you ever actually seen a ghost?" Veronica asked Brixton.

"There are a ton of ghosts all over the place. Not just in spooky old castles. Even here in Portland."

Veronica crossed her arms. "So you haven't."

"Well... not really. I'm sure Dorian has. Especially since he goes around at night. Right?"

Dorian adjusted his wings and wriggled his horns as he considered the question. His visage was modeled after one of the gargoyles that sits high atop the Cathedral of Notre Dame in Paris. An early prototype for *Le Penseur*, the famous grotesque with horns, wings, and a contemplative expression, Dorian appreciated the details his maker had imbued into the stone that was then given life through an ancient book of alchemy.

"I have seen things," Dorian admitted. "I am not certain they were ghosts, yet I remain open-minded. There are more things in this world than I understand. Why are you concerned about this supposed ghost?"

"The girl in the road was identified as Ridley Price." Brixton paused, as if waiting to see if the others recognized the name. "Ridley Price was murdered before we were born. But this week, she came back."

"Is it, perchance, the anniversary of her death?" Dorian asked. He knew a thing or two about hauntings. He did not require sleep, so he had read many books from the library. Hauntings, when they did occur, took place for a reason.

Veronica groaned. "Don't humor him."

Dorian blinked at her. "I do not believe in humoring people. You should realize this, young Veronica. I treat you and your friends with the utmost respect. Far more than many of the adults in your life."

This was true. Zoe herself had forgotten that fifteen-year-olds were once considered adults, even when she and her brother had indeed been on their own since Zoe was sixteen and Thomas fourteen. Yet that was a long time ago.

Dorian Robert-Houdin had never been a proper child. He had been brought to life in 1860, looking as he did now, at three-and-a-half feet tall. He spoke Latin upon his awakening, because of his connection to the alchemical book that had given him life. The first language he learned was French, followed by English—and of course the most important language of all: food. Cooking gourmet food was his passion. No, his *calling*. Though each of these aspects of him was now firmly entrenched, he still remembered the feeling of newness that came with each. The sense of wonder that filled one's soul as one learned new things as a pupil.

"Fine," Veronica said. "Tell us about the ghost girl, Brix."

Brixton looked up from his phone. "Unless it's some weird numerology thing, this isn't an anniversary for her. She was killed at the end of the summer, sixteen years ago. So like sixteen years plus a little more than two months ago. Oh, and I didn't notice this before…"

Veronica's long black hair fell over the boy's slim shoulder as she leaned closer to look at his phone screen.

Instead of looking at whatever the boy had found that was so fascinating, Dorian waited for them to explain. His eyesight was excellent. More so than that of the children. His disdain for modern phones was because their screens were not responsive to the touch of his clawed fingers. He was unable to use modern mobile phones. Even those with physical keys were too small for him to use properly. His device of choice was a typewriter, yet for modern communication he also used a rotary phone that plugged into the wall, and he had learned to type suitably well on Zoe's laptop.

"How terrible." Veronica shuddered. "Her body wasn't found until five years after she was killed, when her bones were found in the woods. She was alone all that time."

"You're the one who said she isn't a ghost," Brixton said. "So what does it matter if she was dumped in the woods?"

"You're such a toad."

"You are both," said Dorian, "failing to get to the point. Why are you so interested in this poor girl in the first place? I sense that it is not simply that you have taken up ghost hunting as a hobby."

"You're right," said Brixton. "There's a reason I'm telling you both about Ghost Girl. An important reason why I need your help."

CHAPTER 3

"Do you believe in ghosts?" Heather repeated the question provocatively, her chin raised in defiance, as if daring me to say *no*.

Blue hadn't found the girl when she ran after her, but she chalked that up to not being quick enough to follow her. Convinced that Heather had suffered a shock, Blue had ushered the two of us into the tiny office in the back of the café and brought us more tea. In paper cups this time, with no teapot in sight. She'd also opened her first aid kit and found a bandage for Heather's bleeding hand. Blue was now back at the register, leaving me and Heather alone in the little room.

"That girl we saw wasn't a ghost," I said. "She can't have been your high school friend."

"You think I don't know my old friend?"

"Hair covered most of the face of the person we saw just now. Your imagination did the rest."

"It was *her*, Zoe."

"I'm so sorry about what happened to your friend." I paused, remembering something. "Why did you say the word *riddle* when you saw her?"

"Ridley Price," Heather said. "She went by the nickname Riddle. Because she loved puzzles."

Heather thrust her phone into my hands. A photo of the girl I'd seen minutes before filled the screen.

"It can't be her." My voice came out in a whisper. Because as I spoke the words, I didn't entirely believe them. The girl in the photograph had brown eyes, not gold, but otherwise *it was her*. She was even wearing the same flannel shirt.

This couldn't be real. It had to be a trick.

"I knew ghosts might exist," Heather said into her cup of tea, "but I've never seen one before." Her head snapped up and she met my gaze with wide eyes. "You saw her too. The girl in this photo. It wasn't my imagination."

"I did. But we saw a solid form. A real person. It's far more likely someone is playing a joke."

"A joke?"

"A cruel one. But people aren't always nice. Is it the anniversary of her death?"

Heather shook her head and took her phone back. "She was killed at the end of the summer, sixteen years ago. Not the beginning. And what kind of anniversary is sixteen years, anyway?"

"Tell me about her—and what happened."

A sad smile formed on Heather's lips. "She'd just finished her junior year of high school. I was a year behind her at school, but that didn't matter. We bonded over our love of nature, especially flowers. I loved picking flowers, even back then, and she could always tell me what the flowers meant—like how my favorite daisies symbolized innocence. I remember one of our first conversations at school. She came up to me because she saw I'd woven daisies into my hair. That was only two years before she..." Heather shook off the memory. "She was one of those girls everyone liked. She was popular, but not in a mean girl way. She was kind to everyone. She was about to turn seventeen. She didn't make it to her birthday."

Sixteen. That's how old I was when my brother and I fled Salem Village to avoid my getting swept up in the witch trials for a talent similar to Ridley's: being much better at bringing plants to life and helping them thrive than those around me. They thought I was a witch.

"I was so jealous she got to spend the summer at a farm in eastern Oregon," Heather continued. "She had a job, a paid internship to learn about permaculture. It's not like we were at a fancy private high school where kids did things like that. We didn't have counselors or parents setting things up for us. She found it and earned it herself. Because she loved the subject and wanted to learn."

"Enterprising."

"Not in an annoying, self-righteous way, you know? Like I said, everyone liked her. Not just those of us who were friends with her. When the school year was about to start, she came home and her parents threw her a welcome home party. The party was at her parents' house, just for close friends and family. That's where it happened. The murder."

"You were there at the party?"

Heather blinked at me, as if she'd forgotten I was there. "Ridley invited me, but I wasn't nearly as mature as she was. I was jealous. Angry about both her summer adventure and the fact that she'd pushed me and other friends away in the months leading up to the internship, when she was so focused on studying. I realized, later, that of course that's what a responsible person would do. She was studying hard, so she'd do a good job and have good experience to talk about in her college applications. And she hadn't broken off all contact with us. She'd simply changed her focus, you know? No longer staying out until midnight talking about boys under the stars. I was so selfish to make it about me... and then she was dead."

"Who—"

"They don't know! That's the worst part. No, not the worst part. The worst was that they didn't find her body for a few years. Knowing she was dead but with that small lingering doubt... But now, *still* not knowing who did it is so frustrating, you know? Knowing someone killed her at that welcome home party, but not *who.*"

Something was bothering me about Heather's story. "How do they know she was killed by someone at the house if they didn't find her body? How did they even know she died that day?"

Heather paled visibly. "They found her blood at the house, and no one saw her again. Everyone looked. God, how they looked. The story was everywhere. I couldn't get away from it. From my failure."

"It wasn't your fault, Heather."

"You don't know that," she snapped. Heather was not a person who snapped at people. "You weren't the one who was supposed to be there for your friend. I was. The search parties... God, why do they call them that? A *party*." She wrinkled her nose. "It's like the opposite of a party. The real party was in their backyard. They were gathered in the back garden for her welcome home party. Only Ridley never came downstairs to join them."

It struck me again that something about Heather's story was off. It was a memory from sixteen years ago. Half a lifetime ago for her.

As Heather continued speaking, her wistful expression told me she was once again barely aware of my presence. "Ridley had always gone by the nickname Riddle, because she'd loved riddles and games her whole life. That summer was no different. She told us she had a riddle for us that day. A riddle for us to solve. A personal one."

"A personal one.... Something that would expose a misdeed of one of the people there?"

"Misdeed," Heather repeated. She broke into a smile for the first time since seeing the supposed ghost of her friend and clasped my hands in hers. "I love that sometimes you talk like you're from another century. That's one of the reasons I think you're an old soul, even though you're younger than me. Riddle talked like that too. When she slipped me and her other friends notes in the high school hallways, they were never about normal stuff. She wrote notes that were folded in intricate patterns and had riddles like, *What building has the most stories?*"

I smiled. "A library."

Heather smiled back. "You would have *loved* her." The smile disappeared. "But then she went too far. *Not only a grand riddle. The grandest game of them all.* That's what she said was going to happen at the party. And then the invitation itself... it was a riddle she said we wouldn't be able to guess. The invitation said she'd reveal the solution at the party."

"You think she was going to expose someone's secret?"

Heather nodded. "I mean, we didn't think so at the time. At least I didn't. That was the theory the police came up with after interviewing everyone. Especially after her diaries went missing. That she'd found out something about one of them and they killed her for it."

"She made the mistake of making it into a game." I shook my head. At sixteen, she hadn't been jaded enough to know how badly such a ploy could turn out. "They never figured out who did it?"

She shook her head. "There was talk that someone on the police force mishandled evidence, losing some important clues. All they know is that it was one of the people at the party. There were seven of them who showed up. It would have been eight if I'd gone. Her mom, dad, and older brother. Her childhood best friend, her boyfriend, and another boy she was good friends with, and... who am I forgetting?" She scrolled on her phone for a few seconds. "That new girl she'd befriended. I'd forgotten about Joona. A quiet girl who'd just moved here from Korea. God, I wonder what happened to her. To all of them."

"You're not in touch with them?"

"We weren't a group of friends, like in movies. Ridley was the sun we all orbited. And it's not the kind of thing you want to relive, you know? I don't know about them, but I ran away from it. It's just so... strange. Seeing her ghost. After all this time. Why *now?*"

"We didn't see her ghost," I insisted. I've seen a lot of things in the more than 300 years I've been alive. Seeing a ghost isn't one of them. I can't be certain they don't exist. But I hadn't seen evidence that day.

There was another explanation for seeing someone the same age they were sixteen years before. The same reason I've looked twenty-eight years old for more than 300 years.

The Elixir of Life. *Alchemy.*

CHAPTER 4

I hadn't seriously considered that Ridley Price might be an alchemist who'd faked her death, because the Elixir of Life isn't something easy to discover. It takes years of study and practice. At twenty-eight, I was young to have found it. I'd accelerated my studies when my brother Thomas fell ill from the plague, in hopes I could find a cure for him. Instead, I accidentally discovered the Elixir for myself. It had taken me centuries to embrace it.

I still look twenty-eight, but my naturally brown hair turned white long ago. Being an alchemist has enabled me to experience many wondrous things in the world, but it's not all positive. Since alchemists who've discovered the Elixir of Life don't age, while those around us do, it can be a lonely life without long-lasting connections. Still, many people have sought it. Only a few have succeeded.

Could Ridley Price have discovered the Elixir of Life at sixteen?

I could imagine it, but I couldn't *believe* it.

Alchemy isn't magic. It's transformation. *Transmutation*, if you want to get technical about the term for transforming elements. Alchemy is a metamorphosis of impure elements into a purer form. Lead into gold. A mortal body into an immortal one. And spiritual alchemy, the inner work to transform ourselves and make us whole.

Each requires rigorous study, the right elements, and the practitioner's intent.

It took years, if not decades, for an alchemist to create their own Elixir of Life. Nicolas and Perenelle Flamel were decades older than I was when they discovered the Elixir. I'd never asked how old they were at the time, and it was entirely possible they no longer remembered. My friend Tobias Freeman had found it at fifty, many years after he'd witnessed me preparing herbal remedies with alchemical intent.

In past centuries, alchemical texts and teachings were hidden away, accessible only to those deemed worthy. Nicolas and Perenelle had both worked to expand access to alchemical teachings: Nicholas by taking in a woman as a pupil (me), which was unheard of at the time, and Perenelle by adding alchemical teachings to her artwork, hoping it would be more widely viewed than books hidden away under lock and key. I could hardly believe I was lucky enough to have them both back in my life after so many years.

"Zoe?" Heather touched my shoulder. "You really look like you've seen a ghost. I told you she—"

"She wasn't a ghost," I insisted.

"You're spooked."

"Not because I think she's a ghost."

"Then what?" Heather raised both of her eyebrows expectantly. With her innocent, open gaze, I doubted she was capable of raising a single eyebrow or forming any other skeptical expression.

I couldn't very well tell her what I really thought. If Heather were to learn I was an alchemist, all of Oregon would know by the next day. No, that wasn't fair. It would probably take two days. Heather meant well. She simply couldn't be trusted with a secret.

"You weren't done telling me about her disappearance," I said instead.

"Murder," Heather corrected. "Her murder."

"You were telling me about what happened at her welcome home party."

"Ridley was in her room getting ready. The rest of them were out back—but each of them had gone inside for *something*. To cook, to get the plates, to charge their phone, to use the bathroom—that kind of thing. Nobody could remember who was where at different times, because they didn't think it was important. They all knew each other, so they were just having a good time. Ridley wasn't someone who spent hours on her hair or makeup, but she loved riddles, so they all assumed she was putting the finishing touches on a game they'd play that day. But when they checked on her, when they wanted to sit down to eat, they got no response. That's when they knew something strange was going on. They didn't find her—they only found blood."

"That doesn't mean she was dead."

"No. But they tested it and it was her blood. And she was never seen alive again. Ever. Even though the police never charged anyone, we all thought her boyfriend did it. Nathaniel Gallo. They had one of those on-again off-again relationships, you know? They were off the day she died. She told him she wanted to focus on her studies. Right. We called him Nathaniel *Gallows* after that. For the gallows that are used to hang people? Joking that he'd be hung for killing her." She shuddered. "Kids can be horrid. I was one of them, Zoe. Oh, God! Do you think that's why she's haunting me? Because I was so cruel to the boy she loved?"

"She's not haunting you. She was in a crowded café, remember? She didn't even look in your direction until you spilled the tea."

Heather blinked at me, considering the question. "You think I'm okay? I'm not being haunted?"

"You're not being haunted. You said her boyfriend wasn't charged, but you all thought he did it?"

"Nathaniel's dad had been in jail before. Prison? Jail? For being a thief, I think. Which didn't help what people thought of him." She grimaced. "It was awful of us. Who *does* that?"

"You said her body was eventually found. How?"

"After a big storm, someone hiking in Forest Park found a skeleton peeking out of the earth. The remains were positively identified as hers. No question. She's dead, Zoe. She didn't escape that house."

A sense of unease crept over me as I thought back on what I'd seen of the girl who so resembled Ridley Price. Two elements of her visit hadn't fully registered with me at the time, but now clicked into place.

"Rosemary," I said. "Rosemary for *remembrance*. That's the symbolism of rosemary. The young woman we saw had flowering rosemary in her pocket."

"Those beautiful purple flowers," said Heather. "That was rosemary?"

"Not only that, but a woman held the door open for her when she came into Blue Sky Teas," I murmured.

"What does that have to do with the rosemary for remembrance?"

"It doesn't." My heart sped up. I wasn't imagining the girl's odd behavior. "Did you see her *touch* anything?"

Alchemists can open doors for themselves. We're human. We aren't even immortal. We stop aging, but we can die just like anyone else. And we can touch and move physical objects. *Unlike a ghost.*

Heather gasped. "You're right. She avoided touching the tree. She was careful to stay clear of the line of people. And two guys held the door open for her when she left."

"It was like—" I broke off, unable to finish my sentence. Her haunting movements. That overwhelming scent of rosemary. And *those eyes.* It wasn't possible. And yet…

"Are you starting to believe me that we saw the ghost of Ridley Price?"

CHAPTER 5

"I need to tell you the whole story," Brixton said. "Then you'll understand why I need help. Hit the lights, V." He shoved his phone into his pocket as he crossed the attic floor and snatched the candle next to Dorian's typewriter.

Veronica simply scowled at the boy. "It's daytime." She pointed at the skylight cut into the sloped ceiling above, through which sunlight streamed and illuminated the attic.

The skylight was a new addition to the Craftsman house. When Zoe had purchased the crumbling Craftsman in desperate need of restoration, the roof above the attic was covered with a tarp to protect the house from a gaping hole caused by storm damage. After Dorian had hidden in Zoe's crates she shipped to Portland from Paris, when he had sought out her help to solve the mystery of why he was turning to stone, he had used the hole in the roof to sneak out under the cover of darkness. He still lived in secrecy from most of the world, yet now he had a proper door to leave the house late at night: the skylight.

"Just turn out the lights," Brixton said. "Um, please? And, um, anyone have a match?"

Veronica acquiesced, flipping the light switch and dimming the bright room perhaps ten percent, and Dorian lit the candle with the long matchsticks from a drawer in his desk. Had it been the witching hour, a candle and moonlight would have created ghostly shadows in the attic. But now? The boy was making a valiant effort to set the scene for his ghost story, yet the sun was working against him.

"Go on," Dorian encouraged.

"The first sighting of Ridley Price's ghost was a few days ago." Brixton sat cross-legged on the floor and held the candle in front of his face. "Ghost Girl appeared in the flower garden in her parents' backyard. The garden *she herself* had planted. When her mom came outside to see how an intruder had gotten into the backyard, she dropped the cup she was carrying. When she looked up, her daughter's ghost had vanished."

Dorian sighed. "A grieving parent. She would, of course, tell others. They would then imagine they had seen her as well."

Brixton shook his head. "Her mom didn't come forward and tell anyone besides her son—her husband died a few years ago—and her son thought the same thing you did. But then, an old friend of Ghost Girl's saw her in a reflection of her kitchen window when she was cooking dinner. Her friends were with her. I don't know if they saw Ridley, but they saw their friend scream. Again, this person didn't say anything publicly at first—not until what happened last night. Which is why we're gathered here today."

"Get on with it already." Veronica kicked his shoe.

Brixton ignored this. "Last night, her old boyfriend drove off the road —to avoid her ghost that appeared in the road." He paused for effect.

Dorian enjoyed the theatrics. His own father had been a stage performer, so he appreciated such flourishes. *Bon!* This was exactly what he needed to allay his feeling of homesickness. Storytelling in the grand sense, as if he were attending a theatrical performance.

As his young friend with a flair for the theatrical continued his story, Dorian smiled at the memory of watching his father, Jean Eugène Robert-Houdin, perform grand illusions as the gargoyle watched from the rafters.

"The guy ended up in the hospital," Brixton continued after a beat. "When he was questioned about the accident, he said he wasn't drunk— they tested him and he wasn't—but he swore he'd seen the ghost of his teenage girlfriend. He was totally freaked out and called a bunch of people. That's when they put the pieces together and learned that others had seen her too. They hadn't imagined Ridley. *They'd all seen her.* My

THE ALCHEMIST OF RIDDLE AND RUIN

question for you is, what does she do next? Did she get a taste for violence, or was the car crash only an accident?"

"The newspapers reported this?" Dorian asked. "I know this country is still somewhat new to me..."

"Not big newspapers," Brixton said. "One of the people who saw her posted it on social earlier this week, and then ghost hunter websites picked up the story. Their reporters interviewed those people. That's where I read this stuff. So what do you think? Is she going to do more damage?"

Dorian sighed. "Ghost hunter reporters? *Alors*, this is fiction after all. *Merci* for the entertaining ghost story. Now, would either of you wish to play a game of chess? And do not forget the platter of snacks."

Dorian never entertained guests without a range of homemade food. What kind of host would he be without that? As it was the start of summer, he used a harvest of apricots for many things, including the muffins he baked for the children. He also included cucumber olive bites (he did not believe Brixton ate enough vegetables).

Brixton scowled at them as both Dorian and Veronica helped themselves to food. "You guys aren't taking this seriously."

"Since when do you care about ghosts, Brix?" Veronica asked. "I mean, beyond telling a good ghost story. You already did that. I don't see how we can help. But we can eat Dorian's feast."

"But she—" Brixton did not complete his own sentence.

Dorian set his plate on the side table. The boy was clearly upset about something. Veronica saw it as well. She placed a hand on his forearm.

"What's going on?" she asked softly.

"Ridley isn't just a random ghost," Brixton mumbled. "She's the ghost of the girl my mom was best friends with when she was my age. If Ghost Girl is getting revenge by coming after people she knew who let her die, my mom is high on that list."

CHAPTER 6

"A mystery is afoot." Dorian looked up from a scattered mess of tea leaves and rested his gray elbows on the worktable in my basement alchemy lab. He'd left me a note on the fridge, letting me know where he'd be.

After my thwarted breakfast with Heather, I'd walked her home before heading home myself. Heather's son Brixton wasn't there when we got to her house, and I knew her husband Abel was working out of town that summer, but she assured me she was fine on her own. Back in her own surroundings, she no longer looked as distressed from our ghost sighting. I left after she promised to call if she needed me. An accomplished artist, she was already sorting through charcoal pencils. I expected she'd work out her fears with her art.

"You're stuck perfecting this gift for Max?" I pointed at the misshapen ball of clay next to Dorian on the table. He'd come up with the thoughtful idea of creating an alchemical gift to give Max for the opening of The Alchemy of Tea next week. Dorian had already given Max one of his antique typewriters, which was a nice addition to the shop, and I'd crafted a homemade hand cream for Max to soothe his scratches from his work harvesting tea plants. Dorian's new idea was far bigger.

"I am using all of my intent, as well as the proper ingredients, yet the clay will not transform as I command it!"

Dorian had pointed out that small businesses had a hard time making it, especially at first, so he wished to give Max a gift that would help The Alchemy of Tea survive. He insisted that neither the quality of Max's alchemy-infused tea leaves nor the hand-selected tea-related products would be enough for a new small business to survive. An additional gimmick was necessary. Dorian was working on something to fill this void, but he hadn't yet told me exactly what it was.

"But this is not the mystery of which I speak." Dorian brushed the tea leaves aside, a sulfurous aroma rising as he did so. "I merely thought the meditative practice of alchemy would help me think."

"Do you need help? If you told me what you're—"

"Never mind my failures. You have distracted me. I was waiting for you to return home. I wished to tell you about our latest case we must solve."

I crossed my arms. "We're not detectives. As I've told you. Repeatedly."

"Yet working together, we have solved many mysteries—"

"Only because we had to—"

"To save ourselves. Yes, yes. I am aware of this fact." He waved a clawed hand dismissively.

My stomach gave an involuntary growl. Since Heather and I hadn't eaten after seeing the possible ghost, I was famished.

"Ah!" Dorian exclaimed. "Why did you not tell me you were famished? This is why you are behaving as a cranky alchemist. Let us depart from this dank and dusty alchemy laboratory and retire to my kitchen."

Dorian had been my roommate since the day I'd moved in. An unintentional one at first, but now I couldn't imagine living in this big drafty Craftsman house without my dear friend. He was the baker for Blue Sky Teas, where he baked before sunrise each morning. He always brought home the misshapen pastries, which tasted just as good, but he couldn't bear to have himself associated with food that was less than perfect on any scale. Dorian had been aching to get back to being a chef, which he'd been in France, though always behind the scenes and never letting anyone see him. Here in Portland, Blue Sky Teas was now known as much for its baked goods as its tea. Blue didn't mind in the least. Often called our Hawthorne neighborhood's mom, she was one of the most mellow people you'd ever meet. She hadn't always been that way, but after starting a new life in Portland, she took up the lease on a storefront nobody else wanted. In doing so, Blue saved both the indoor tree and herself.

Two minutes later, I was seated at my cozy kitchen table, eating the most delicious apricot muffin I'd ever tasted in my life. I told Dorian as much.

"I apologize for the fact that the muffin top resembles a cartoon monster with vampiric teeth," Dorian said as he swept invisible crumbs. "This was not my intent of the shape and placement of the chunks of fruit."

I tasted ginger along with the fresh chunks of apricots. Ginger is generally thought of as a warming spice for winter, but it was the perfect addition to these muffins. "The flavor combination is perfect. You've outdone yourself."

"*Merci.* It is the first crop of fresh summer apricots that has made it possible. I normally am not so humble, but in this case the apricots elevate it—*bof!* You have distracted me once more."

"What did you want to tell me?" I popped the rest of the muffin into my mouth.

"You were dismissive because you believe me to be a busybody. But no. This case I speak of *does* relate to us."

"It does?"

"Aha. I have your attention now? *Bon.* I have information that pertains to your friend Heather Taylor."

I stared at the gargoyle. "You saw the ghost of Ridley Price too?"

Dorian blinked at me. "You already know of this mystery?"

"Heather and I *saw her* at Blue Sky Teas this morning."

"She visited my café?"

I nodded. "It wasn't her… only it was." The girl had to be an alchemist, not a ghost. But those strange movements, her avoidance of touching anything, and the impossibility of someone so young being mature enough to discover the Elixir of Life. It didn't make sense.

Dorian's black eyes watched me intently. "You wonder the same thing as I do. If she is not a ghost, then a sixteen-year-old girl discovered the Elixir of Life. If she is an alchemist, she must be quite lonely. We must befriend her. Or, if she is a violent ghost, we will assist Brixton and Heather, and by doing so, contribute a great deal to science."

"She's not a violent ghost."

He shrugged his wings. "Then you and I are in a unique position to help her if she is indeed an alchemist. Eat another muffin. Afterward, you will tell me everything you know. And then, the great Dorian Robert-Houdin will concoct a plan to find the truth about Ridley Price!"

I ate another muffin. Not because Dorian had suggested it, but because the muffin called to me. I took a plate and my mug of green tea to the living room, where a portrait of me and my brother Thomas now hung above the hearth. Perenelle Flamel had painted it without my knowing she'd done so, not long before Thomas died. The painting had been lost to us for centuries, but it had recently been returned to me. My house felt even more like a home with Thomas's mischievous grin here with me.

A confusing mix of joy and despair overcame me. Sitting on my green velvet couch in front of the unlit hearth with my treasured brother looking down at me, my best friend smiling as I ate his delectable muffin, the loving couple who thought of me as daughter now living down the street, so many dear friends nearby, a thriving vegetable and herb garden in my backyard, and my beloved Max coming home to Portland next week.... I knew I could be happy growing old here. And yet, I knew that could never happen.

"This muffin," Dorian said cautiously. "It is not as good as the first? It is the last of this recipe, but there is more food—"

"The muffin is perfect."

"*Très bon.* Then you are ready to tell me more of the ghost—or alchemist—you have seen." Dorian hopped up onto the armchair on the other side of the hearth.

I kept my curtains drawn most of the time so that prying eyes wouldn't see that my roommate was a gargoyle. This way, Dorian could have the run of the house during the day, before he crept out at night under cover of darkness. In a city, there was never any time that was truly empty of people, but Dorian wore a hooded cape, so if he was ever spotted, the three-and-a-half-foot gargoyle would look like a child in a Halloween costume who was out later than the observer thought was a good idea. They'd tell their friends about what bad parents the child must have, not run screaming from a living gargoyle.

"I'm not going to tell you my impressions at first," I said. "Only exactly what I saw."

I told Dorian what Heather and I had seen, wondering yet again what exactly I had seen. As promised, I kept my description to my observations, not my impressions of them, until the end.

"Everything about it was so odd," I concluded. "Her movements, and how she didn't touch anything. She even waited for someone to let her out. If she wanted to run away from Heather, she could have left more quickly if she'd just opened the door."

"Aha. The ghost theory is even more credible." Dorian jumped off the chair and began pacing in front of the fireplace.

"Aren't ghosts supposed to be able to walk through walls?"

"*Oui.* Yet then, people would have known she was a ghost."

"The rest of her behavior did that well enough." I shivered. "You didn't tell me why you said she's dangerous."

"She caused a traffic accident. She has been visiting the people with her on the day she was murdered. Then, last night, she stepped in front of the car of her boyfriend, Nathaniel Gallo. He was gravely injured."

"The girl we saw this morning didn't have any injuries." Or did she? Was that why she was walking awkwardly? I relaxed. Her movements made sense now.

Before a smile could form on my lips, I realized the problem with that explanation. She'd walked gracefully when I first saw her.

"Oh no," I said. "Please don't tell me he drove right through her."

"I wish this were the case. It would prove beyond a reasonable doubt that she was indeed a ghost. Unfortunately, he swerved to avoid hitting her. He recognized her as his old girlfriend. She could be attempting to kill people she thinks betrayed her. Brixton is quite worried."

"Brixton?" I groaned. "You told Brixton?"

Dorian cleared his throat. "*Assumptions*, Zoe. The boy is the one who brought this story to me. He is quite concerned for the well-being of his mother. The ghost of his mother's friend has returned—and is harming people she once knew."

I wasn't worried that a ghost would haunt Heather. But a person with a grudge? That was a completely different—and far more dangerous—proposition.

CHAPTER 7

"Zoe and your mother have seen the ghost as well," Dorian informed Brixton. He was speaking on the land line phone in his attic.

His concise summary was met with the sound of shuffling and mild swearing.

"Ridley entered Blue Sky Teas this morning," Dorian continued. "She said nothing. She *touched* nothing. She could not even open the door for herself. She had to wait for others to do so for her."

"No way." It was Veronica, not Brixton, who spoke.

"I put you on speakerphone so V could hear," Brixton added. "See. I told you she was really a ghost. Why didn't my mom tell me?"

"Where are you now?" Dorian asked.

"Not at home, but she could have texted me." Brixton sounded hurt.

"It's not the kind of thing you tell someone by text," Veronica said. "I'm sure she'll tell you later."

"Can you return to my attic," Dorian asked, "so we can plan our investigation?"

"We'll be there in ten."

Dorian drummed his clawed fingers together after hanging up the receiver. He hoped they would arrive shortly. Zoe had left for the market to buy groceries. She walked, rather than taking her truck, yet she would not be gone too long. Zoe would not be worried that Brixton and Veronica were visiting with Dorian. It was the subject of their conversation that would disturb her, if she were to return home and join them. She never approved of involving the young people in investigating. But what else was he to do?

Fifteen minutes later, Veronica popped another chocolate blackberry bite into her mouth. Dorian did not think of it as bribery. Not at all. He was simply a good host to provide varied sustenance even though it was their second visit in as many hours.

"She's really a ghost," Brixton whispered. The boy had repeated the words many times since arriving. "I thought so, but I didn't *really* think so. She's really a ghost."

"You really need to try one of these, Brix," Veronica said.

"Where were you two when I telephoned?" Dorian passed the platter to Brixton.

"Researching Oregon ghost stories."

"I hope the library staff did not reprimand you for speaking with me. You swore a tremendous amount when I first informed you of the situation. I would hate for your library cards to be revoked." Zoe's library card had been voided for the crime of defacing library books. Dorian had wished her to fight the charges. Yes, he had written notes in each of the cookbooks Zoe had checked out from the library. But he was making the recipes *better!* Could the provincial people of Oregon not understand this?

"We weren't at the library." Veronica held up her phone.

Dorian sighed. The world had changed so much since his youth.

"If we tell Ethan he can go ghost hunting with us once he's back from staying with his grandparents," Brixton said, "I bet he'd buy us the ghost hunting equipment we need."

Veronica rolled her eyes. "He's our friend. Not just some guy we can ask to buy us stuff."

"He has a ton of money. It's not like he doesn't offer to buy things when we need stuff."

"Yeah, but that's different. You can't *ask* him to buy whatever you—"

Dorian held up a clawed hand. "We do not require ghost hunting equipment, *mes amies*. The ghost of Ridley Price is already visible to people. *Alors*, we do not need ghost hunting glasses." He paused and tapped the side of his gray head. "What we need is our little gray cells. We must use our intelligence to discover where she will go next."

"Back to the first guy she tried to kill?" Brixton suggested

"You don't know she was trying to kill him," Veronica said. She was correct, of course. They did not yet have enough evidence.

"He ended up in the hospital," Brixton growled. "I don't want that to happen to my mom."

"It's not like she grabbed his steering wheel. She's probably confused. If she can't touch things and she can't talk, she's just trying to communicate with people she used to know… God, that's terrible. She must be so frustrated!"

"Frustrated enough to try to kill that guy."

"Nathaniel Gallo," Dorian interjected. "I wonder if he is still being held at the hospital. If so, he would be a captive audience. You could pepper him with our questions."

The teenagers looked at each other.

"Um, Dorian," said Brixton. "We're fifteen. How are we going to get through the doctors and nurses, and then get that guy to talk to us?"

"When I was born, fifteen was considered an adult." It was not exactly accurate, yet far more true than it was in the twenty-first century.

"Yeah, but it's not like that today," Veronica said. "We can't tell the hospital staff we're detectives. It's not like I'm Nancy Drew."

Dorian pursed his gray lips. "The annoying girl who strings along her poor beau Ned and is a bad influence on her curiously named friend George?"

Veronica narrowed her eyes. "Nancy is *not* annoying."

"Yet she—"

"Don't." Brixton held up a hand. "You're not going to win this argument."

Dorian did not win arguments for the sake of emerging victorious. Yet when he was certain he was in the right, why would he not say so? "Veronica," he began in what he deemed a less confrontational voice, "you are far, far more sensible than—"

"I'm *sensible*?" Veronica's cheeks turned a shade of scarlet that was quite alarming. "That's what you think of me? That I'm the sensible one?"

Dorian blinked at her. "This is accurate, no?"

Brixton's eyes were closed, and he was shaking his head.

Dorian was suddenly aware that teenagers could be very strange creatures, indeed.

"I am *not* sensible." Veronica grabbed her bag and stormed out of the attic.

"I am confused," Dorian stated as he and Brixton faced the empty doorway. "What has transpired?"

"She thinks sensible means boring."

Dorian turned toward the boy. "But this is untrue. Why did you not tell her so?"

Brixton shrugged. "That would be worse."

Dorian narrowed his eyes. Learning English was quite easy compared to learning to decipher the subtext of fifteen-year-olds. "How so?"

"Dunno. I just know it would be bad."

CHAPTER 8

"Have you ever seen a ghost?" I asked Nicolas and Perenelle Flamel from my seat at their kitchen table. I needed a walk to think clearly, and Dorian had requested groceries, so I stopped at the Flamels' new home on a walk to the market.

Many years ago, Nicolas was my mentor. He and Perenelle were only recently back in my life after I'd lost them for far too long. The two of them were the closest thing to nurturing parents I'd ever had. I was overjoyed to have them back—and almost as pleased that they were no longer living in my house. Though I loved them dearly, they were…a handful. The famous alchemists had moved into a house a couple of blocks away from me, which they bought with gold Nicolas had created through alchemy once he recovered from an earlier injury.

Nicolas and Perenelle were the ones who taught me that alchemy can mean many things, but at its core, it boils down to one thing: transforming the impure into the pure. Though alchemy's most well-known attributes are turning metals such as lead into gold and creating the Elixir of Life, it also encompasses plant alchemy, called *spagyrics*, which is what I excel at.

Hundreds of years ago, Nicolas Flamel was a scribe and book-seller—one who stumbled across a book that taught him alchemy.

Perenelle took the hapless alchemist as her second husband, and together they became two of the most powerful alchemists in all of Europe. They both excelled at transmuting metals, which enabled them to donate large sums of gold to charities in France. Only when people became suspicious did they pretend to age and die. In truth, they faked their deaths. They went all out, even digging graves and having tombstones erected. When their graves were exhumed many years later, once sightings of Nicolas were too numerous to ignore, their coffins were found to be empty.

"There's no such thing as ghosts," Perenelle said. "You're not drinking your smoothie." Her thick old-French accent had softened slightly since she and Nicolas had arrived in Portland, but the charming accent still helped make the woman who was the utterly unique Perenelle Flamel.

I pushed aside the sickly green mass with chunky, dark-colored flecks of something that definitely shouldn't have been in there. "I'm not thirsty." Perenelle was a brilliant alchemist and master artisan, but she couldn't cook. Or, apparently, mix a drink.

"Is it not good?" she asked. "The recipe book that came with the blender recommended these ingredients."

"I believe," said Nicolas, "we were supposed to remove the skin and stone of the avocado. Not simply add the entire fruit into this machine."

"There's avocado skin and pit inside here?" I grimaced as I held up the glass. That explained it.

"Why didn't the directions *say* so?" Perenelle plucked the glass from my hands and dumped the contents down the drain. "I don't know why I let Nicolas talk me into purchasing this blender. It's far more dangerous than anything in our alchemy laboratories. Do you see how quickly these blades spin? It isn't safe. I need to retain all of my fingers for both alchemy and artwork."

"You don't stick your hand *inside*, my dear." Nicolas moved the blender carafe away from her delicate hands.

The Flamels had been in captivity so long that they'd only caught glimpses of modern technology. Nicolas was the one to adapt more quickly. He was eager to try new things. Which, it appeared, meant absolutely *everything*. They had arrived in Portland with only the clothes on their backs, but now their new home was filled with nearly as many objects as my own.

Which is saying a lot, since I run an online antiques store, Elixir, and keep the wares in my attic. I've always been terrible at turning lead into gold. Plant alchemy is my calling and what I truly excel at. While it keeps me well fed with delicious healthy food I mostly grow myself in my backyard kitchen garden, it doesn't pay the vast array of bills that exist in the modern world.

Take, for example, their small living room, which was visible from the kitchen in the open floor plan home. Two video game consoles (one with classic games and one with the more modern games), one recliner that vibrated, another chair that looked like a throne for a king, a precariously high stack of board games, three bookshelves filled with books on assorted subjects from their frequent trips to Powell's Books, a bicycle and scooter resting next to the front door, and enough artfully curated potted plants that it looked like a college student's apartment.

"So neither of you has ever seen a ghost before?" I asked again.

They exchanged a look.

"What?" I asked.

"You're thinking of Jacques?" Nicolas asked his wife.

"Of course."

"Who's Jacques?" I looked from Nicolas to Perenelle and back again.

"I still think that was simply a trick of the light. Or perhaps a trick with glass—Zoe, have you heard of Pepper's Ghost? I was reading a book on stage magic I found at the bookstore. This store does not charge nearly enough for the wealth of information in the pages of their books!"

"Yes, dear." Perenelle patted his arm. "Back to Jacques." She turned to me. "He was a farmer we knew in France. He died after a long illness, but people swore they still saw him walking in the hills. Only ever his shadow, though. We dismissed the rumors. Until we saw him outside our cottage. But as Nicolas said, it was through a window. Glass windows were quite new at the time, though. So I'm not sure how someone would have known to make a trick with them. It was either Jacques, or...."

"Or his ghost?" I asked.

Nicolas chuckled. "Or the wine! I was making my own mead, and as I recall, that night we imbibed a particularly strong brew. I expect we got caught up in our reminiscences. There is no such thing as ghosts, Zoe. Come now! I'll make you a proper beverage."

I smiled at Nicolas's enthusiasm. One thing that never fails to amuse me is that the image that history captured of Nicolas Flamel is completely wrong. One particular sketch, of a serious man with a long beard, has been referenced again and again. Yet it was a drawing made centuries after Nicolas had lived openly, sketched by a man who had never met him. The real Nicolas has wild hair, a curious expression, and is usually smiling—if he can sit still enough for anyone to see it.

"Why don't you pick out a board game while I make you a cup of tea?" Nicolas pointed at the precarious stack I'd noticed upon my arrival.

"I need to get to the market. Dorian has a few things on his list I can't harvest from the backyard."

If I hadn't been trying to hide in plain sight, I could have grown even more food in my backyard. Because of my "plant whispering," as Brixton calls it, I don't need as much space as most people to grow a wide array of crops. I can coax a few square feet of red winter wheat into a harvest of enough wheat to bake dozens of loaves of bread, or one tomato plant into producing hundreds of tomatoes across the entire summer season and beyond.

I was worried about Dorian. When he'd first arrived in Portland, in my shipping crates from France, he'd been terribly homesick. But we had a lot more to worry about then. Life-threatening concerns took precedence. There was no time for him to feel maudlin.

But now that we'd both settled into a life of normalcy, at least for a short time, here in Portland, it was easier to be thrown off balance by simple things. That was one reason I never liked visiting Massachusetts. The people I'd known as a child were long gone, and the landscape unrecognizable from what I'd known in the first years of my life, but so many of the regional plants were the same. No matter how much time passed, I'd recognize the sight and smell of them anywhere. Green friends I'd spent solitary time with as a young girl in the vast fields outside Salem Village, when people thought of me as a simpler. I knew how to commune with the natural world from a young age. It wasn't magic or witchcraft. It was simply a natural aptitude. One that's been stifled in so many people. Back then, it was suppressed out of fear. Now, it's the lack of forests and fields in urban areas that makes it difficult to play in nature.

I had my garden, alchemy lab, online business, Max, and many friends. Dorian had his cooking and a few friends, but I could tell he felt something was missing. I hoped he wouldn't do anything rash, but I expected I was fooling myself to think anything less. I was expecting a gift for him to arrive in the mail sometime this week. I hoped it would cheer him up.

Perenelle took my hand in hers. "You were always a serious, old soul, even when you were young. Take it from someone who's made all the mistakes of several lifetimes. You have many people who love you. Don't forget to enjoy that."

"I won't." I wasn't lying. My problem was the exact opposite. After pushing people away for so many years, I loved too fiercely here. It was Dorian I was worried about. With nothing to lose, what would he do?

CHAPTER 9

Dorian tapped at the keys of his one working typewriter. Additional typewriters were nestled in crates in one corner of his attic. The broken remains of delicate metal reminded him that the world had moved on. It seemed that every few meters, a shop existed to sell or repair a miniature computer. Yet few people existed who could fix his beautiful machines.

He typed another sentence on the Smith Corona, then reread the words embossed on the sheet of paper.

He had already typed a page filled with notes about Ghost Girl, but his little gray cells had failed him thus far. What did he wish to do next? He had no focus. It was not good practice to force one's mind to come up with answers when none presented themselves. Instead, he had turned to one of his many projects. He knew, like his literary twin Poirot (who spoke loquaciously about the little gray cells of his mind), Dorian would solve the case once the literally gray cells of his mind had rested.

"*Zut,*" he muttered to himself. The words he had written were dull. Lifeless! Where was the passion that had filled his soul when he began working on his masterpiece? He had been inspired to write a brilliant work of Gothic fiction after visiting the Witch's Castle, a mysterious pile of moss-covered stone ruins deep within Forest Park.

Dorian had not bothered to research the true history of the ruins. He feared the truth would ruin his literary creativity. He knew the structure had not originally been called the Witch's Castle. That was a name given by locals after the original building had burned to the ground. Such a mysterious name should certainly inspire a brilliant ghost story. At least this is what Dorian had felt at first. But now?

Shaking his head, he jumped off the chair, clasped his hands behind his back, and paced the floor. His Gothic novel was going nowhere. His gift for Max was a failure. And now, his attempts at solving the mystery that would help Brixton could go no further from a theoretical place of armchair detecting.

Sunlight shone through the skylight above, yet another reminder that Dorian was a prisoner in this house during daylight.

There was not much room to pace. The attic was not entirely his room. It was also the storage area for the antique wares Zoe sold through her online business, Elixir. It was a half-hearted endeavor, mainly so people would not become suspicious about how she generated her income. Though in truth, Zoe was also quite terrible at transmuting lead into gold. She did rely on selling a few expensive antiques each month to provide money to live on. In that, Zoe Faust was savvy. She had an eye for what might become valuable in the future. Zoe was modest, yet she admitted this skill came not from knowing objects, but people. She had great insight into both plants and people. This is how she had survived for more than 300 years without being exposed.

Dorian, too, was used to hiding. This was nothing new. In fact, since arriving in Portland and solving the mystery ailment that had been slowly turning him to stone, he had felt freer than he ever had in his over 150 years on earth. Before meeting Zoe, Dorian had survived by working across France as a personal chef and assistant to people who had lost their sight. Because Zoe and a few others knew he existed, he did not need to hide within the walls of this house. Zoe was even considerate enough to keep the curtains drawn in the rooms he frequented, so he could roam freely without fear of being seen from the outside. And once night had fallen, he donned a cape and both explored and baked pastries in the pre-dawn hours at Blue Sky Teas.

He had freedom, a small number of friendships, even a fulfilling job where he could put his culinary skills to good use.

And yet...

THE ALCHEMIST OF RIDDLE AND RUIN

He feared he was homesick.

This had been a minor issue when he first arrived, easily remedied by having free rein of the kitchen along with a subscription to *Le Monde* (he was an educated gargoyle, after all).

It had been triggered, he decided, when he and Zoe had traveled to Paris* (**The Lost Gargoyle of Paris*) after the tragic fire that had swept through the Cathedral of Notre Dame. They had been worried that alchemical forces might have attempted to destroy the majestic cathedral. Thankfully, this turned out not to be the case, but they had indeed caught a dastardly criminal while there.

Traversing the familiar historic streets of Paris had reminded him of all he'd given up to find the cure for his terrifying affliction that was causing him to turn to stone. He knew he had also gained much here in his new life in Portland. Why, then, did he feel restless?

Zut alors! This maudlin attitude would never do.

A rare wooden clock from the early 1800s caught his eyes. *Magnifique!* The hour was later than he thought. He could begin preparing lunch. This would undoubtedly cheer his mood.

When he cooked, his little gray cells would figure out what should be the next steps in discovering the truth behind Ghost Girl's strange actions. Were not many other great detectives confined to their homes, or even a hospital room in Tey's *Daughter of Time*? Dorian Robert-Houdin might be a prisoner during daylight hours, yet he would solve the mystery that would both help his young friend Brixton and rid him of his own disquieting thoughts.

Dorian scampered down the two flights of stairs and into his kitchen. Yes, the great Dorian Robert-Houdin would be the force behind unmasking Ghost Girl's secrets. As soon as he was done preparing lunch.

CHAPTER 10

Pushing aside my overblown worries of what Dorian might do, I walked over to the stack of games in the living room while Nicolas and Perenelle good-naturedly bantered about who would wash the dangerous carafe.

On top of the stack of games sat the tenth-anniversary edition of Crimson Fish, its cover askew.

"You've been playing Crimson Fish?" I asked.

"The concept is most ingenious." Nicolas's wild eyebrows came alive as he spoke enthusiastically.

"It's somewhat similar to the 'Clue' game beneath it," Perenelle added, "in that you're solving a mystery, yet it's filled with so much more color!" She left Nicolas to deal with washing up and fixing tea, and joined me in front of the impressive collection of games. She lifted the lid and unfolded the colorful board that represented the ocean. The gold of hidden caves sparkled, the bright blue schoolhouse filled with young fish visually popped off the cardboard, and the bright red of the eponymous crimson fish in the center of the board shone brightly. A silver question mark twisted through the shape of the fish with its dot ending in the fish's curled tail.

I had a fond place in my heart for the game as well. Friends I'd met in Albuquerque a decade ago, when I was living out of my Airstream trailer there, had introduced me to it when it was a new game. I enjoyed the beautiful visual elements like Perenelle did, but my favorite thing about it was that you could play on your own. It worked best with a group, but even for a solitary player, you could follow the clues and red herrings to reach a satisfying solution. The term "red herring," meaning a distraction that leads away from the main question at hand, was of course how the clever board game creators came up with the name Crimson Fish.

"What an age this is to be alive," Perenelle continued as she ran her fingertips over the blue bubbles. "You can reproduce this vibrant cerulean pigment on a mass-produced scale. Brilliant. Absolutely brilliant."

"Of course my dear wife would enjoy the colors more than the mystery of the game." The kettle whistled and Nicolas poured hot water into an iron teapot that made me smile. Though Max's shop, The Alchemy of Tea, wasn't yet open to the public, he'd been selecting and sourcing stock, and running his choices by me and a few others. Nicolas had fallen in love with one of the cast iron teapot samples, so Max had insisted the Flamels take it.

"The supposed ghost I saw loved games like this," I said.

Perenelle looked up from the colorful board. "Your question of ghosts was not a theoretical one?"

"We knew that, didn't we, dear?" Nicolas looked from one cupboard shelf to the next. "Why do modern people keep their wares hidden away behind cabinet doors?"

Perenelle lifted her ample skirts to crouch in front of me. "Who did you believe you saw?"

"I don't actually believe she was a ghost," I said. "I saw a young woman behaving strangely, but Heather swears she's someone she knew when they were schoolgirls together. The girl's nickname was Riddle because she loved riddles and games. She was murdered sixteen years ago, but she showed up this morning. She hasn't aged a day."

"Your witness is Ms. Heather Taylor?" Nicolas chuckled from the kitchen, still searching for teacups. "I wouldn't place too much stock in her words."

Perenelle *tssked*. "Heather is brilliant in her own way. Her artistic vision is well beyond most people who study art for decades. Because she truly *sees*. If she says it's the same woman, it is. You of all people know how this could be done. She could be..."

I knew very well where she was going. "She could have found the Elixir of Life. She could be an alchemist."

Perenelle gave the hint of a nod. "How old was Riddle when she supposedly died?"

"Sixteen. She could have faked her death like you two did."

"Unlikely at that age that she could have found the Elixir," Perenelle said. "In that case my esteemed husband is most likely correct. Heather's imagination—"

"I saw the girl, too."

Perenelle frowned. "But you didn't know her in the past. How could you—"

"Technology." I held up my phone. "This is a photograph of the young woman who looks like the one we saw this morning."

"Interesting," Perenelle murmured. "Perhaps she's a prodigy. I said it was *unlikely* for anyone to find the Elixir at such a young age, though not impossible."

"She was also good with plants, like I was at that age," I said. "So good she got an internship—that's like an apprenticeship—to learn more."

"Indeed?" Nicolas scratched his chin. "What was she called? Her proper name."

"Ridley Price."

"Ridley Price," he repeated. "You've looked her up on the computer in your hand?"

"She was murdered in Portland sixteen years ago. If it wasn't for the fact that photos of her look identical to the young woman I saw this morning, I wouldn't have even considered that she could be the same person—either as an alchemist or a ghost."

"If she's as good as you were when we found you," Nicolas added, "I'd say it's quite possible that with proper guidance, she may have found the Elixir of Life so young. But guidance would be necessary. A mentor."

"And why choose to disappear from her life in such a dramatic fashion?" I shook my head. "Something doesn't feel right about that."

"You didn't know her," Perenelle said softly. "We all have different demons. Heather knew the young woman?"

"She was good friends with her," I explained. "Heather was supposed to be at the party where Ridley was killed. That's why she was so shaken."

"How awful. I should bring her some flowers. My pigment garden is thriving. I believe she'd appreciate the madder and yarrow."

"That's a lovely idea," I said. "I'm sure she'd appreciate it."

"If Ridley Price faked her own death and is an alchemist," Nicolas said, "then the question becomes, why is she back now?"

"And," I said, *"what does she want?"*

CHAPTER 11

I stood on the threshold of Heather's front door and hoped she'd hear me out. "I believe you're right that someone is back to get answers about what happened to Ridley Price. But we didn't see a ghost."

"What do you mean 'someone is back'? Please don't start speaking in riddles, Zoe. It was an annoying yet endearing quality of Ridley's when we were kids. I don't need it right now."

"I don't mean to be cryptic, but I need you to trust me."

I'd hurried to the market after meeting with Nicolas and Perenelle, dropping off groceries for Dorian before heading to see Heather once more. She didn't always think things through, so I wanted to make sure nothing was spinning out of control in the few hours since I'd left her.

Heather stared at me. "You know something? How do you know something? Oh! Is Max feeding you information he isn't supposed to have? I get it. I won't say anything. I trust you. Come inside."

She and Brixton lived on the other side of the Hawthorne district, walkable but only if I had time, so today after dropping off groceries at home, I drove my truck to Heather's house. When I first met Heather and her family, they lived in an apartment a short walk from my house. Now, along with Brixton's step-father Abel, they lived in a modest house near Hawthorne Bridge.

I stopped short as soon as I stepped inside. A circle of eight sketches adorned her living room wall. These were rough sketches, done in ink and watercolor wash, the edges of the paper torn from a notebook and sloppily taped to a beige wall with blue painter's tape. Even so, these were powerful renderings that captured the essence of the people.

Seven images encircled a central sketch. It wasn't the largest illustration. It wasn't even the most complete. Yet it was the most haunting. Swirls of brown hair filled the page around an angelic face. No. Angelic wasn't the right word. Large brown eyes followed me as I stepped across the room to get a closer look. These were haunted eyes that held secrets.

Ridley Price.

The young woman we had seen that morning.

"These," said Heather as she swept her paint-flecked arm in a circle around Ridley's image, "are the people who were there at Ridley's party that day."

Curling tape held up the faces of two teenage girls on the wall below Ridley. A young woman with black hair and what at first glance appeared to be a shy smile but was much more of an enigmatic one. Next to her, a young woman with waves of blonde hair, curled eyelashes, and lips shaped in a flirtatious pucker.

"Those are Ridley's friends Joona Kim and Amber Cook. I wasn't close to Joona. She was pretty quiet, and I didn't get to know her well. Lots of people called her June instead of Joona. I knew Amber better, but she made me feel like an outsider because she'd been friends with Ridley so much longer."

Above Ridley were a forty-something man and woman. The man had sparkling blue eyes, but the rest of his face was dull. I wondered if Heather hadn't selected the right color for his sickly skin, but the ink lines that showed through the watercolor accentuated an impression of illness on his face. The woman held her chin high. Even in the form of a rough sketch, her violet eyes looked down at me as if I was being judged by the queen. The blue-eyed man with a dimple in his chin was far friendlier.

I leaned in closer. "Are those test tubes floating around his head?"

"Riddle's parents, Tess and John Price." Heather smiled as she tapped on one of the test tubes. "Before he died, Mr. Price was a chemistry teacher at the high school."

"Chemistry?" Chemistry was the modern branch of alchemy that had survived. Could that be how Ridley had learned about alchemy so young?

"Both her parents were chemists. Her mom was a flavorist. She probably still is."

I looked back at the regal woman who looked so incongruent next to the friendly, dimpled man. "Flavorist?" I pride myself on keeping up with modern vernacular and other changes with the world, but I'd never heard the word.

Heather disappeared into her kitchen and returned with a bag of chips labeled that they were dill pickle flavored. "The ingredients don't mention dill pickles."

"Ah. Using chemistry to create flavors that taste like other things."

While Heather tossed the chips aside, I inspected the illustrations to the left of Ridley's parents. Two teenage boys. One with unkempt black curls and a friendly yet cocky smile, the other with a mop of chestnut hair and an enigmatic smile that mirrored Ridley's. The chestnut-haired boy wore round copper-colored glasses that reminded me of the 1920s.

"Emilio Acosta and Nathaniel Gallo," Heather said, following my gaze. "Emilio was one of Ridley's oldest childhood friends, along with Amber. The three of them were a pack since elementary school. Emilio was the first boy Ridley ever kissed. But they weren't a couple by the time I met Ridley. Amber and Emilio ended up getting married a few years after high school, but they got divorced. And Amber is maybe a scientist now? I remember Ridley's mom loved that she was interested in science, unlike her own kids. Joona and me—wait, that's supposed to be Joona and *I*, isn't it?—anyway, we met Ridley at the start of high school. That's when Ridley met her boyfriend Nathaniel."

"The boy people thought was guilty of her murder."

Heather nodded. "Nathaniel *Gallows*. You know, I wouldn't really blame the universe for sending Riddle's ghost back to haunt me for being so cruel when I was a teenager."

"All kids are cruel." I looked more closely at Nathaniel Gallo. Heather had used a metallic colored pencil for both his glasses and a few strands of his hair, capturing both the impression of sun-kissed highlights and the suggestion of movement with only a few strokes in the rough pencil sketch. More than the skillfully drawn features, though, I was drawn to the boy's expression. When Heather drew anyone, she seemed to capture their very soul.

I looked up from the sketch. "You didn't sketch Nathaniel as a killer."

"I don't imagine him as one..." She bit her lip. "Is that weird? I mean, on one level, I know he did it. That's what we were told. I just don't know..."

"This last person is her brother?" I asked, moving to the last sketch, to the right of Ridley. The twenty-something young man looked so much like Ridley that at first glance I wondered if it wasn't a second attempted sketch of Ridley that Heather hadn't gotten quite right. It was similar but more masculine than the center sketch of Ridley Price.

"Roman Price. Her older brother. He was in grad school getting his MFA."

"Handsome." In a clean-cut 1950s boy band kind of way. With his half-tamed wavy brown hair, there was an innocence about him, but also a spark of creativity.

Heather tucked a strand of hair behind her ear. Was she blushing? "I had a crush on him for about two seconds. He's a poet. You might've heard of him. His first collection of poetry won some big award. He wanted to be an English Literature professor. I heard he ended up doing it, but I'm not really sure. He looked a lot like his sister, so I kinda didn't want to look him up again, in case he still looks so much like her that I'd cry."

I took a few deep breaths as I thought about what she'd just said and looked at Heather's sketches once more. Ridley surrounded by old friends and new, her parents and her brother. Seven people surrounding her central image. In spite of the chemistry connection, there was a far simpler explanation than either an alchemist who faked her death or a ghost who was back to haunt them. An explanation that was staring out at me from the wall.

"Heather."

Though I'd spoken her name softly, she jumped at the sound of her name, as if she'd been in her own universe of memories.

"Could it have been her brother *Roman* we saw this morning?" I asked. "In disguise, of course. I bet he had access to his sister's old clothes. And he could have gotten a wig, assuming he still cuts his hair short."

Heather blinked at me for a few seconds, then burst into laughter. "Oh, Zoe! Roman is over six feet tall! He didn't look too much older than us, but he must have been around six years older. Even if he'd stopped aging the day she died—like that's even possible!—it couldn't have been him."

"No. You're right." The person we'd seen was both young and nowhere close to six feet tall. Or were they? I hadn't stood next to the person we thought was Ridley. Was it possible Roman selected tall people to stand next to? In a controlled environment, like on a movie set or even a theater stage, it would have been possible. But at the café this morning? It would have been nearly impossible to fake.

Heather reached out and tugged on the tape at the edge of Roman's sketch, but stopped before she'd pulled it off. "Not dry yet. I'd better leave them up."

"You made these *today?*" I reached out and touched a lifelike strand of Ridley's hair. Only a few hours had passed since I'd left Heather. "Wow."

"I couldn't imagine doing anything else after we got back from Blue's."

"They're so lifelike."

"That moment has stayed with me. I haven't seen any of them in years, but I remember them. I didn't realize how close to the surface my memories were. I buried them to get by, you know?"

"Things like that are never too far from the surface," I murmured, unable to pull my gaze from Ridley's face.

"I don't know what to do, Zoe. One of them killed her."

CHAPTER 12

Alchemist. Ghost. A sibling impersonating their sister.

Which one was the answer?

Whatever was going on, Heather's story about Ridley's murder was filtered both by her not having attended the fateful party and the passage of time.

"If they're sure someone in the house killed her," I said to Heather, "where was the body hidden? Why didn't they find it for so long? It had to have been somewhere."

Heather wrapped her arms around herself. "There was so much blood. After they found that... it was chaos. They called the police, but it's not like they stayed together. Before that, the front door was locked. Mrs. Price always kept it locked. But after they found the blood, Amber told me everyone split up and did different things. There was screaming and running."

"So in the chaos, anyone could have slipped out and hidden her body where it wasn't found for years."

Heather nodded. "Yeah. It's *possible* a serial killer who hated happy teenage girls slipped over the fence or something. But how likely is that? It had to be one of them. They were the people in her life. And her diaries were gone."

"The secret you mentioned."

"The police figured she knew a secret about one of them that she was going to reveal. Her riddle." Heather's voice shook. "And I wasn't there for her."

"It's not your fault," another voice said. Brixton walked in from the kitchen. He must have come in through the back door, where he often left his bike.

"It's not polite to eavesdrop, Brix," Heather said, but her voice wasn't sharp.

"This is her?" He walked up to the sketches and touched the tape around the edges of the Ridley illustration before turning around to face us. "I want to help."

"Help with what?" I asked him.

Brixton rolled his eyes. "To catch the ghost before she hurts my mom."

Heather let out a sigh. "Thank goodness! I thought you were going to say you wanted to help catch her killer. That's why she has to be back, but I don't want you anywhere near that mess. It's way too dangerous."

I groaned silently. If there was a way to make sure Brixton would get involved, that was it.

"Ridley's ghost isn't going to hurt me," Heather continued. "Why would she come back after all these years to hurt me?"

"You don't know how ghost time works," Brixton said.

How did one argue with that?

Brixton was hovering between the existence of a child and an adult. He was too intelligent for me to speak down to him, but not mature enough to necessarily make the right decisions.

His well-meaning mom was also oblivious to the difficult experiences Brixton would undoubtedly face as a young man with dark hair and ethnically ambiguous features. Especially one with a juvenile record, never mind that it was for breaking the arm of a man hurting his mom. I was glad he had Abel, the doting stepdad who'd entered their lives just a few years ago, but who loved Brixton fiercely.

"Ghost time." Heather repeated the words. "You have such a clever way of thinking, Brix! What do you think, Zoe? Maybe she's just confused. She must feel so alone."

"She might be alone," I said, "but she's not a ghost."

"Then what did we see at Blue's this morning?"

"A living person," I said, "who wants to rattle people. A person who wants us to believe they're a ghost."

"But why would someone do that?" Heather asked. "Why now?"

"Something must have changed. You don't keep up with the people here on the wall, right? So you don't know if someone was… oh, I don't know, arrested for something new and says they have information about Ridley's murder in exchange for leniency."

Brixton smirked. "That's more far-fetched than a ghost. You've really never seen a ghost in all your years alive?"

"Brix!" Heather snapped.

"It's okay." I smiled at Heather, then gave Brixton a warning glance.

I had to tread carefully. Though Brixton had accidentally learned about my identity as an alchemist the day I moved into my house, Heather didn't know the whole truth about me. She was a dear friend, but one who was utterly incapable of keeping secrets. While I was getting settled into life in Portland, she told me how gratifying it was to think of herself as a big sister.

"See?" Brixton said. "You can't say for sure that ghosts don't exist."

"It wasn't a ghost your mom and I saw this morning."

"Whatever," Brixton said. "Whatever she is, she's not getting to my mom. I'm not a kid anymore, Mom. I can help."

Heather squeezed him tight. The top of her head only came up to his nose. "You don't need to protect me. That's my job to protect you." She squeezed harder. "You forget about all this. Zoe and I will take care of it."

Brixton shrugged out of her embrace and stepped to the wall of sketches. "You think Ridley's mom killed her?"

Heather gasped. "Why did you say that?"

I'd had the same thought. Not a rationally thought-out reaction, but an emotional one. Tess Price's harsh gaze was clearly rendered in confident black lines and a few messy splashes of watercolor. Brixton was right in what he saw.

"He's right," I said. "This isn't the sketch of a good person."

"Everyone else on the wall is sketched like...I dunno." Brixton shrugged. "Like they're real people. Except for her."

"You drew these with the eyes of your fifteen-year-old self." I saw hints of my own mother in those cold eyes. But as I'd learned only recently from Perenelle, my brother Thomas told her some things that made me wonder if there was more to my mother than I'd thought. She hadn't wanted to condemn me, but was herself trapped. "This isn't reality, but perception."

"Ridley's mom hated me," Heather said. "But she loved Ridley. I don't think she killed her daughter."

"But one of them did." He stooped to look more closely at the haunting sketches.

Heather tugged on his arm to pull him back. "You shouldn't be thinking about that. Leave this to the adults."

"I can help—"

"Really, Brix."

He stared at his mom for a moment before speaking. "Whatever," he mumbled, then slipped back into the kitchen.

"Don't you want lunch?" Heather called after him.

"I'll be at V's," Brixton said through the door.

"Veronica always cheers him up," Heather said, but not like she meant it. "As long as he's really going to her house, he's fine."

I wasn't worried. Veronica was the sensible one.

Heather stood with her hands on her hips, her attention back to the wall of her hastily sketched artwork. "I know what's missing."

She ran to her bedroom. I didn't follow, but heard drawers opening.

"Here it is." She pulled a folded sheet of textured paper from an envelope and unfolded the card. "The invitation to Ridley's party. I'm glad I didn't think of this before Brix came home. He'd want to solve the riddle."

"You saved it all these years?"

She handed me the card. "The invitation to her party."

On the front, the date and time were printed underneath the words, *Join me for my welcome home party and see the riddle solved*. On the inside of the folded card, a pressed white chrysanthemum was glued in place next to four rows of text.

> *A springtime daisy means you'll keep a secret,*
> *whether for a moment or a lifetime of regret.*
> *Tear off the petals, deep in thought:*
> *will this be the beginning or will it not?*

I read the riddle silently to myself, then read it once more aloud. "Did you each get a different piece of the riddle?"

Heather shook her head. "We all got the same one. The police asked about that." She rubbed her hands over her arms at the distressing memory.

I frowned at the strange riddle. "But the party was in the summer, not spring."

"It was. But it's a riddle."

"Daisies bloom in both the spring and summer."

Heather shrugged. "Riddles aren't supposed to be straightforward."

"Something from that summer sixteen years ago has to connect to today," I said. "You didn't stay in touch with the people who were there…"

"No. Only what I heard through others. Like Emilio being in the army, and Ridley's dad passing away."

"What do you know about her internship?"

"It was a permaculture internship on an Oregon farm. Messenger Farm. I remember that since it's a funny name. Sounds like a cult, doesn't it? Anyway, they questioned the woman on the farm. Aggie Messenger. That was her name. She had a solid alibi."

"Alibis aren't always what they seem," I said.

"She worked as a midwife," Heather said. "She was delivering a baby. The new mother and her whole family confirmed it."

I had to admit that was a good alibi.

But Aggie Messenger combined two professions often associated with witchcraft—a crime I was accused of for my aptitude with plants. I had to know more about this woman.

CHAPTER 13

Dorian's phone rang as he finished preparing lunch.

He did not mind the interruption. His mood was already much improved. Between the backyard bounty and the local market, Zoe had obtained many of the fresh ingredients he sought to prepare today's feast. Cooking with the French philosophy of *mis en place* (gathering all of his ingredients together on the counter), had already restored his mood.

He switched off the burner and scampered to the corner of the room, where one of the land line telephones was plugged in. Unlike the older model he preferred in his attic, this was a plastic monstrosity from the 1980s. He shuddered as he recalled the colorful styles from that hideous decade.

He understood that Zoe loved the color green, because it reminded her of her beloved plants, yet the shiny sea-foam green hurt his very soul. Still, he did not wish to miss the caller, in case it was someone wishing to speak with him. He disdainfully plucked the hideous fluorescent receiver from its base.

"*Allô?*"

"Oh, good." Brixton's voice. "You're at home."

"Where else would I be during the daylight hours?"

"Are you, um, making lunch? *What was that for?*" The second question did not appear to be directed at Dorian, and the boy's voice became muffled as he continued. "Why are you scowling at me like that, V? Why can't I ask Dorian if he's making lunch?"

Dorian chuckled. "I would be most pleased to cook lunch for you and young Veronica. You will have to make do without chanterelle mushrooms in the sauce I'm preparing, because a certain owner of this home did not seek them out elsewhere when they were not easily obtainable."

"K. See you in a few."

Ten minutes later, the laminated floor of Dorian's kitchen squeaked rhythmically as Brixton tapped his foot on the tiles. "My mom and Zoe don't want me involved in figuring out what's up with Ghost Girl."

"And Veronica?" Dorian asked. "What do your parents think?"

"I haven't told them. Obviously."

"They do not respect your maturity and intelligence as I do." Dorian paused as he stirred caramelized onions on a cast iron skillet. "What do *you* wish to do?"

"I'm in." Veronica grinned. It was a different expression than Dorian was used to seeing on the girl's face. Defiant, almost. No, that could not be the case. Despite her protestations, Veronica was indeed the sensible one.

"And you?" Dorian scooped the perfectly crisped onions onto the tops of three open-faced sandwiches and faced Brixton.

"Do you even have to ask?" Brixton smiled so enthusiastically that his dark curls tumbled over his eyes. Dorian was of the impression that the boy desperately needed a haircut, but he knew better than to point this out.

"*Bon*," Dorian said instead. "I have been thinking over this situation. We must set a trap to catch her. This is the only way for us to discover if she is truly a ghost."

"See," Brixton said to Veronica. "We do need ghost-hunting equipment—*ouch*. Seriously, V? Dorian just said—"

"Even with equipment," Veronica said, "catching a ghost is complicated. It doesn't matter what we have. Dorian knows that. He doesn't think she's a ghost."

"Of course he…" Brixton's voice trailed off. He swore. "Neither of you thinks she's a ghost? But you were looking up all that Portland ghost haunting history with me, V."

"It's fascinating stuff. Why is it always old hotels that are haunted? I mean, is it just because more people are there to report things, rather than one person in a house who nobody'd believe? Or is it being away from home that makes people more likely to be scared by strange noises and drafts? Or maybe—" Veronica paused and her mischievous grin was back. "Maybe it's that historic hotels are super old, and old things just make us feel like believing in a ghost story."

Brixton was unmoved by her speech. "But my mom was so sure of it. She didn't imagine a breeze and creaking floor was her dead friend. Dorian, you really don't believe me either?"

"I am an open-minded gargoyle. You may be correct that she is not of this world. And yet... I believe it is more likely she is a mortal who has discovered the Elixir of Life."

Veronica gasped. "But she's only like a year older than us. I thought learning alchemy took forever. Like going to med school. Oh—you mean she was a prodigy?"

"We do not yet know the truth," Dorian assured her. "Yet it is a reasonable theory, is it not? Someone wished her harm. *Alors*, she used her plant alchemy training to transform herself and escape harm."

"Then why is she back?" Brixton crossed his arms and stared at them. "No answer from either of you, huh? Because it doesn't. Make. Any. Sense."

"Maybe she wanted to come home," Veronica said softly. "If she left because someone wanted to kill her, they could still kill her now if she came home. Alchemists aren't immortal. Zoe and Dorian have explained that. They stop aging, but they can still die."

"We must speak with her," Dorian said. "This is the only way to find out what she truly is. And why she has returned. Therefore, we must set a trap."

"You have a plan?" Veronica asked.

"When Ethan insisted upon calling me 'Scooby' earlier this year," Dorian paused and adjusted his tucked wings to regain his dignity, "I wondered about this reference you insisted was complimentary. I learned many things." He steepled his clawed fingers together. "The self-appointed leader of the group of friends, a fellow called Fred, loved creating traps. His traps did not adhere to the laws of physics much of the time, but no matter. He got away with it since he was a cartoon. I, however, have the inkling of a much better trap. One that will adhere to the laws of physics and work successfully in reality."

"What is it?" Brixton asked.

"It will take me a short time to perfect my trap. I will explain everything once I have it ready."

"Will that be today?" Veronica asked.

Dorian considered this. "Perhaps, but not until quite late."

"Good. Because I know what Brixton and I need to do today."

"You do?" Brixton asked.

Veronica gave them a devious smile that Dorian would hardly have recognized as that of the innocent girl he had met the previous year.

"Listen carefully," she said. "This is what we need to do."

CHAPTER 14

Sitting in the bucket seat of my 1942 Chevy truck in front of Heather's house, I called Dorian's phone, which was the land line of my Craftsman house.

Cell phone screens don't respond to Dorian's clawed fingertips, so I'd plugged in one of my antique phones in the attic. The phone and my laptop computer were his connections to the outside world while he was in the house. He was a terrible typist on the flat keys of the laptop, and much preferred writing on his typewriter, but aside from the typed shopping lists he'd leave me in the kitchen, the typewriter didn't do much good when it came to communicating.

Now that Dorian was the baker for Blue Sky Teas, baking pastries in the teashop's kitchen in the pre-dawn hours of the morning, he made his own money for online purchases. Which was helpful, since he'd maxed out my own credit card multiple times before he got a proper job.

At least Dorian was no longer fiscally irresponsible. Not because he was using his own money, but because he didn't enjoy shopping for the sake of it. He required certain commodities (usually for the kitchen), but once obtained, he didn't shop for the sake of shopping.

"*Allô?*" Dorian picked up on the second ring.

"It's me."

Dorian clicked his tongue. "I appreciate that you change your vocabulary to keep up with the times. Yet simply saying 'me' is not clear. What if someone answered the telephone who did not know your voice?"

"You're the only one who answers this line. And you *do* know my voice. You'd know it even if I switched to French."

"Or Czech."

"You're learning Czech?"

"This is not the point, Zoe. I take it you are calling because you realized you forgot to procure chanterelle mushrooms? It is no matter. Lunch is over. I was creative in my substitutions. Still, I would appreciate more careful consideration in the future."

"There weren't any at the market. It'll be the season for them soon, when it warms up a little more, but it's a bit early."

"If that is not the purpose of your call—?"

"Is Brixton with you?" I asked.

"You only telephoned because you wish to speak to the boy?" Dorian grumbled. "He has his own mobile phone."

"He didn't pick up when I tried him. He's upset about the situation with Ridley Price."

"Ah. The Ghost Girl."

I winced. "Please stop calling her that. You know perfectly well it's more likely she's an alchemist than a ghost."

"Do I?" Dorian chuckled. "Anything is possible, *n'est-ce pas?*"

"Her parents were chemists."

"Chemists! You have been withholding key information. You have—"

"I found out five minutes ago. You didn't answer me about Brixton."

"No. The boy is not here. He is with Veronica."

I was relieved that he was with Veronica. She'd keep him from making any bad decisions. She was the sensible one.

I was due at Max's mom's house in Astoria in the late afternoon for an early barbecue dinner. He was staying with his mom, Mary, while harvesting and preparing tea from the yard where the plants had been growing since he and his apothecary grandmother planted them when he was a toddler. He was due back in Portland in a day or so, but he requested I come to Astoria first. He wouldn't tell me why, but I didn't need convincing to spend more time with Max.

It would take me two hours to get there, with a one-hour detour to get to Messenger Farm. That would leave me enough time to explore for a couple of hours and still arrive at Mary's house before five o'clock. Luckily, it was nearly the height of summer, so the sun would be out for several hours after that. I could enjoy a couple of hours with Max and his mom, then drive home safely. I'm so sensitive to the natural world around me that I grow tired as soon as the sun sets, and I get antsy if I'm away from nature for too long. I counted my blessings that my afternoon and evening would be filled with nature. As would my night. My bedroom overlooked my backyard garden, and I slept with my window open. Though I can't exactly hear my plants, I can feel their presence. It was the roses I felt most strongly right now. They were nearly at their peak. In a few days, they would shine brightest, then fade. I had never grown roses before, but now that I was in Portland, the City of Roses, it felt appropriate to try.

After looking up Messenger Farm's location on my phone, I studied the paper map in the glove box of my truck. Though I'm not as curious about modern technology as Nicolas, I do appreciate my computer and cell phone. I don't keep the phone with me at all times, nor do I check it hundreds of times a day, but I admit it comes in handy.

I filled up my truck and bought a green smoothie and granola bar at a tiny café near the gas station. I'm not someone who can skip meals, but I also was careful about what I selected from the menu, knowing how different ingredients affect me. I can only tolerate the smallest amount of caffeine, so I never drink coffee, but I added cacao nibs to my smoothie order. The chocolate would provide just the right amount of caffeine to fuel my long drive.

I wasn't able to find much information about Aggie Messenger or her farm online. She was a very private person. That made me even more curious to see if I would sense any alchemical practices on the premises.

I got on the highway to the Oregon farm where Ridley Price had apprenticed sixteen years ago. If Ridley was an alchemist who'd faked her own death, she'd been practicing alchemy at that farm.

The sun blazed overhead, and the roads were dotted with cars filled with Oregonians enjoying the beautiful day, but traffic rarely slowed. I reached the farm in a little over an hour. Only… it wasn't a proper farm. This was a homestead.

A hand-painted sign swinging in the wind at the edge of the dirt driveway proclaimed this to be "Messenger Farm," but this was no farmland. It was a small permaculture haven. Heather had mentioned the word permaculture when she spoke of Ridley's internship. I had assumed she heard the word that was becoming more widespread lately and was using it to talk about farming and gardening in general. But that wasn't the case.

There were no rows of crops in this half-acre plot of land. Instead, the earth was filled with seemingly haphazard fruit trees giving shade to smaller shrubs and herbs that the casual observer might assume were weeds. The property was enclosed not by a constructed fence, but by a border of hedges. American hornbeam, by the look of it. With several smaller shrubs and more delicate herbs underneath.

A plume of dust gathered in my wake as I drove up the dirt driveway leading to the modest farmhouse. Before stepping out of my truck, I sat in silence for a full minute. Unsure of what I was waiting for, I listened. I didn't see or hear anything aside from the hum of bees and the chirping of birds. A keyhole garden to one side of the house assured me the homestead was being actively managed.

Stepping out of my truck, I felt as if I'd stepped back in time. Gravel crunched under my feet as I walked the few feet to the porch. Unlike mine, it didn't creak underfoot. I knocked on the front door, but was met with silence. I knocked again. Again, nobody answered. There was no fence, so I walked to the keyhole garden. It was a collection of raised garden beds planted not in rows but in a circle with one line for the gardener to walk inside, thus forming the shape of a keyhole. The soil was healthy but not damp. Nobody had watered it recently, but with the mulch and mix of tall and short herbs and plants, these plants didn't need frequent watering.

I continued around to the back of the house. An herb garden immediately behind the two-story house was planted in a spiral shape, with the center of the spiral a few feet higher than the bottom. These edible gardens next to the house were large for a single-family home kitchen garden, but too small for commercial farming. I wondered if Aggie Messenger had named her homestead a farm because she sold produce at her local farmer's market. The plants were thriving. Aggie was clearly someone who cared lovingly for her plants—and they loved her back.

At the same time, these plants had an edge to them. They were tough. Nearly wild. Though they were well-loved, it was also clear that with the way they were arranged in harmony with each other, they didn't need a person to tend to them regularly to survive.

The scent of dust was the strongest odor I could detect. That made sense, since I'd stirred up dirt on the unpaved road. I expected I'd also smell the scent of the natural chemicals that are released when plants are harvested. Yet I smelled nothing now. Nobody had harvested any of these plants in quite some time.

Not a soul was present, so I tried the doors and windows. They were all closed and locked. I wasn't going to break in… but I could do something else. I hopped onto the side of what looked like a storage shed that was also fitted with equipment to catch rainwater, and heaved myself onto the roof. I went straight for the single chimney. If nothing else, a furnace would tell me if someone had practiced alchemy there.

Nothing alchemical had been coming out of it in recent years, if ever. If Ridley Price had practiced alchemy here, it wasn't as part of a larger scheme to train alchemists.

"What's your game, Ridley Price?" I murmured as I looked over the farm before getting down from the roof. "Why are you back? If you're alive, what made you disappear in the first place?"

CHAPTER 15

I got back in my truck and found the Main Street of the small town. Driving slowly, I passed a general market with a diner attached to it, a large hardware store, two tiny antique stores, and then what I was after. I parked in front of a small building with a sign declaring it both City Hall and Library.

"I'm trying to find information on Aggie Messenger of Messenger Farm," I asked the woman at the front desk of city hall.

Her smile disappeared. "I'm so sorry, hon. The memorial service was last week."

"Memorial service?"

The woman winced. "I'm so sorry. I shouldn't have opened my big bazooka. I assumed that's why you're an out-of-towner asking. Aggie passed away two weeks ago."

I closed my eyes. My one lead was gone.

"I'm so sorry," the woman said again. "Were you close?"

I opened my eyes. I've been told I'm terrible at lying. Best to stick to the truth. "We shared a love of how we grow plants."

The woman nodded. "She was our local magician."

My surprise must have shown on my face, because she laughed before clarifying, "She got bountiful crops years that much larger farmers struggled. It looks like a mess over there, with so many trees and bushes planted all on top of each other, but she knew what she was doing with the land. She had a way with plants. She loved that homestead so much."

That sounded a lot like what I'd done in Salem Village. But that was before I'd found alchemy. I was simply following what came naturally to me. Had Aggie Messenger found alchemy, or was she simply a plant whisperer?

"What happened?" I asked.

"You don't know?" The woman twisted a pen between her hands. "I probably shouldn't say."

"So she *was* murdered."

The woman's eyes bulged. "What?" she sputtered. "I didn't mean... I only meant that she was such a private person. She didn't like other people outside the community knowing her business. Why would you say that? Murder? Here?"

I thought quickly. "I only meant that since you said there was no public notice about her memorial, I wondered if that's because the police were investigating—"

"Oh, no." She let out a sigh of relief. "Aggie requested that. No public obituary. She was a really private person. I guess you didn't know that, if you two only talked about plants." She eyed my hands suspiciously.

I smiled at her observation. "My hands spend a lot of time in the dirt, but I take care of them." I lifted a salve from my bag and handed it to her. "This salve is great for gardening scrapes." Of which she had many on her hands and wrists.

"Homemade?"

"It is. I'm not trying to sell it to you. You can have it. I've got plenty more at home. If you like it, I'll send you the recipe so you can make it yourself."

I handed her my business card for Elixir, which included an email address. I no longer sold tinctures like I had a century ago, but I made enough that I could give them away whenever someone might benefit from them. Like Aggie Messenger, I was a private person. Selling antiques online was easier than maintaining a public storefront for herbal remedies. Besides, the people of Portland already had wonderful options for herbal remedies.

The woman's eyes lit up as she smoothed some of the healing balm over her hands. "It's probably just my imagination, but I swear my sinuses can breathe more easily now too."

"Eucalyptus essential oil is one of the elements in there."

"It was an accident."

"Aggie?"

She nodded. "She didn't use a tractor on her own little plot of land, but she was helping another local farmer on her land. Those things can be dangerous."

"Nothing suspicious about the accident?"

The woman gave me a look that told me as clearly as if she'd spoken that *I* was the suspicious one. She held her cell phone in her hand. I flinched, preparing myself for the police to come through the door to question the strange white-haired woman inquiring about murder in their small town.

"Ooooh," she said instead, looking up from her screen. "I looked up Elixir. You sell creepy old stuff, like a vampire-hunting kit from Victorian England. Now I get it."

"You do?"

"I understand why you want to see a mystery where there isn't one. I'm sorry your friend passed away. But it was simply a farming accident." She shook her head. "If you're still wondering, I can put your mind at ease. When she was first injured, she told folks what happened, and it really was simply an accident. She didn't finger a killer or anything like that. But sadly, her injuries were bad. She died two weeks ago."

Aggie Messenger of Messenger Farm died only two weeks ago. She didn't die right away, yet she didn't accuse anyone of killing her, so she hadn't been murdered. But the timing was so close to when Ridley's ghost sightings began. Was it connected? Aggie lived long enough to tell people about her accident. That meant she lived long enough to do a lot of other things.

What had happened that summer sixteen years ago? Whatever it was, had Aggie's recent death set things in motion?

CHAPTER 16

I arrived in Astoria half an hour early.

"You look lovely, darlin'," Max's mom Mary said in her Texas drawl. "You didn't need to bring flowers, but they're beautiful. *Prickly*, but beautiful. Trying to tell me something?" She gave me a wink.

"They're Canada Thistles. They symbolize bravery and determination, but that's not why I picked these pink beauties. They were growing wild in a field I passed by on my way here, and this handful was spilling out onto the cracked road. I hated to see them trampled by a car."

"Ha! Practical. I love it. Let me find a vase."

Mary Jasper was a hoot. Raised on a ranch in Texas by a father from a long line of Texan ranchers and a Chinese American mother whose parents had emigrated, she'd been in Oregon for more than half her life, but still spoke like a Texan and could always be seen wearing a pair of her assorted and beloved cowboy boots.

"How about this empty bottle of wine for the flowers?" Mary lifted a bottle from a side cabinet filled with photos of Max and his sister Mina when they were kids. "Nah, the neck is too scrawny."

"Max is outside with the tea plants?"

"That's my guess. And that he's lost track of the time. Why don't you go fetch him?"

Max had left home after high school, and his mom still lived in the home where he'd grown up. Treasured memories from Max's childhood were abundant in this house, especially the backyard. That's where his grandfather had buried a treasure for him to find and where he'd learned about gardening from his apothecary grandmother.

As a toddler, Max had planted rows of tea plants with his grandmother before she died. *Camellia sinensis.* The species of plant that made all the tea that's officially "tea" as opposed to an herbal infusion or tisane. They'd put their love into those plants, and the plants had responded in kind. They thrived, and more than 40 years later, Max was harvesting leaves for his new business venture, The Alchemy of Tea.

I spotted the rows of tea plants before I found Max. As it turned out, he was the one to find me. Arms wrapped around my waist from behind and soft lips brushed against my neck.

"I missed you," Max said.

"Missed you more." I spun around. Max was a few inches taller than me, but we stood on sloped ground that left us eye to eye. "You're still planning to be back in the next day or so?"

"I hope so. I've still got a lot left to finish before the summer solstice opening of the shop."

Our hands were intertwined, and I rested my forehead on his. Max's lush black hair was growing longer and fell past his eyebrows. In the afternoon breeze, my white hair mingled with his dark locks. We stood together in companionable silence for a few moments, feeling each other's warmth and breath.

Max had only recently embraced his plant alchemy potential, though he hadn't found—or even tried to find—the Elixir of Life. Even knowing the truth about me and the Flamels, he hadn't expressed any desire to stop his cells from deteriorating to cease aging. I understood his position. I never would have sought it out if not for foolishly thinking I could save my brother from the plague. Nicolas Flamel warned me that I couldn't save Thomas, but when you love a person as much as I loved my brother, you don't listen to reason. I hadn't let myself love anyone for a long time after losing my brother so young. But I'd learned a lot since then. Grown wiser, if not visibly older. I had forty wonderful years with my first love, Ambrose, before he died. Nearly a century later, I found Max, who had also lost his first love. Without realizing it, I'd fallen in love with him. I wished more than anything that we could grow old together.

"You going to tell me why you invited me today?"

He grinned as he ran his thumb across my bottom lip. "Is it that bad to see me 24 hours earlier than you would have otherwise?"

I knew what would happen if I didn't pull away, and it would mean missing dinner as well as whatever it was he'd mysteriously invited me to Astoria for. I forced myself to take a step back, but I kept hold of his hands. Max was still smiling at me, but I knew it wasn't only my visit that made him happy. He looked so contented here in this garden and with his next step in life.

"I'd follow you to the ends of the earth, Max Liu, but I don't think that's why you invited me here."

"Patience. All will be revealed in good time."

"Just because you've had to be patient to get The Alchemy of Tea established, it's cruel of you to make me wait to find out."

After his grandfather's death and then retiring from his job as a detective, it had taken Max months longer than he'd expected to get the permits in order for his new shop. That gave him time to make additional trips to his childhood home in Astoria, where he was picking and preparing the tea he would sell as a small part of his selections of tea, as well as replenishing the plants and soil. It also gave him time to order inventory and design the interior of the shop in Portland. He was having far more fun with the layout than I'd imagined, picking out the perfect wooden shelves and display cases for both tea and tea accessories, and designing the décor to make it a peaceful spot where customers would enjoy spending time. He wanted it to embody the harmony of Cha Dao, a term his grandmother had explained to him as "the way of tea."

The shop would soon celebrate its grand opening in the Hawthorne neighborhood, the quirky area in southeast Portland where we both lived. The storefront was directly next to Blue Sky Teas. Max was excited to be starting this second career in his 40s, and he and Blue would help each other's businesses. Blue would be able to direct her customers next door if they liked the tea they enjoyed at her café, and Max would recommend the cozy café next door as a restful place to enjoy a cup of tea while sitting under a living tree at a tree ring table. Opening Blue Sky Teas had been perfect for a new phase of life for our friend Blue, and I hoped The Alchemy of Tea would prove the same for Max.

He'd known soon after I met him that I *claimed* to be an alchemist, but it was only recently that he understood what that truly meant. He also now realized that what he thought he'd only imagined his apothecary grandmother practicing when he was a boy was indeed real. He was now working on his own form of plant alchemy with the tea plants he'd lovingly planted as a child. That's why it was necessary for him to be here with the living plants while he made his preparations.

"Why do you look like there's something you're not telling me as well?" Max kept hold of my hands.

"Because you know me too well, Max Liu. You ready to come inside? Your mom sent me to get you." I knew why he loved it out here. He'd grown up with these plants in this bountiful yard. The houses in Astoria had more land than those in central Portland. The earth smelled fresh and raw, as if he had been digging as well as harvesting.

Max didn't budge. "Spill."

He was horribly sexy when he was pretend-angry. The tilt of his parted lips made me want to do something else besides talk. I felt a pang of regret that we wouldn't have time to ourselves tonight.

"Have you ever heard of a girl named Ridley Price?"

Max dropped my hands. His expression faltered. "Where did you hear that name?"

"It's a funny story—"

"There's nothing funny about what happened to her." The joy in his voice from moments before was gone.

"You knew her?"

He gave a single shake of his head. "Not while she was alive. But after she disappeared… everyone in Portland knew her name. And her face. Have they finally caught the monster—?" He shoved his hand into his pocket for his cell phone.

I put my hand on his arm. "Nobody has been arrested. But… her ghost has been seen all over our neighborhood the past couple of days."

Max's shoulders relaxed. "Ah. The urban legend that sprang up after they found her bones. It pops up again every so often."

"Max," I said softly. "Heather and I saw her. This morning. At Blue Sky Teas."

"That's impossible."

"I know… But only if she's really dead. I was thinking—"

"That she's an alchemist?" A half-smile ticked up his lips. "I've been immersed in the alchemy of tea for months and all I have to show for it is a bit of plant magic to coax extra flavor from these leaves…" He shook his head. "I'd say she was the world's smartest sixteen-year-old if she found the Elixir of Life so young."

"You're not *looking* for the Elixir of Life," I pointed out.

"Neither were you." Max brushed a strand of white hair out of my face. I missed these intimate gestures. I couldn't wait until he was back in Portland full-time to open The Alchemy of Tea.

"Not for myself, but I was still looking."

"Even if it were possible that she found the Elixir of Life so young, they found her body, Zoe."

"Her *skeleton*. Bones that nobody could identify—"

"It was her. DNA tests confirmed it."

"Oh." I kept up with modern science as much as the next person, but my assumptions sometimes defaulted to what I'd known when I was young.

As a young woman studying with the Flamels in the French countryside in the early 1700s, I could imagine an airplane, because Da Vinci had imagined it centuries before my birth and half a millennia before it became a reality. I also understood the foundations of modern chemistry, because alchemy was a branch of medieval chemistry—one that was later discredited because of so many con men claiming to possess the ability to create gold. But genetic sequencing? Until recently, I never imagined that could be possible.

"Then you think I saw a ghost?" I asked. "Do you believe—"

"I believe," said Max, "that the person responsible for Ridley Price's death is a cold, calculating sociopath. They killed a teenage girl and hid her body so well that it wasn't found for years. It required cunning and planning to get her out of that house. You didn't see a ghost, Zoe. You saw the ongoing twisted game of a monster. I don't know who the girl is that you saw. But I know who's pulling the strings. Nathaniel Gallo."

CHAPTER 17

"We're hoping we could ask you a few questions about what happened to you," Veronica said to the man whose front door had creaked open. The man recently released from the hospital after crashing his car because of the appearance of his high school girlfriend's ghost.

Nathaniel Gallo.

Dorian raised the volume of the computer to better hear Veronica and Brixton. He was listening to what was being said on Veronica's phone, while looking at a photograph Veronica found online of Nathaniel Gallo. The photograph on Dorian's computer screen showed the man as he was sixteen years ago, when he was not much older than Brixton and Veronica. A boy with a rebellious expression peered at the camera lens from behind round spectacles.

They had decided it best not to reveal Brixton's true relationship to the Ghost Girl, lest they unleash the wrath of the blackguard, so Veronica would be the lead investigator. It was, in fact, young Veronica's idea to question the man, now that he was home from the hospital. Dorian had swelled with pride when she presented her plan. He liked to think of himself as something of a mentor to the intelligent young woman.

"You're teenage detectives like Nancy Drew?" asked Nathaniel Gallo.

Veronica's phone was inside her bag, so Dorian was unable to see the girl's face, but he imagined her reddening.

"We're exploring possibly supernatural occurrences in the local area," Veronica answered. Her voice betrayed nothing. "Your experience caught our attention."

"I'm not doing any more interviews." The man's voice was resigned.

"We won't take much of your time," Veronica pressed. "And it'll really help our project."

"A project on ghosts." Skepticism. This man was not a believer! Yet he was the one who had seen the ghost. Most curious.

"We're not taking a position," Veronica said. "We're simply gathering evidence."

"Evidence." The man snorted.

"I'm really sorry about your broken arm. I'm Veronica."

"I'm Brixton," the boy added, causing Dorian to flinch. The plan had been for Brixton to remain as silent as possible, including not divulging his name voluntarily. The tenor of his voice made Dorian worry the boy wished to say even more.

This was the type of sleuthing Zoe would have frowned upon. Sending the children to the home of a man who most likely murdered a young woman their age. Yet it was Veronica's idea! Dorian did not wish to stifle her growth. He acted as the responsible adult, making sure someone knew where they were going (Dorian himself knew this) and that the two of them stayed together. What could this man possibly do if they were together?

Nathaniel Gallo did not immediately answer. When he did, Dorian wished the boy had listened to him and stayed silent.

"Brixton?" Nathaniel Gallo said. "You don't hear that name too often. It makes me think of someone I haven't thought of in a long time."

"Um, yeah," Brixton said. "Funny about names. So, will you talk to us?"

"It would really help our project," Veronica added sweetly.

A sigh. "I shouldn't invite you two inside, but you can join me on the porch."

Dorian was pleased the man had not invited them inside. If he had, Brixton's job was to remind the man that other people knew they were at his home.

For a few moments, no words were spoken. Only a squeak and click (the front door, he imagined) and a faint scraping sound (chairs being rearranged, he hoped).

"Thanks for talking to us," Veronica said.

"Um, yeah. We appreciate it," Brixton added.

"What can I tell you?"

"We read about what happened to you." Veronica paused. "But social media muddles things, you know?"

"Which is why I shouldn't be talking to you. Or anyone."

"We've read about other ghosts around here," Brixton said. "That's what we want to understand. It's hard to tell what's real and what's not."

"Not really," said Nathaniel Gallo. "Until last night, I could have poked holes in any ghostly sighting you'd ever read about. Ghosts aren't real. I was so sure..." The silence stretched out so long that Dorian was worried the phone connection had been dropped. "Until I saw her."

"Your old girlfriend, Ridley Price." Veronica's voice was soft. Empathetic.

"Riddle. She loved it when people called her Riddle."

For the first time since they had made their plan, Dorian found himself surprised. There was *love* in the man's voice. He would swear to it.

"You really saw her?" Veronica's voice was almost a whisper.

"I don't know. Yes...no. I could have sworn it was her. But she died—she was *murdered*—so many years ago. It can't have been her."

"How did you even recognize her while you were driving at night?" Brixton asked.

"You two rode your bike and skateboard up this long private driveway, right? You remember the curve at the start? That's where I saw her. I was leaving, and at that curve my headlights flashed on her. I wasn't going too fast, but the sight of her scared me. But because it was *her*, I swerved and went into the ditch. I was so freaked out I didn't hit the brakes when I swerved to avoid her." The man chuckled sadly. "I was hiking with Riddle the first time I got a broken arm. And now she gave me the second broken arm of my life."

"Did you pass out?"

"No. But when I looked back, she was gone."

"Why would she be back now?" Brixton asked. "It's not like it's an anniversary—"

"It's. Not. Anything." Nathaniel's voice was angry. "Because she's not real."

For the first time in this conversation, Dorian questioned their plan. It was daytime, so Dorian could not travel with them to be nearby if anything untoward occurred.

"But you just said—" Brixton began. "*Ouch.*"

Dorian chuckled to himself. Veronica must have stopped the boy from aggravating their host.

"I hit my head," Nathaniel said. "I got a concussion. Maybe I'm not remembering things like I think I was. It's funny... when they told me I had a concussion and asked if I had someone who could look after me for a couple of days, my first thought was that Riddle could do it. She was so caring like that. And we were going to spend our lives together."

"I thought you two had broken—"

"That's so romantic," Veronica's voice cut off Brixton. "It's no wonder she was your true love. But we read that other people had seen her too. Is that right?"

"That's what has me so confused. After my accident, her old friend Amber called me and said she'd seen her too. And even though I'm not in touch with Riddle's mom, for obvious reasons—"

"Obvious?" Brixton asked.

A pause. "Tess Price believes I killed her daughter."

"That's terrible," Veronica said. "I'm sorry that all these painful memories have been brought back."

"They never left me. I think about her every day. I don't know if getting closure is a real thing that helps, but I never got that. And I can't imagine anyone filling that hole she left. I'm sorry. I don't know why I'm pouring out my life story to you two. It's just that you seem like such a nice young couple."

"We're n—" Brixton began, but Veronica must have silenced him again.

"You're just around the age we were," Nathaniel continued, "when everything fell apart. But that's not what you're here for. You said you're investigating whether or not ghosts exist. I can't help you. I don't know what I saw, but multiple other people she knew saw her as well. Maybe they're saying that because they hate me. They believe I killed her and was never punished, so they could be lying to torment me."

"Do you really believe that?"

"What I believe is.... No. What I *know*. What I know is that someone murdered the love of my life sixteen years ago. I'm sorry I couldn't help you with your story. But the truth doesn't always tell you what you want it to."

The sound of rustling. The man must have stood up. He was ending the interview.

"Could I use your restroom before we head home?" Veronica asked.

Another pause. Nathaniel Gallo did not appear to be slow to comprehend information. No. He was measuring his words. Why did he not wish for the girl to go inside?

"It's in the hall on the left," he said finally.

Only after Veronica said "thanks" did Dorian realize the full extent of why this cautious man might be wary of having her inside his house.

A door creaked open and shut.

Whatever was about to happen, Dorian was helpless to prevent it.

"Did your mother send you, Brixton?" Nathaniel Gallo asked.

"Um..."

"Even though your skin and hair are darker than hers, you look a lot like your mom. Heather Taylor. It took me a minute to figure out why you looked vaguely familiar. But when you said your name was Brixton, I knew exactly who you were. So tell me, why are you really here?"

CHAPTER 18

"You think Nathaniel Gallo killed her?" I asked Max.

"He loved riddles, just like Ridley did. The whole case is one big riddle. He even became a board game designer. He created that popular game Crimson Fish after he killed her."

I gaped at Max as I processed this information. "The prime suspect in her murder created that game?"

Max nodded. "Have you played it? It's filled with so many false motives and dead ends. It's a lot more complicated than an average board game. The mind that created those twists—"

"Red herrings," I said. "Five years after her death."

"What?"

"It was five years after she disappeared that the game came out. I remember the ten-year anniversary edition came out last year. That means it came out after they found her bones."

"I know. It's why I hate that game."

"How can you hate Crimson Fish? I love that game." I used to play it with a couple of kids who lived in the RV park where I parked my Airstream trailer when I lived in New Mexico. "The characters have delightful names like Colonel Carp, Doctor Dover, and Sir Seaweed. And there are so many puzzles to think about."

"Maybe it's fun for a game or two, but the investigating officer brought a copy to the station when she was looking into whether Gallo had hidden a confession as a riddle in the clues or illustrations."

"I take it he didn't."

"Nope. No hidden confession. But that game stayed around the station for years afterward. It was a good idea, thinking there might be a connection. Since the game only came out after something changed—after they found her bones."

"Oh no..."

"What are you thinking?"

"Max, I know what changed *now*. Heather was so upset this morning that I looked into something she said."

Max groaned.

"Don't worry," I added. "I haven't done anything. Not really. I've only figured out what changed. I think this is what set things in motion. But I don't yet know what it means."

Max pinched the bridge of his nose. "What changed?"

"The summer Ridley was killed, she had an internship at a homestead. Messenger Farm, owned by Aggie Messenger. Aggie died just a couple of weeks ago, from injuries sustained in a farming accident. When I learned that, I thought maybe it was related somehow. I couldn't think how, but now—"

"Messenger wasn't a suspect for long," Max said. "I remember her. She was hours away that day, with numerous witnesses."

"I don't mean that she killed Ridley. I think she *knew something*."

"And left a dying message?"

I nodded.

Max sighed. "You could be onto something. Deathbed confessions are real. People regret so many things in life when they know they're going to die. Secrets they want to get off their chests."

"And Ridley had a secret she was going to reveal sixteen years ago," I said. "Heather told me her diaries were stolen. That she was making a game of something that was much more than a game to one of those seven people. She might have told someone she trusted. Someone who wasn't involved with her family and friends back home."

"Someone like Aggie Messenger."

"Aggie could have told someone else about it before she died."

"What are you two doing out here with these boring old tea plants?" Mary asked, startling us both. "The sun'll be setting soon. Let's get grilling."

After barbecuing skewers of homegrown vegetables and black bean sweet potato burgers with Max and his mom, the sun was getting lower in the near-summer sky. Mary carried an empty platter inside, leaving me and Max alone at the well-worn deck table.

"I think it's time." Max stood and turned to the western horizon.

"I finally get to learn why I'm here?"

"I thought you might like to help me take cuttings of the tea plants, so we can bring them back to Portland with us."

"You already know how to make cuttings to propagate new plants."

He shrugged. "I do. But then the plants wouldn't have both of our energies."

"For our first shared garden?" I whispered.

Max grinned. "It's nearly the summer solstice, and there's over an hour of sunlight left…"

"Oh, Max." I leapt up and kissed him. "That's why you've been poking around the plant roots."

"You really like the idea?" Both of Max's eyebrows were raised in a hesitant expression.

"I love it." And I loved Max. Taking plant cuttings together might seem like a small thing, but for most of my life, I felt closer to plants than people. For the years I'd been an herbalist, I used plants to help people. To get the preparations right, I had to get to know the plants as well as I knew myself. But I rarely had the same deep connection to the people I helped.

Max and I spent the next hour taking cuttings of *camellia sinensis* plants, after telling Mary we'd be in at sunset to help with the dishes (which she insisted wasn't necessary). Max had scoped out the heartiest plants, but we selected the cuttings together.

The new tea plants we planted wouldn't be ready to harvest for a few years, and today was the first step, but what a wonderful one it was. Max was finding himself as a plant alchemist, and it was something we could do together.

"It looks like you prepared land over on the south-facing hillside," I said. "Were you originally thinking of planting more here?"

He shook his head. "Mom loves the flowers from the *camellia sasanqua* plants. Since she looks after the *camellia sinensis* plants my grandmother and I planted decades ago, I thought it was the least I could do to add the variety she loves."

The *camellia sinensis* variety of tea plant has the leaves that are used for brewing tea, but its sister variety *camellia sasanqua* can't be used for tea. However, it would give Mary vibrant pink flowers on the ornamental plants. With our cuttings completed, we planted the flowering tea plants for Mary.

The sun had dipped below the horizon by the time we were done. Max walked me out to my truck.

"Don't," Max said.

"Don't what?"

"If someone is really pretending to be the ghost of Ridley Price, they're up to something dangerous."

"Something involving Heather—"

"Which is why I already made a few phone calls."

"I knew you were taking a long time when you said you had to close up the back shed!"

"The door really *was* sticking. But while I was fixing it, I also called a couple of old friends who worked the case. They're already looking into it."

"Thank you, Max."

He rested his forehead on mine. "See you soon."

"I can hardly wait."

"Really, Zoe. Whatever you're thinking of doing, don't. Nathaniel Gallo is dangerous."

I wasn't sure what I was going to say, but the sound of my ringing phone saved me.

"Is Brixton with you?" Heather asked when I picked up.

"No. Why?"

"He's not answering his phone. I'm sure it's nothing, but… remember the last time that happened?"

I did. And it wasn't good.

CHAPTER 19

"Mom saw Ridley's ghost, too," Brixton said to Nathaniel Gallo.

Nathaniel swore. "Is she okay?"

"Like you care."

"I haven't seen Heather since she dropped out of high school, but I was happy to hear you were both doing well. I gave money for the stroller some of the girls at school were collecting donations for. I had to give anonymously, since they thought I killed Ridley. Half the time, I wanted to drop out myself. I was envious Heather had really done it."

"Mom got her GED last year."

"I'm glad to hear she's doing well."

"She was until this morning."

Nathaniel swore again. "Did Riddle's ghost come to your house? Is she hurt—"

"Ridley's ghost found my mom at our favorite local café. It was in public. The ghost didn't do anything to her. But Mom is freaked out."

"She should be. If Riddle has something in mind from beyond the grave, you can be certain it's a riddle of epic proportions."

"So you *do* think she's a ghost?"

Nathaniel Gallo did not answer immediately. When he spoke again, his voice sounded like that of a much older man. One who was tired. So very tired. "I don't know what to think. I could never guess what was

THE ALCHEMIST OF RIDDLE AND RUIN

going through that brilliant mind of hers. She didn't... She didn't say anything to your mom, did she? Or communicate a message...in some way?"

"I seriously have no idea what you're trying to say."

Nathaniel Gallo laughed, but it was a nervous sort of laughter. "Never mind."

"Um...did Ridley say anything to you? Were you trying to say she told you something, but you didn't tell anyone about it because it sounded weird?"

This, Dorian considered, was an interesting development, if true.

"No. Never mind. I still don't know if I imagined her. Yeah, I must have imagined it."

Dorian gripped the edge of the table holding the computer, willing Brixton to press him further.

"Wait," the boy said, and Dorian's anticipation rose. "Did she—"

"Whatever she's up to, it's best to get out of her way. I learned that the hard way."

The sound of a door slamming shut followed Nathaniel Gallo's words.

"Thanks for your time, Mr. Gallo." Veronica's voice was sharp. "I didn't realize how late it was. My parents are expecting me for dinner. Come on, Brix. Thanks again, Mr. Gallo."

Shuffling.

Rattling.

Muffled voices.

Oh, how the waiting was excruciating! Had the villain kidnapped the children?

No. The sound of skateboard tires on asphalt came through the phone. Brixton and Veronica were leaving of their own accord.

Dorian would have been pleased by how much his little gray cells were improving their investigatory observations even with the lack of one of his key senses, had he not been so worried about the children.

What had Veronica seen that caused her to react so violently?

After another minute, the sound of screeching tires. Those must have been Brixton's bicycle. The skateboard wheels ceased and a thump of it being flipped into her hand.

"What the hell, V?"

"Further." Veronica was out of breath. "We need to get back to Zoe's house."

The sound of skateboard wheels on asphalt resumed, but he could not hear Brixton's bicycle.

Dorian unmuted himself and spoke loudly, "Be sure to stay together."

Brixton exclaimed words not fit for sensitive ears. "Don't *do* that. I'm freaked out enough as it is."

"Omigod," Veronica said at the same time. "I forgot you were on the phone."

"Whatever you saw in the house, you can tell me when you arrive. Get more distance between yourselves and that man. Go."

∽

They arrived at Dorian's house half an hour later. Yes, he was well aware everyone in their acquaintance thought of the Craftsman abode as "Zoe's house," yet did he not live there as well? Was it not he who fed the children? Was it not he who they were working with to solve the mystery of the Ghost Girl?

Dorian had comfort food waiting for them. Iced cocoa, as even though it was evening, it was too warm a day for hot cocoa. He had also made summer fruit popsicles with coconut milk and fresh berries and herbs from the garden. The addition of basil was a genius touch, if he did say so himself.

Zoe was not yet home from her evening with Max at his childhood home.

"My mom is going to kill me for not returning her calls and not being at Veronica's house like I said I'd be." Brixton bit into his strawberry popsicle as he spoke. "I called her back, but I need to be home for dinner like... five minutes ago."

"We will be brief," Dorian said. "I only wish to hear what young Veronica saw inside, when she left her bag on the porch."

"I should have taken my phone inside with me," Veronica said, "but I knew Dorian would want to hear whatever Brix and Mr. Gallo talked about."

"What did you see in his home?" Dorian asked.

"First, it's creepy that it was filled with board games, even though there's no sign of kids in that house. Just him. It's like he's stuck sixteen years ago. But it gets even weirder. He has a shrine to Ridley."

"A shrine?"

"Dozens of photos of her in this little nook! But that's not even the weirdest thing."

"Yes?" Dorian prompted.

"There's a locked room." Veronica spoke slowly and waited for their reaction.

"I gotta say," Brixton said, "that one's not so weird. Everyone deserves privacy."

"From who? He's the only one who lives there. Who keeps a room locked up in their house when they live alone?"

Dorian gasped. "You believe he has a prisoner?"

Veronica gasped back. "I wasn't even thinking about that possibility."

"Someone would have noticed if he was a creepy kidnapper." Brixton gulped. "Right?"

"I didn't get a kidnapper vibe." Veronica shook her head. "But it's like he's got something important locked up. Something he wants to be sure nobody sees."

Dorian drummed his fingers together. "*Oui*. This is a most important discovery. What does *monsieur* Gallo have locked away in his home?"

CHAPTER 20

Heather called me back a few minutes later, apologizing for worrying too much. Brixton had called her back and said he and Veronica had lost track of time and he hadn't remembered to plug in his phone.

I wondered if that's all it was, but as long as he was safe, I was glad. I started telling her what I'd learned about Aggie, how the farmer might have known something about Ridley's death that she shared before she died, but Heather was distracted by waiting for Brixton, who would be home at any moment. It could wait.

I reached home not long after sunset.

"You have visitors in the backyard," Dorian informed me.

Nicolas and Perenelle were sitting on the back porch, eating a dessert platter that must have come from Dorian.

"We solved your riddle," Nicolas said as he inspected a chocolate-covered strawberry.

"He means we know how she faked her own death," Perenelle explained.

"She couldn't have," I said. "I know you two did a great job at faking your deaths in the past, but things are different now. There was DNA evidence that proved it was her."

"Remind me once more what *Dee Enay* means?" Nicolas popped the strawberry into his mouth and smiled like a man who's never tasted chocolate before. To be fair, a chocolate-covered strawberry was still a novelty for his tastebuds.

"I believe it is the letters DNA," Perenelle answered. "Though I don't remember what they stand for. Zoe?"

"I'm not sure of the scientific name, but it's the genetic testing that can precisely identify a person—showing if a person was at a certain location, touched something, or testing their remains if they're not identifiable by sight."

"They need to test it *against* something, though," Nicolas said. "This is what someone who loves riddles would consider."

"Yes, otherwise it would be an unknown person. But in Ridley Price's case, they had many things to test it against. An official lab tested her remains. It was definitely her."

"Zoe." Nicolas raised his wild eyebrows. "Think about the lessons you learned when you were my apprentice."

"I think of them often." It was true. Nicolas was the only person who saw my aptitude and didn't care that I was a woman. Even Perenelle was initially wary of taking me in, because she knew first-hand the difficulties that came with a woman trying to break free from society's dictates. She didn't want me to suffer the same trials she had.

"Then think critically," Nicolas said. "Think about what you truly know—and what you do not."

"I don't know if there was contamination." Was that what he meant?

"Even more basic." Nicolas grinned at me. "I suppose I shouldn't be disappointed. You haven't faked your death, as we have. I understand it to be more difficult these days. But even in our time, we had to think about what people would look for. What they would suspect versus what they would believe. This is the riddle I believe I have solved."

"You're having far too much fun stringing Zoe along, dear." Perenelle gave him a wry smile.

"I am a teacher," Nicolas insisted. "Forgive me, Zoe, if I still feel you are my apprentice, even now that you have grown up. *Think.* Ridley Price is a child of this era. She would know what people would look for when they found a skeleton."

"DNA." I groaned. The idea was so simple. "She could have gone to the source. She could have switched the data on file from her missing person's case with that of a different skeleton."

It would take effort to execute, but if someone wanted to fake their own death, it was possible.

Nicolas grinned as he ate the last chocolate-covered strawberry.

"We wanted you to stop worrying about a ghost," Perenelle said. "Now you only need to worry about an alchemist with a devious plan."

∽

The Flamels took their leave, and I brought their dishes inside.

"They finished my desserts," Dorian beamed. "I can make you more, if you are in need of sustenance after your long drive."

"I'm exhausted and full, but thank you. Oh, before I go to bed, I should warn you not to go over to Nathaniel Gallo's house tonight."

Dorian blinked at me. "Why would you surmise I had such a plan?"

"I know you want to catch what Brixton thinks is a ghost, and she was seen at his house."

"She told you?" Dorian sputtered.

"What? No, the ghost didn't talk to me. She's not even a ghost."

"Ah, yes." Dorian was calmer now. "The ghost who was seen at Nathaniel Gallo's home."

"What else would I be talking about?"

"Nothing. Do continue."

"I know she's not a ghost—because she's an alchemist."

Dorian frowned. "This is what you and the Flamels were discussing? Yet they did not think to bring *me* into their confidence for your discussion?"

"Nicolas wanted to have a mentor moment with me. He wouldn't tell me his theory outright, but he helped me think through the possibilities. We already knew it was far-fetched for her to be a ghost.

Now I'm even more convinced she's not. There are ways, even in the modern world, to fake one's death."

"But if it is an alchemist with an unknown plan whom we fear, why would you tell me to stay away from *monsieur* Gallo's home? If Ridley Price is not dead, then Nathaniel Gallo is no killer."

I considered the question. He was right, of course. But there was something unsettling in Max's description of the man.

"Just stay away from him," I said. "And don't encourage Brixton to investigate."

"I will not encourage the boy to visit this person."

Why did I get the feeling Dorian had chosen his words carefully?

I was working on a solar infusion of herbal tea on my back porch. Dried rosehips and hibiscus flowers steeping in a glass mason jar with the energy of the summer sun. I went to bring it inside, now that the sun had gone down, and as I did so my phone rang.

I winced. I shouldn't have had my phone with me while I was working so closely with my plants. The thing about alchemy is that even when you're not aiming for something as complicated as a transmutation of metal or an elixir of immortality, the maker's energy and intent matters. An herbal infusion can be good if it's mass produced with exact measurements and clocks, but it can be *spectacular* when the person who created it by hand is truly paying attention. People who work with plants directly can listen to the ingredients rather than measuring them. Observing what the sun had bestowed on the ingredients in my jar, I could judge whether it had enough time or needed more—but not when I was being interrupted by the ringing phone. Heather's name showed on the screen. I hit the button to answer, hoping Brixton hadn't run off again.

"Blue came by," said Heather.

"Is everything all right?"

"I don't know… Someone had left a note for me at Blue Sky Teas. They want me to meet them at the Lone Fir Cemetery at sunrise. At Ridley's grave."

Ridley's grave? "Who's it from?"

"It's the strangest thing. It's not signed. Not only that, but it's like the paper is old. Really old."

"Charred?"

"How did you know?"

It was the paper I'd seen float down to the floor of the café when leaves of the weeping fig tree fell to the floor. When the supposed ghost of Ridley Price had walked by.

CHAPTER 21

I pulled up in front of Heather's house as the first rays of dawn peeked above the horizon. I was late. Sunrise would be here soon. Luckily, we didn't have far to go.

My body is so attuned to planetary cycles that when the sun goes down, my body slows and craves sleep, and when the sun rises, so do I, regardless of how much sleep I've had. But getting up *before* sunrise? I wasn't at my best, and hadn't been since bolting awake twenty minutes ago to the sound of an alarm clock instead of sunlight shining through my window.

The street was silent when I reached Heather's house. I had expected her to be waiting on the porch, since I was late, but there was no sign of life. I gave a start as three seven-foot-high sunflowers swayed in the pre-dawn twilight. Foolish of me to have been startled. I knew Heather had planted the sunflowers, and a chilly breeze stirred up the towering flowers. I cinched my silver raincoat around my waist to shield me from the chill.

Only after I knocked for a second time did Heather appear. A light blue cardigan sweater hung loosely on her arms over a wrinkled white sun dress. Her eyes were bloodshot, and her hair tangled.

"Didn't sleep?" I asked.

"How could I? What am I supposed to say to Ridley's ghost? That has to be who it's from."

"You don't know that." I did suspect it was a note from either alchemist Ridley Price or whoever wanted us to believe Ridley's ghost was back. I hadn't told my suspicions to Heather, though. I'd simply told her it was a bad idea to meet the note-writer alone. Heather was flighty, not stupid. She agreed it was a good idea for me to go with her. But now, in the breaking light of a new day, I wondered whether we should be going at all. We crossed the small lawn and climbed into my truck in silence.

"What's that thing?" Heather pointed at the small glass mason jar filled with a bright red liquid.

"Sun tea."

She scrunched up her face as I took a sip. "But it looks so strong. Nothing like real tea."

"It's an herbal infusion I made by brewing it in the sun. I needed sunlight in some form, since it's barely after five o'clock in the morning." If I couldn't wake up with the sun, I'd bring the sun to me to wake up. It was the rosehips and hibiscus solar infusion I'd made the previous day and strained into four smaller jars.

"Before you start the car—" Heather put a hand on mine to stop me from turning the key. "There's something else I wanted to ask. Not about that weird drink."

I waited for her to say more.

"Never mind," she said after several seconds of silence. "You'll think I've lost my mind."

"Now you really have to tell me." I laughed, but the sound fell flat.

She lifted something small from the handwoven bag she carried, and held what looked like the fragment of an old piece of paper—not in front of me to look at, but under my nose. I knew immediately what it was. The scent was so faint that I hadn't noticed it when the note had fallen to the floor with the tree leaves the previous morning. But now that it was an inch from my nose, it was clear.

"Brimstone."

Heather pulled her hand back and choked. "Brimstone. Oh God, you're right. That's what sulfur is. Does that mean Ridley escaped from—"

"It's simply sulfur." I mentally kicked myself. Nobody used the term brimstone anymore. It was simply a chemical compound, and one I should have referred to as sulfur. Not a word associated strongly with Hell.

"I recognized the scent of sulfur from mixing paints." Heather tucked the note into the tiny cross-shoulder bag she clutched in her lap.

"We don't have to go—"

"I'm fine. Let's go or we'll be late."

I started the engine and pulled onto the sleepy road.

Heather tossed her bag at her feet and turned on the radio. She gasped as static crackled over the airwaves. "Spirits interfere with electronics. They—"

"It's not a ghost. I don't usually listen to the radio while driving. If I want music, I play a tape."

"A tape?" Heather giggled. "You're three waves of technology behind. Sorry! I forgot you grew up in a strict family that didn't use a lot of modern technology. I didn't mean to—"

"It's fine. Really." I told the truth whenever possible. Heather knew the truth that my parents had been quite strict, skeptical of my love of plants as a viable career path, and that we didn't have modern conveniences in my home. I simply withheld the fact that it was the late 1600s.

"I'll play you a song from this year. Where's the port where I can plug in my phone?"

"We'll be there in less than five minutes."

"Plenty of time for a song."

"It's an old truck. No cell phone port." I didn't add that the tape deck was even older than the type of tape Heather probably remembered her parents having when she was a kid. I'd installed an 8-Track two decades after I first bought the truck new.

The streets were nearly empty at this early hour, and we reached the cemetery in just a couple of minutes. Heather bounded out of the car as I turned off the headlights and locked the doors.

My silver coat billowed behind me as I hurried to catch up with Heather. She walked with purpose, like she knew where she was going. I knew as well: Ridley Price's grave.

The cemetery had existed since the mid-1800s and was filled with some of Portland's oldest families. Though new burials were few, families that had purchased large plots still had space for family members who died in the present day to join them in the beautiful setting.

Stepping through the historic graveyard, I was reminded of Paris cemeteries. Massive granite tombstones served as heartfelt memorials to loved ones. In between the forest of trees, stone carvers had added details to tombstones in all shapes and sizes. I stepped past a patch of yarrow growing wild. I was glad the cemetery caretakers had let it grow rather than razing it as a weed, as was often done.

I fell further behind Heather. It was partly because I was lollygagging at the historical grave markers, many of which were filled with lovingly carved symbols, but also because my ankle was stiff. I'd sprained it quite badly earlier that year, and it still periodically gave me grief at the start of the day.

I paused to stretch my ankle, and that's when I saw them.

Two figures, both dressed in raincoats like I was. Though it was summer, it was a misty morning in Portland, so the raincoats themselves weren't suspicious. Yet both of their hoods were up, completely covering their faces. They moved silently toward a small mausoleum, where they vanished.

I knew of rumors that the Lone Fir Cemetery was haunted, but I couldn't imagine ghosts wearing red raincoats. They were simply two people who'd stepped beyond my field of view behind a mausoleum. I hurried in their direction and caught sight of them once more. Should I run to catch up with them? No, there was no reason to suspect they had anything to do with our assignation. Until the hood of one of them fell back, revealing a profile I knew, because it was as if one of Heather's sketches had come to life. Ridley's old friend Emilio Acosta.

"Heather," I whispered. But she was nowhere in sight. I had only a moment before I'd surely lose them for sure. I ran after them.

"Emilio," I said when I was a few feet away from them.

The petite person with him gave a stifled scream. She spun around, and I recognized her long eyelashes and expressive face. Amber Cook. Hadn't Heather said they'd gotten divorced? They weren't holding hands, but they were walking together and wearing matching raincoats.

"Hi." Emilio's voice was friendly, though his expression reserved and his body language tense. He wasn't a large man, but he held himself like a fighter.

"You got a note too?" Amber asked.

"*Shh.*" Emilio shot her a look. "We don't know who she—"

"I'm a friend of Heather's. She got a note. That's why we're here."

"Where's Heather?" Emilio looked accusingly over my shoulder.

"I must have lost her."

"I don't like it here." Amber followed Emilio's gaze to something behind me. But in her face, I didn't see skepticism. I saw something else. *Fear.*

I spun around. There was no one there. Only a solitary crow observing us from a tree branch. It cocked its head and looked at me. *Caw*, it said, then flapped its wings and flew away.

When I turned back around, Emilio and Amber were gone.

Damn. I took a few steps in the direction I'd seen them going, but they must have been purposefully hiding from me. There were certainly enough places to do so. Old growth trees with thick trunks, towering stone statues over graves, and mausoleums.

A hand grabbed my arm.

"Heather," I whisper-screamed.

"You okay? I thought I lost you. Ridley's grave is this way."

I gave one glance back at where Amber and Emilio might have gone, then followed her. "Heather, I just ran into—"

She clasped my arm once more. "Look!"

She didn't have to point. I already saw where she was looking. The girl from the previous day appeared.

I use the term "appeared" literally. I wasn't sure where she'd come from. It wasn't from behind a gravestone, as plentiful as they were. She stood apart from them, in a small clearing. She wasn't far from a giant cedar tree. That must have been where she had been hiding. She faced our direction but wasn't looking at us.

She wasn't nearly close enough for us to see her face clearly, but there's an energy that accompanies a person's gaze. I didn't feel that from Ridley. Unless she really was a—No, I pushed irrational thoughts aside. This wasn't a ghost. Yet as her gold eyes caught the light of the sunrise, I admit that gave me momentary pause. With the sunlight just beginning to filter through the trees and memorials of generations of loved ones around us, it was a dramatic place to make an appearance. Like it was staged. Which is exactly what this was.

I shook off my hesitation and took a step forward—but Heather held me back.

"What does she want?" Heather whispered.

"That's what we're here to find out."

The figure turned gracefully, without acknowledging our presence. I followed. Heather didn't keep pace with me, but a few seconds later, I felt her behind me.

The cemetery was relatively flat but filled with trees. Pink camellia blossoms blocked out the light as I followed. We followed the silent young woman through linden, fir, and chestnut trees. The figure had reached a clearing. She had nowhere else to hide.

We were almost to the clearing ourselves—when the sound of an arrow whizzing by pierced the air and ended with a *thunk*. Heather screamed and collapsed.

CHAPTER 22

Heather screamed again.

I knelt at her side. "Are you all right?"

She nodded. The arrow hadn't struck her, but she'd wisely ducked as it flew by.

I looked around frantically. I didn't see anyone, but I spotted the arrow high in the trunk of a Douglas fir tree only feet from where we stood.

"Stay here." I ran toward the clearing.

"Zoe, you can't—"

I reached the clearing. I knew it was a risk, but I didn't think our quarry would fire again. She wanted to be seen but not caught. We must have gotten too close.

I assumed it was the girl, and that she had shot the arrow because she hadn't wanted us to get too close. But what if I was wrong? Where had Emilio and Amber gone? I couldn't imagine the frightened Amber shooting an arrow, but looks could be deceiving. With how dense the trees were in this sprawling cemetery, it would have been easy for more people to be hiding. Not all of the suspects in Ridley's murder had revealed themselves this morning.

Back to what I did know with certainty. The girl who'd invited people to the cemetery couldn't have simply vanished. The trees were thinner here, but three tombstones were gathered closely together. I hurried to them. But when I peeked behind them, no one was there. Where had she gone?

I hadn't been looking carefully at the front of the graves, but now that I'd reassured myself there was nobody there, my eyes fell on the name of one of the gravestones. Ridley Price.

Above a granite headstone, a sandstone statue of a young angel stood carrying an open book and a pen in her hand.

"Where did she go?" a voice called out. It wasn't Heather. It was the deeper voice of a man. A frustrated one. The voice wasn't either Emilio or Amber. *Someone else was looking for Ridley.*

I hurried back to Heather, who was now standing underneath the arrow. She jumped up, trying to reach it and failing.

"We should leave it," I said. "Did you see or hear someone else?"

"All I can hear is the sound of my heart thudding in my ears." Heather pressed fists to her ears. "I can't reach the arrow anyway. I didn't realize it was so high. How did a ghost shoot an arrow?"

"Because it wasn't a ghost." I shivered. I had wanted to support Heather, but I hadn't thought the assignation could turn deadly so quickly. "She's gone now, but I don't know if the arrow was shot by the person we're thinking of as the ghost. When you and I lost each other a few minutes ago, I saw Emilio and Amber."

"They're *here*?"

"I don't know if they're still here, but they were. Dressed in matching red raincoats."

"Where did you go?" Another voice I didn't recognize. How many people were lurking about the cemetery this morning?

I couldn't see this person either, but at the sound of it, Heather gasped and grabbed the collar of my silver raincoat, dragging me behind the wide trunk of the fir tree.

"That's Ridley's mom," Heather hissed. "Ridley must have left her a note, too."

"Then why are we hiding?" I whispered back.

"I can't see Riddle's mom! Not like this. I can't—"

"Heather Taylor, is that you?" A woman I recognized from Heather's sketch stepped into view. Her hair was now much shorter, but her dark blue eyes gazed upon me with the same royal air Heather had captured so accurately. Tess Price.

"Now I've lost both of you." The man's voice was further away now. "Mother, where did you go?"

"Over by the fir tree." Tess raised her voice as she called to her son, but her gaze didn't leave Heather. "You haven't changed a bit." Accompanied by the look she gave Heather, it was clear the words weren't a compliment.

"There you are." A man in his mid-thirties joined us next to the grand tree. Heather's sketch had done him justice as well. Roman Price was older than Heather's memory had drawn him, but his delicate features hadn't changed much in the intervening years. If he hadn't been over six feet tall, I would have thought it entirely possible for him to have impersonated his sister. But he couldn't have been our ghost.

"Oh," he continued, startled as he realized his mother wasn't alone. "Did you two happen to hear a scream and see a girl who disappeared right over—Heather? Heather Taylor?"

Heather gave him a meek smile.

A range of emotions came over Roman's expressive face before he found his voice once more. I wondered for a moment if he'd had a crush on her as she'd admitted having on him as a teenager, but his words made clear the reason he was flustered. "You've seen my sister's ghost, too?"

"She's angry at me," Heather whispered as she pointed up at the arrow. "I didn't protect her when she was my friend. So she tried to kill me."

"What are you saying?" Roman choked out. "That can't really be —" He broke off and reached over his head. He was taller than the rest of us and easily reached the arrow. With two sharp tugs, he wrestled it out of the bark. He stared at it, unbelieving.

"For God's sake," said Tess Price. "Heather is hysterical. My daughter isn't a ghost. We haven't seen her ghost."

"But Roman said he'd seen her too," Heather protested.

Roman was still staring at the arrow. "I didn't think—I didn't really think—*Ouch.*" He jerked the tip of the arrow away from his hand. A line of blood appeared on his palm. The arrow was sharp. If it had been a few feet closer…I shuddered at the thought.

"Oh, do finish your sentences, Roman." Tess Price's words made her son redden, but also had the effect of shaking him from his fixation on the arrow. "If my son isn't going to speak coherently, at least introduce me to your companion, Heather."

"I'm Zoe," I said, when it was clear Heather wasn't doing any better than Roman. "Zoe Faust."

"Tess Price," said Tess. "This is my son, Roman. I take it that you two received a similar note from the cruel person who's pretending to be my daughter?"

"Heather did," I answered. "I came with her this morning so she wouldn't be alone."

"Pleased to meet you," Roman said, but the words were perfunctory. His attention was on the arrow.

"It might have been Emilio and Amber who shot it," Heather said. "Did you see them? They're in bright red raincoats."

Both Roman and his mother gaped at her. Heather shrank back.

"They're here?" Tess snarled at Heather. "Why didn't you say so? What about Nathaniel? He must be here, too. He's gathering us all here—"

"We haven't seen him," I said.

"But there are so many places to hide here." Roman looked upward, into the thick canopy of trees as a few drops of blood dripped from his palm.

"I saw a patch of yarrow a little way from here," I said, already tracing my steps back to where I'd seen the plant that could help stop bleeding.

"What's she talking about?" Tess asked one of the others.

"You shouldn't be on your own," Roman called after me.

"I'll go with her," said Heather, and she caught up with me a few seconds later. "Are you looking for where Nathaniel and the others could be hiding?"

"I'm going after this." I plucked a few stalks of wild yarrow. *Soldier's Woundwart*, it had once been called, because of how it was used to staunch bleeding on the battlefield. I returned to Roman's side and pressed a quick preparation to his hand, where the tissue he'd applied had already soaked through.

"Don't worry," Heather said. "She knows what she's doing. She's an herbalist."

"I have proper dressings at my house," Tess said. "It's not far from here. But Heather, I'm not done talking to you. Do you remember where I live?"

Heather nodded.

"Meet us at my house," said Tess. It wasn't a question.

CHAPTER 23

"Was that a scream?" Veronica asked.

"Probably a bird," Brixton replied, though he looked far from certain.

Dorian held his tongue. Like Veronica, he, too, thought the shriek sounded like that of a human. Yet he did not wish them to turn back.

"Maybe this is a terrible idea," Brixton continued. "Zoe and my mom will see us."

"They're so distracted they didn't even notice we were in the back of Zoe's truck," Veronica pointed out.

"*C'est vrai*," Dorian added. "This is true. They did not notice us at all. Nor will they notice our approach."

Dorian was dressed in his cape, looking like a child in a costume. The thick woods of the cemetery would further protect him from view. Dorian's only sense of unease was that the roles of the children were not as he expected. Should it not be Veronica who was cautious?

Brixton yawned. *Bon*. This explained the boy's hesitance. He was tired and therefore not his usual self. Dorian understood it was not normal for Brixton and Veronica to be awake before six o'clock in the morning. Dorian himself did not need sleep, so he had already returned from the Blue Sky Teas kitchen, where he had baked dozens of delectable pastries for that morning's patrons. Therefore, he was already back at home when

Zoe's pre-dawn alarm sounded. This was quite unusual. Dorian knew with certainty that the game was afoot!

He was unsure of the exact nature of the game, until Zoe called Heather to say she would probably be late. Late? For a sunrise assignation?

After overhearing this conversation, Dorian had called Brixton's mobile phone and roused the boy, telling him he must be ready for action, and to have Veronica arrive at his home posthaste (a term the boy was unfamiliar with, yet he understood the urgency). Dorian had then crept into the back of Zoe's truck, underneath the tarp, with a bag of implements he had been gathering. He was not certain he would have the opportunity to use them now, yet he expected it might be the case. When Zoe arrived at Heather's house and went to the front door, Brixton and Veronica snuck into the back of the truck with Dorian.

Now, the three stowaways crept out of their hiding spot. At a distance, they followed Zoe and Heather through the dim light filtering through the graveyard's thick trees.

Brixton was a few paces behind Dorian and Veronica.

"He's scared because the cemetery is supposed to be haunted," Veronica whispered to Dorian.

Brixton caught up with them and grabbed Veronica's arm. "That looks like Ridley's mom over there." The boy protectively pulled them further behind an outgrowth of trees. "You were right, Dorian. Something is going down this morning. Why else would they all be here at the exact same time."

Veronica gasped. "Look," she whispered. "That's why they're here."

At the crest of the gentle hillside, the ghost of Ridley Price appeared. Standing between two trees of blooming flowers that looked as if they sprouted from her shoulders, she resembled the stone angel standing above her grave.

Nobody moved. Not Dorian and his compatriots. Not the Ghost Girl. Not Zoe, Brixton's mother, nor the dead girl's mother and the younger man she was with.

"She's beautiful," Brixton said.

Veronica scowled.

The girl's face became a visage of fury! And now... she was moving away. Surely the others saw this as well.

"Why are the others not following Ghost Girl?" Dorian asked.

"Zoe and Brix's mom are talking to those other two people," Veronica whispered. "But where did..."

"There." Dorian pointed. "Ghost Girl has moved quickly." Giving up cover, he scampered forward, his cape rippling behind him.

Where was the girl? He caught sight of her once more. But then—she vanished.

"What the—" Brixton was at his side.

Could the creature truly be a ghost? Dorian shook himself. "She has appeared once more. Hurry. We must implement our trap."

Dorian knew where she was going. This path led out of the cemetery. He ran ahead of Brixton and Veronica on clawed feet. Though modern technology did not favor his skin and claws, here in the outdoors he was in his element. He ran more quickly than others on grass, dirt, and stone, even with the bag he carried. He also climbed quickly on vertical surfaces, unencumbered by ropes and harnesses.

He was ahead of Ghost Girl and the children. The grand elm tree on the girl's predicted path was as easy as pie (an expression Dorian had come to love after baking eight pies as a special order for Blue Sky Teas, which he completed in record time). In mere moments, he scaled the trunk and was several meters high, his clawed feet gripping the bark of a massive branch.

"Where did she go?" Brixton's faint voice called, though Dorian could no longer see him.

Ghost Girl kept running. She was in Dorian's sight, running in the direction he expected. A few more steps. Yes. There.

He dropped the net.

The girl screamed. "Get it off! Get it off!"

As Dorian watched silently from above, Veronica reached her first. "It's only an old fishing net. It's not going to hurt you."

"Stay away from me."

As the girl squirmed in the antique net, Dorian himself squirmed. It was an antique net from a Victorian magic show, catalogued in Zoe's antique collection and offered online. He hoped the girl would not

THE ALCHEMIST OF RIDDLE AND RUIN

damage it. Dorian would have purchased a less valuable net online had he known in advance he would need such a trap. But he had no time to plan! When Zoe was leaving to bring Heather to a dawn sighting of the ghost, the great Dorian Robert-Houdin knew he must act.

Yet recrimination was only a secondary concern. He had caught Ghost Girl! His simple trap was far superior to the overly complex mechanisms of the blond cartoon character Fred. And why did the cartoon young man wear an ascot? This was another thing that baffled him about this strange television show he had learned about after Brixton's friend Ethan referred to Dorian as "Scooby."

Dorian winced as the girl continued to squirm. It was inadvisable for him to climb down the tree and reveal himself, even in his hooded cape. Yet he would have felt better if Brixton had reached the side of young Veronica. Where was the boy? Ah. *Bon.* The running boy approached from behind a thicket of trees.

"You're not a ghost." Brixton was out of breath as he reached the two young women.

"Where were you?" Veronica asked him.

"I didn't see where you went. I went another way. He got—I mean, *we* got her."

"Stay. Away. From. Me." Ghost Girl's voice was different. Darker and more mysterious. Dorian chuckled. She had recovered from her initial shock and was attempting to recover her mysterious persona.

"This trap wouldn't have worked," Brixton said, "if you were a ghost."

"How do you know what ghosts are capable of?" she asked defiantly.

"Ghosts," Veronica said, "could easily get out of that net. They also don't have stomachs that growl. I'm pretty sure that was your stomach, not mine. If you're anything like me, you *hate* being hungry. You want to join us for breakfast?"

The girl who was not a ghost was silent for a moment, then laughed. Once she began, she did not appear capable of ceasing her laughter. "I admit nothing. But... I wouldn't mind breakfast."

"We have a friend who can see to that," Brixton said. "We can take the bus over to the house."

The girl hesitated. "How do I get out of this net?"

"Um," Brixton said. "V?"

Dorian swore inwardly. He had not explained to the children how to remove the net without damaging it! In truth, he was unaware of how to extricate a person from a tangled net. He should have asked Veronica to look up the information online.

"I'm on it," Veronica said, her phone already in her hand.

Dorian swelled with an emotion not unlike paternal pride. Veronica was growing into such an intelligent young woman. She had been the one to greet him with the most civilized reaction when she learned of his existence, and she continued to show such maturity and intelligence in all of her actions.

"Lift that thingy there," Veronica instructed Brixton. "No, the *edge* thingy."

Well, intelligence in most of her actions.

The girl in the net shrank away as Brixton approached.

"We don't want to hurt you," Veronica said. "But you really freaked out Brixton's mom. We want to know why."

In the confines of the net, the girl froze. "Your mom?"

"Heather Taylor. She saw you at Blue Sky Teas. I'm Brixton. This is Veronica."

"I expect you already know who I am," she said softly.

"Ridley Price." As Veronica spoke the name, a gust of wind swept her dark hair around her face.

Surely the girl could not control the wind, even if she were an alchemist. Dorian knew it must have been a coincidence, but the effect was chilling. Brixton felt it too. He stumbled backward and only barely escaped the gnarled roots of a sycamore tree. Dorian wondered if he was mistaken about her being an alchemist and she was truly a ghost. He did not believe so, yet he did wonder. *Non.* Dorian Robert-Houdin was a rational gargoyle.

"Ridley Price," the girl said, as if the name was foreign on her tongue. "That was once my name."

That was too much for Brixton. He grabbed Veronica's hand and pulled her away from Ridley, yet she twisted her arm and evaded his grasp.

"Her shiny eyes are contact lenses, Brix," said Veronica. "She's flesh and blood. And we promised her breakfast. I'm going to help her with the net."

"Thank you," the girl said. "I don't know why I take corporeal form sometimes, but other times I don't."

Dorian chuckled silently. The alchemist Ridley Price was a good actor. Pretending to be a ghost! It was quite an effective performance.

"I'm sorry I frightened your mother, Brixton," she continued. "That must have been in the old neighborhood teashop." Her voice turned to a whisper and Dorian had to listen carefully to hear her. "I shouldn't have gone. It was too much…too risky. But I wanted everything to be perfect."

"Perfect for what?" Veronica asked as she lifted the net off.

"Trapping my killer."

CHAPTER 24

Roman Price was the one who opened the door of his mother's home for us. His hand was now wound with strips of gauze. An astringent smell hit my nostrils. He must have used iodine to clean his wound.

I felt myself instinctively thinking about another herbal preparation would help the wound as it healed, but reminded myself he was a grown man who was perfectly capable of cleaning his own wound, as he'd done.

"We were worried," Roman said. "Glad to see she didn't run you off the road like she did Nathaniel a few days ago."

"The trees on your street are different than I remembered." Heather pushed me through the door ahead of her. "We made a couple of wrong turns."

"My mother is in the back garden. Let me go get her."

"We'd be happy to join her outside," I said. I always loved seeing other people's gardens. Not only was it usually a more tranquil place to talk, but a garden could tell you a lot about a person. But so could this house. The walls themselves were barely visible. Nearly every inch of space was filled with either bookcases or a unique style of artwork: chemical molecules. An illustration of a chocolate bar showed the chemical bonds that created chocolate. In another framed print, caffeine molecules were drawn as steam rising from a painting of a mug of coffee. The glass coffee table was stacked with books, along with a glass vase that held bright blue forget-me-nots.

"Thanks." Roman led us through the crowded living room toward French doors that opened to the backyard. "She likes it out there. She sits by Ridley's garden."

We found Tess Price sitting on a cushioned wicker chair in a section of the yard filled with flowers. When she looked up, her eyes were red-rimmed. Still, she inspected Heather with the same critical gaze she had at the cemetery.

"Forgot where we lived?"

"Mother, that's hardly necessary." Roman turned from his mother to us. "Coffee?"

"Not for her." Heather pointed her thumb at me. "She'll be bouncing off your walls if she has that much caffeine."

"I'll make tea." As Tess stood, she brushed her fingertips over the stem of a chrysanthemum plant that hadn't yet bloomed. "I've got both herbal and English black tea. Then you can tell me what you know about the person trying to make us think she's my daughter."

"You were one of the people who saw her earlier this week?" I asked.

Tess snapped the stem of the chrysanthemums and swore. "I kept this part of the garden exactly as she created it," she said. "I wanted to honor her memory that way. Whoever is doing this to us knows how much I miss my daughter. They're playing into my weaker, irrational impulses."

"Riddle Garden," I read from the letter painted with green paint on the side of a raised bed of flowers.

"Riddle's Garden," said Tess. "She painted that sign when she created that mix of flowers. She loved plants, especially flowers. She didn't have a violent bone in her body. Shooting that arrow at us was a mistake. There's no way my Riddle would have done that, not in life or in death. Now let me make that tea and you'll tell me what you've seen as well."

Something in the garden pulled me closer. "Do you mind if I look at these flowers another minute before I follow you all inside?"

"Sorry about my friend." Heather gave me an embarrassed glance.

But my awkward request had the opposite effect I'd expected.

"I don't mind at all." Tess gave me what appeared to be a genuine smile. "Make yourself at home in the garden. I'm so pleased it's being enjoyed. Most purists think it's an odd mix, but my Riddle created it, so I love it."

Chrysanthemum, forget-me-nots, oleander, fern, and bittersweet. The periwinkle forget-me-nots, deep purple vining bittersweet, and pink oleander were in bloom, but the chrysanthemums hadn't yet flowered; they were fall-blooming and wouldn't flower for a few months. An old walnut tree with plentiful moss shielded the planter box from direct sunlight. In addition to mulch, beautiful smooth stones were sprinkled throughout the bed. I touched one, wondering if it might have held any alchemical energy. It didn't. It was simply a decorative rock.

Tess was right. There was something odd about this flower garden Ridley had planted. The flowers were a strange assortment. Not just in their appearance, but toxicity. Had her mother really maintained the garden exactly as Ridley had created it? If so, was there an alchemical significance to the flowers? She could have been growing flowers with specific energies. But again, I didn't sense anything special about these flowers. Of course, many years had passed since Ridley's hands had touched the garden bed. These flowers couldn't have been the same ones she'd planted.

It was such a strange—and dangerous—combination of flowers, and a curious spot hidden in the shade. I looked again at the painted sign. *Riddle's Garden*, Tess had said. But the words were actually *Riddle Garden*. I looked more closely to see if something had caused the paint of an "s" to fade. I reached forward, but a voice called out from behind me.

"Water's boiling," Tess called from the kitchen window. "Come pick out which tea you'd like." Had she seen me examining the bed more closely? The oleander wasn't safe to touch without gloves, which she must have known since she'd maintained the flowers safely for years.

When Nicolas was tutoring me in plant alchemy, he had encouraged me to grow a poisoned garden, to learn about the power of plants. Was there something powerful in this mix of plants that I wasn't sensing? Or something Tess didn't want me to see? I pulled myself away from the strange garden bed.

I stepped back into the house through the open French doors, where Heather met me with a basket of individually wrapped packets of tea. I picked out a lightly caffeinated green tea. A bit strong for my usual taste, but this was a strange day.

As Heather disappeared back into the kitchen, I noticed that Roman's book of poetry, HANSEL, had pride of place on the coffee table. Tess might be prickly, but she was a proud mother. I spotted Roman's follow-ups, SNOW and FOREST, on a nearby bookcase. Each of the three volumes was based on a fairy tale theme. When reading up on the family, I'd read that neither of his later collections had been as well-received as HANSEL. I'd read his most famous poem before, but not in years. I cracked the spine and read the lead poem.

HANSEL

Hansel is alone in the forest, Gretel-less.
Perhaps there was a sister once but she wandered off
and was smothered by silence.
That is the first change in the myth.
An abusive father, a dead mother.
He's never been any good at relationships.

Hansel was not led into the forest
and abandoned. He left on his own,
stealing bread and a flask of water,
slipping out of his attic bedroom,
pushing aside spiders and setting the doves cooing,
his feet bare on the dew-slippery weeds.

Hansel was not protecting anyone.
He was not misled. In fact, he was trying
to get lost. He has an inbuilt sense of direction,

*a compass with its point fixed in an arbitrary beginning
while his heart heads out, extending
toward a horizon he imagines.*

*The forest gathers round. He can only
place one foot in front of the other. He scatters
bread crumbs not to find his way back
but to watch them disappear (all those hungry birds)
and for a few seconds he can imagine
what it might be like to be found.*

*Is it important to imagine the forest?
Let it be dark with splotches of light,
the path uneven, which requires him to pay attention.
This not a stroll through a park
but a blundering and stumbling,
much stubbing of toes and stomach grumbling*

*(why did he crumble the bread instead
of eating it? When did he drop his flask? Now
he must drop to the forest floor, suck water
from puddles, let the twigs and spiders
rearrange his errant hair). He can hear breathing
in the darkness now, no longer sure it's his own.*

*Let us say Hansel gets eaten. We could stop
there and draw an easy moral: children, stay home,
do not wander far. Apportion your bread,
use it wisely. Always travel with a companion.
Or we could raise a question: Do stories deserve to end?
Or do they wander off and lurk, ready to begin again?*

"Oh, do put that down." Roman plucked the book from my hands. The words weren't spoken sharply. There was more embarrassment in his voice than anything.

"It's a great poem," I said. "My favorite part is the last two lines: *Do stories deserve to end? Or do they wander off and lurk, ready to begin again?"*

"Youthful exploration."

"Then you're an old soul."

He blushed at the compliment as Tess and Heather each carried two cups of tea out to us. With the tap of a button on his phone, classical music began to play on its speaker. Mendelssohn's A Midsummer Night's Dream. He lowered the volume and set the phone on the coffee table.

Roman frowned at the cup his mother handed him. "I haven't seen these teacups in a while."

"You remember them, though."

Roman's frown deepened. "From Mother's Day the year Ridley died. I joked with her that her gift to you was a hideous puke-green, but she insisted the teacups were a beautiful moss-green."

"These were her last gift to you?" Heather quickly placed the delicate cup on the coffee table.

Tess placed it back in her hands. "If there's one upside of Nathaniel's cruel joke, it's that he's reminded me to spend more time with what Ridley left behind. I don't want these teacups to gather dust on the shelf. I don't care if they break. I need to use them. Drink."

Heather did as instructed.

"You think it was Nathaniel?" I asked. "He couldn't have been the girl."

"But he could have hired an actress," Tess said. "Modern technology makes it easy to find people who look like someone else. That has to have been what he did. I wasn't expecting that arrow, though."

"No," I agreed. "We must have gotten too close to her."

"Which would have ruined the plan, so she had to scare us off."

"No." Heather set her shaking teacup down before she spilled it. "It was *Ridley*. Don't you remember, Zoe? She was so close to us at Blue's—"

"How close?" Roman's face was pale. "I couldn't get close to her this morning. Do you really think it was my sister?" He swallowed hard.

"We didn't get that close to her." I tried to keep my voice calm, even though I wanted to shake Heather's shoulders.

Instead, my eyes were drawn to the beautiful display of forget-me-not flowers on the coffee table. The flowers... What was it about those flowers in the garden?

"Roman," said Tess. "Did you learn nothing by being raised by two scientists? That wasn't a ghost. Your sister's killer hired someone to impersonate her. Nathaniel must be behind it."

"I know you're right. The rational part of my brain knows you're right. But it looked so much like her." Roman stood and began to pace as he spoke. The rapid movement dispersed the scent of the forget-me-nots on the coffee table.

Of course.

The "Riddle Garden" was exactly that. Not "Ridley's Garden," but a garden that was *itself* a riddle. Chrysanthemum, forget-me-nots, oleander, fern, and bittersweet, next to moss.

Ridley had left a message through the secret language of flowers. Flowers have been used for hundreds of years, if not thousands, to convey secret meanings through floriology. I was most familiar with the Victorian Language of Flowers. If I applied that to the flowers Ridley had planted—chrysanthemum, forget-me-nots, oleander, fern, bittersweet, and moss—those flowers spelled out truth, true love, caution, a secret bond of love, truth, and maternal love.

After my visit to Aggie Messenger's farm and what Max and Heather had each told me about Ridley's life and death, the flowers told me the rest of what I needed to know.

I knew who was haunting the people at Ridley's party.

CHAPTER 25

Dorian reached the house before the others. He opted for speed rather than stealth, and thus had one close call in which he was nearly observed. When a strong gust of wind momentarily lifted the hood of his cape, an elderly man glimpsed his face. Luckily, the man simply cleaned the lenses of his glasses with a handkerchief and seemed pleased with the result. People, Dorian had found, saw what their belief systems allowed them to see. Nobody expected to see a formerly stone gargoyle running through the streets of Portland in a Little Red Riding Hood cape.

Upon entering the house, Dorian left the front door unlocked. He'd had a brief moment to tell Brixton as much at the cemetery, when the boy hung back to gather the net as Veronica and Ridley walked ahead.

Now he was preparing a delicious breakfast in the kitchen as he awaited their arrival. They would go directly to the attic, where Dorian could call Brixton's mobile phone from one of the land line phones of the house and speak with all of them.

Yet now, he heard voices approaching from the backyard! Dorian made sure the back door was locked.

"Huh," Brixton said. "I thought Zoe had left this open for us."

"You don't knock when you arrive at your friend's house?" Ridley asked.

In the kitchen, Dorian remained motionless.

"She's probably caught up in making breakfast," Veronica said in a stilted voice. "I told you she must have left the *front* door open for us."

Their voices grew softer. A few moments later, the front door clicked open. Dorian turned off the burners and prepared himself to take stone form in case it was not Veronica or Brixton who stepped through the kitchen door to retrieve their breakfast. But it was only Veronica who pushed through the swinging door.

"Sorry about Brix," she said. "I knew I should have been the one to coordinate with you."

"All is well that ends well, *n'est-ce pas*?"

"*Oui!*" Veronica smiled. "She still insists she's a ghost, but she has to be an alchemist, right? We never talked about how to bring that up with her. I don't want to reveal anything about you or Ms. Faust."

Dorian gathered breakfast items onto a silver platter as he replied. "Ridley desires to speak with someone. She wishes to bare her soul. I do not suspect that this is the only way she can obtain a satisfying *petit-déjeuner. Non*. She wants more than breakfast. She wishes to speak with people who will understand her purpose. Let her speak. See where it leads you." He handed her the platter. "I will call Brixton's mobile phone in one minute."

"Not mine?" She frowned as she accepted the platter.

"I wish you to have your phone available for any necessary research."

She grinned as she departed for the attic.

Dorian wiped down the counters and gathered items to be washed in the deep sink. Precisely one minute later, he lifted the receiver of the kitchen phone and dialed Brixton's mobile phone.

"You're on speaker, Dorian," Brixton said. "We're here with the ghost of Ridley Price, like we talked about."

"I'm pleased to make your acquaintance, Ridley," Dorian said.

"Not only do you have a friend who cooks the best crepes I've ever tasted," Ridley said, "but you also have your own Poirot?"

Dorian beamed. "*Oui, mademoiselle. Exactement.* This is exactly what I am. I am a great detective. An advisor who has solved many mysteries." He wished he could also admit to being the chef who had cooked the crepes she praised, yet he could not admit he was inside the house, or she would surely wish to meet him in person.

THE ALCHEMIST OF RIDDLE AND RUIN

"You can help me find out what really happened?" she asked through a mouthful.

"Perhaps," Dorian said. "But first, you must be honest with us. You must tell us what is truly happening."

"You need to be honest with me first. Why did you shoot an arrow? Was it to scare off everyone I'd invited?"

Veronica gasped. "I knew I heard a scream. You shot an arrow? Did it hit someone?"

"It wasn't me. It only hit a tree, but it ruined my disappearance. I wanted to scare the people I'd invited. Not with anything really dangerous, but by freaking them out. Then you came along—"

"The arrow wasn't us either," Brixton said. "We weren't even inside the cemetery yet."

"Really?" The girl's voice was filled with skepticism.

Dorian hoped it was not simply that she was a talented actor. If someone had indeed shot an arrow in the cemetery, he hoped it was not done by the girl now sitting in his attic with Brixton and Veronica. Ah! But she would not have brought it up if she were the one to have shot it. Unless she thought they were already aware of the arrow... *Bof!* This was a muddle, indeed.

"We know nothing of an arrow," Dorian assured her. "We simply wished to talk with you. We mean you no harm."

There was no answer for quite some time. Perhaps she was enjoying his crepes? Yes, this must have been the case. In spite of his rush, he had created perfect crepes.

"It's really okay," Veronica said. "You can trust him."

"And you can trust us," Brixton added.

"Not helpful, Brix," Veronica said.

"What? You were just telling Ridley she could trust Dorian."

"You can't say it about yourself, though. Geez. It only works when you say it about someone else."

"But if she doesn't know us either," Brixton said, "why does our saying we trust Dorian make it any more believable?"

"Hey," Ridley said. "Do either of you want the last crepe? This chocolate apricot combination is phenomenal."

"All yours," Veronica said.

"You can have the rest of mine too, if you want it," Brixton added.

"Eww," Veronica said. "You've already eaten like half of it."

"So she can have the other half."

Dorian pinched the bridge of his snout. "*Pardon*," he said. "I am glad you are enjoying breakfast, yet may we return to the matter at hand?"

Ridley laughed. "Thanks. I miss laughing with friends. I can see how much you all care about each other. I miss that... I miss so many things."

Dorian gripped the receiver. Had there been another noise in the house? Surely Veronica would have locked the front door. There was no further noise. He must have imagined it.

He considered the advice he had given Veronica. He did think Ridley was eager to speak, even if she would not reveal that she was an alchemist instead of a ghost. But she also wished to connect with others and solve her attempted murder. Should he press her?

"You must have been really hungry," Veronica said.

"This is so much better than the dry granola bars I've been eating. So. Good."

Dorian beamed and puffed up his chest, even though nobody could see him through the receiver.

"So you don't need to eat as a ghost, but you still enjoy food?" Brixton asked through a mouthful.

"She's not a ghost," a new voice said. Zoe! She had returned home. This was the noise he had heard moments before. Now she stepped into the attic.

"This isn't Ridley Price," Zoe said. "She's Ridley's daughter."

CHAPTER 26

"How did you figure out I'm Ridley's daughter?" asked the young woman.

"Zoe is right?" Brixton gaped at her.

"What's your name?" I asked her.

She didn't answer right away. When she did, she rubbed her eyes as she spoke. "Give me just a sec first." She looked up and glanced around the attic. "Don't worry. I'm not running. I just need to do something first." She pointed at the antique folding screen. It added ornamentation to the room rather than being used as a room divider. I hadn't listed it on Elixir's website because it would have been difficult to package and ship. All right. I also admit it's because it's a beautifully carved piece of furniture.

"I'm going behind that thing," the girl said.

"I don't even understand what's happening," Brixton whispered as the girl disappeared behind the screen.

Veronica scowled at him.

"We're about to understand a lot more," I said.

Less than a minute later, the girl emerged. She no longer looked like someone who could be called Ghost Girl. And she no longer looked like Ridley.

Her brown hair was no longer long and flowing, but was pulled into a ponytail at the base of her neck. The flannel shirt she'd worn open and billowing over a T-shirt was now buttoned neatly. She'd removed the contact lenses that made her eyes look like gold. Instead, brown eyes watched us defiantly through thick, tortoise-shell glasses. The frames sat on the bridge of her nose, slightly askew, as if they'd been squashed. Which they probably had been. She didn't appear to have a bag with her. At least not a big one we could see through the baggy shirt.

Her skin was darker, too. She held a tissue with smudges of a light-colored pigment. Foundation to lighten the shade of her skin. The structure of her face looked different as well. As she tilted her face, I spotted what had caused the effect. There were still traces of makeup on the left side of her nose and cheek. She'd used makeup to create contours to make herself look more like Ridley.

"I'm Eve," she said. "Like you said…I'm Ridley's daughter. But *how did you know?*"

"Several things," I said. "Aggie Messenger was a midwife in addition to farmer. Ridley pushed her friends away around the time she would have begun to show being pregnant. And then there were the flowers."

"Flowers?"

"The language of flowers. Coded messages—riddles—written in the symbolism of flowers. I'll show you." I flipped through the books on the shelf of Victorian era trinkets. I knew it was here somewhere.

"Here." I lifted a small, faded booklet from the shelf and handed it to Eve. "This little book decodes the language of flowers. Ridley's garden has chrysanthemum, forget-me-nots, oleander, fern, bittersweet, and moss. Together, they tell the story of a hidden love, caution, maternal love, and truth."

"Whoa," Brixton murmured.

"Isn't that why you used a sprig of rosemary in your hair?" I asked Eve.

She held the booklet in one hand and tugged at a lock of her hair with the other. "Rosemary for remembrance. I know about flowers and plants of all kinds from Aggie. But it doesn't surprise me that

Ridley would use flowers as even more of a riddle. From what I've learned about her, she loved riddles."

"Ms. Faust?" Veronica said softly. "Brix and I have no idea what's going on, but it sounds like you know a lot more?"

I looked from Eve to the bewildered teenagers. "How did you two meet up with Eve?"

"And their friend Dorian," Eve added.

I felt my blood pressure rising, but I kept my voice calm. Well, as calm as I could. "You met Dorian, too?"

"He's, um, on the phone." Brixton pointed at the cell phone resting on a side table next to a haphazard pile of plates that had once contained a sweet-smelling breakfast. The plates were licked so clean I could only guess by smell that it had been chocolate berry crepes.

"Dorian?" Veronica said in the direction of the phone, but there was no answer. "Weird. He must have hung up. Please don't be mad, Ms. Faust. We found her at the cemetery."

"Eve didn't run away from you?" My own ankle was sore from chasing after her at the cemetery. Ever since I'd sprained it badly when running from a killer, it gave me occasional pangs if I didn't stretch it before running.

"Um, does it really matter how we met up?" Brixton eyed something in the corner while he spoke.

I followed his gaze to the antique net used in a Victorian stage magician's show. It was not nearly as neatly folded as it had been before. It must have been Dorian's idea to use it to trap Eve. He'd begun watching episodes of Scooby Doo on my laptop after being compared to the crime-solving talking dog.

"Never mind," I said. "You can tell me about borrowing that net without my permission later."

Brixton's eyes bulged as Veronica scowled at him. "I didn't say—!"

"Eve," I continued, "did you already explain why you're here?"

"I didn't even tell them my name," Eve said with the hint of a smile. "Even after I ate two crepes, they still thought I was a ghost."

"We called Dorian," Brixton added, "so he could convince her we could help."

"It's a strange feeling," Eve said. "There's power in being a ghost. I didn't realize how much I could affect these people. Ridley's family and old friends…I didn't know anything until Mom—my real mom, the woman who raised me, Aggie Messenger—had an accident about a month ago. It was bad. We didn't know if she'd survive, and she didn't in the end. But before she died, she told me the truth about my birth. That's how I know my biological mother was murdered—and how I found out that this whole time, everyone has been wrong about what happened to Ridley."

CHAPTER 27

"You know what really happened?" I asked Eve.

"Some of it." Eve tugged at her ponytail again. "My biological mother, Ridley Price, was almost seventeen when I was born. She was the perfect daughter, so she didn't tell anyone she was pregnant. She threw herself into her studies instead, knowing after I was born, she'd be busy for a while. She found Mom—Aggie Messenger—through an online permaculture discussion group and convinced her to take her on as an apprentice that summer. It was something she usually only did for college students.

"The timing worked out that she could hide her pregnancy under bulky clothing for a while, and then she told Mom—Aggie—when she arrived at her homestead. Ridley knew that Mom was also a midwife, so Ridley knew she was in good hands both to learn and to have someone delivery her baby—me.

"At first, Mom said no to doing all of that in secret, but Ridley swore she'd run away if she told anyone. Mom finally consented— especially since Ridley promised she'd tell her whole family about me once I was born. That was the plan all along.

"A few weeks after I was born, Ridley went home to her parents' house. She planned to make my birth a big, joyful surprise. She was going to reveal it like a riddle, because she loved those. And then

Mom was going to bring me to Portland a day or so later, after Ridley saw how they reacted and if she'd still be welcome at home.

"But she never called Mom. Local police came to the homestead, since Aggie was one of the last people to see Ridley before she went home. By then they knew Ridley was dead, so Mom was scared to death that whoever killed her would also kill me. She pretended I was her own child. She was a really private person, and never wore form-fitting clothes, so even though people were a little surprised when I arrived, they didn't question it. It was just the 'weird plant lady's' way. That's how they thought of her, so it allowed her to keep me. And keep me safe."

"She never told you?" Brixton asked.

Eve shook her head. "When I was old enough to ask why it was just the two of us instead of bigger families like my friends, she told me there was someone who loved me more than the sun and the moon and every single plant and organism in our little homestead, but they'd died. But it *wasn't* just the two of us. I felt Ridley's presence without realizing it. Whenever I worked with Mom in the garden, I could feel the love of someone absent. Mom said it was the time they put into it with their hands many years before."

I understood the feeling. For most of the years of my life, it was plants that gave me the most love. I suppose that might sound sad, but it's not. Being connected to the world through nature is a magical feeling. It's even more magical when there are people to share it with.

"I assumed Mom meant a dad who'd died," Eve continued, "but I only learned this spring that she meant Ridley and the summer she spent on the farm. I never knew until…" She wiped a tear from her cheek.

"The farming accident," I whispered.

She nodded. "Mom was helping a friend on her farm, and there was an accident with the tractor. Her internal injuries were bad, but she was stable enough to convince the doctors to let her come home from the hospital. She never thought she was okay, though. She could feel she was dying. But she wanted to do something more important. She gathered everything together about Ridley and the people questioned about her murder. She'd always planned on telling me one day when I was old enough, and she also had the information in an envelope to be given to me upon her death if she died unexpectedly. But now, she had a chance to tell me herself, just not on the timeline she'd hoped."

"Aggie Messenger kidnapped you," Veronica said.

Eve scowled. "She kept me safe. She gave me a loving home and the best childhood anyone could ask for. She was my Mom. Ridley loved me, but Mom said Ridley was already scared of what would happen if people knew about me. Mom never thought someone would kill Ridley, or she wouldn't have let her go. But she let her go. And Ridley never came back. The police handled the investigation really badly, so they never arrested the person who killed her. Mom wasn't going to let her killer get to me."

Eve fell silent.

"After your mom died this spring," I began gently, "you wanted to find out what really happened to Ridley when you were a baby."

"I was sure it was Nathaniel Gallo—my biological father—so I came up with a plan to prove it. From everything I could find, people knew he did it, but just couldn't prove it. I thought since everyone else had stopped trying to solve Ridley's murder, but it was brand new to me, that maybe I could solve it. I was so angry and hurt and confused… And I had a whole summer with nothing to do before the new school year started. I knew I had to do something.

"Mom left the farm to me in her will, but I'm only sixteen. There's no other family. She ran away from her own bad situation when she was around my age, so it was always just us. The plan Mom worked out was for me to finish my last two years of high school living with the elderly couple who live nearby, who already treat me like I'm their grandchild. I told them I was staying with distant relatives this summer and would be back before the school year started. That gave me a couple of months to prove it. Even though Mom told me how everyone was convinced Nathaniel Gallo killed her but the police messed up the investigation, she also taught me to be openminded."

"That's why you were 'haunting' everyone," I said.

She nodded. "Like I already told Brix and Veronica, I've been busy since I got here."

"Don't you think shooting an arrow was going too far?"

"What? No!"

"I know you didn't mean to hurt anyone. You intentionally shot the arrow too high, so it would just scare—"

"No," Eve said again. More calmly this time, but even more firmly. "I meant that the arrow *wasn't me*. One of the people I invited must not have wanted my plan to work. I invited everyone who was at the party. I wanted to get close enough to all of them, in my disguise, so everyone would all think I was Ridley. I found a perfect place in that wooded cemetery where it would look like I disappeared like a ghost—an ancient tree with an opening in its trunk. I even prepared a piece of brown fabric ahead of time, so I could hide there invisibly if anyone walked by after I vanished. But I had to get you all to Ridley's grave for it to work. I *wanted* people to follow me and think I was a ghost—I thought it would scare people so I could continue to act as the ghost while I investigated. I had zero reason to shoot an arrow. That totally messed up my plan."

"You didn't see who could have done it?" I asked.

She shook her head. "I only heard Brix's mom scream. The reason I was haunting people in the first place wasn't just to spook them, but to get into their houses without them calling the police, since they would think I was a ghost and not a thief. It didn't work. And they didn't all show up this morning, even though I left notes for everyone. Ask your friends. I didn't have a bow with me when they caught me."

"She didn't," Brixton confirmed.

"So…who shot the arrow?" Veronica asked.

None of us had an answer. I was inclined to believe Eve. Which was unfortunate, because it meant someone out there was dangerous—and we had no idea who it was.

"We need to get the authorities involved," I said. "There's a dangerous—"

"They messed up the first investigation so badly that there was even an internal investigation about the mishandling of evidence. They haven't caught Ridley's killer the entire time I've been alive. What makes you think I can trust them to do better now?"

"There's more information now," I said. "You."

"Shouldn't they have figured that out sixteen years ago?" Veronica asked. "I mean, a baby's kind of a big deal."

"If local police interviewed Aggie and she had an alibi," I said, "why would they question that her baby wasn't hers? Nobody thought there was a missing baby."

"And if Eve is exposed," Brixton added, "she could be in even more danger, right?"

"I can take care of myself." Eve took a few quick steps toward the attic door. "I don't have to stay here with all of you. I don't—"

"I won't call the police," I said. "I promise." I didn't promise I wouldn't call Max. It was a deceitful parsing of words, but I was the adult in this situation. I had to think of Eve's safety. Of keeping all of them safe. But I believed Eve was telling the truth when she said she'd run away if she felt backed into a corner. And Heather had also mentioned the mishandling of the case.

"You swear it wasn't you who shot the arrow?" Veronica asked.

"That arrow ruined my plans."

"Your plans to scare people? Like how you scared Nathaniel and he broke his arm?"

"I didn't mean for him to crash." Eve didn't meet Veronica's gaze. "I didn't know he was leaving. My idea was to dress up like Ridley and go into the bushes by the windows of his house, to have him come outside and chase me, so I could circle back and get into his house. I thought I'd steal his keys and then break in when he wasn't home. But because he passed out when he swerved, I stole the keys then."

"Didn't you care that he was injured?" Veronica asked.

Eve glared at her. "I thought he was a murderer. But I'm not a killer. I could tell he was fine. I know first aid from growing up pretty isolated. I checked his vitals when I took his keys." Her expression softened and her bottom lip quivered. "That's how I learned everyone was wrong about who killed my biological mother. Zoe is right. We have more information now. I have evidence that Nathaniel Gallo didn't kill Ridley Price."

CHAPTER 28

Dorian watched the discussion unfolding from a slit in the attic door. When Zoe arrived home, he had hung up the receiver and followed her up the attic stairs. Zoe had left the crooked attic door ajar, as that was the door's natural state, giving him the perfect vantage point.

"How do you know Nathaniel is innocent?" Zoe asked the girl who was not actually Ghost Girl.

"There's a locked room in his house," Eve said.

Veronica gasped. "We know. Do you know what was in there?"

"I do."

"You got in?"

"It wasn't what I expected." She shook her head and laughed. It was a strange laugh, though. Neither happy nor sad. *Confused.* She ripped the tissue clenched in her hand, then appeared surprised as a mess of tissue fragments floated to the floor. Everything about the poor creature was confused.

"What was inside?" Brixton whispered, transfixed by the girl.

"Nothing about Nathaniel Gallo was what I expected," the girl whispered back. Dorian worried he would be unable to hear the rest of what Eve said, but fortunately, she regained her normal volume and timbre when she continued.

"All the stuff Mom told me Ridley loved..." Eve paused. "His house was filled with it too. And in that locked room, he'd created a lifetime's worth of research into Ridley's murder. He's been looking for Ridley's killer for sixteen years."

The words hung in the air.

"Why would he do that if he killed her?" Brixton asked.

"He wouldn't," Veronica said. "That's what she means. That leaves six suspects. Six people besides Mr. Gallo who were at the house that day. One of them killed Eve's mom."

"I don't think of Ridley as my mom," Eve said. "Aggie is Mom to me. The best mom anyone could have. Ridley was a kid with a lot of potential and her whole life ahead of her. She loved me and she gave me life. I want to learn more about her and find out what really happened to her."

Zoe looked as if she wished to speak, but she held her tongue. Why was she being so cautious? This was unlike her. No, that was not strictly true. She was cautious when it came to acting upon Dorian's brilliantly crafted plans to catch marauders and other miscreants. Yet she was not generally cautious when it came to speaking her mind.

"Where are you staying?" Zoe asked gently.

Ah! This explained her caution. Sixteen was considered "under age." If Dorian Robert-Houdin were appointed as a head of government, he would make a distinction between children and near-adults. Older adults did not give enough credit to those in their teens, yet they were far more capable than many so-called adults. And far better people than many adults. He stole a glance at the portrait of Edward Kelley that hung on the attic wall. For a time, he had kept the painting facing the wall, lest Dorian be reminded of the con man who had nearly killed people close to Zoe, but he had decided it best to monitor the devilish man.

"I'm fine," Eve snapped. "You don't need to worry. Mom taught me to be self-reliant. I could survive in the woods on my own if I had to."

Did the girl mean to imply she was sleeping in the woods? Dorian did not believe this to be the case. Neither her appearance nor her scent indicated she had not bathed.

"You understand." Eve looked at Zoe as she spoke. Her expression was not one of anger now, but of shared understanding. "We came through your garden when we first tried to come inside by the back door. Brix told me you're a plant whisperer. Like Mom. She taught me a lot of what she knew, but I'm not as good as you two."

Dorian observed Veronica bristle as Eve used Brixton's nickname once more.

"It takes time to learn all of their secrets," Zoe said. Again, her voice was far gentler than usual. She did not wish to spook the girl, he imagined. "You have your whole life ahead of you to learn, if you want to. That's why we want you to be safe. Like you said, there's a killer—"

"Do you need somewhere to stay?" Brixton cut in.

Dorian shifted his gaze from Eve and Zoe to the boy. His cheeks were red. Veronica noticed this as well, and frowned at him.

"It doesn't matter where I stay!" Eve leapt up, causing Dorian to jump backwards, fearing she would run toward the exit of the attic. Yet she did not. She simply stood with her fists clenched. "What matters is that I get back inside Nathaniel Gallo's house to get the information he's gathered."

"The police—" Zoe began.

"You don't understand." Eve shook her head furiously. "It's evidence, but it's not *evidence*. It's more creative than that. It's a riddle."

"A riddle?" Veronica asked.

"Mom told me he and Ridley loved games. He's a board game designer now. That's how he's researching what happened to Ridley."

"Through a board game?" Brixton stared at her.

"He's the inventor of that board game Crimson Fish. It has eight characters. Miss Fisher, the flirt. Colonel Carp, an army guy. Professor Blowfish, a longwinded professor. Mr. Octopus, a thief—that's why he has so many arms. Dr. Dover, who sees into souls—a pun for Dover Sole. Sir Seaweed, who goes with the flow. And Ms. Mackerel, the suspicious fish who hides in the seaweed and judges the others. That makes seven, and the eighth character is the missing crimson fish."

Dorian could not fathom why the girl was relaying the board game details. His heart went out to this poor creature who had suffered so much loss. She was truly confused. He hoped Zoe would find her a good home. But also that it would not be *his* home. For he knew Zoe would not approve of him showing his true visage to the girl.

"They're the seven suspects in Ridley's death," Zoe said.

Eve nodded. "Exactly. The seven suspects *each corresponded to one of the Crimson Fish characters*. That's how Nathaniel's mind works. He created this popular mystery board game to work out all the possibilities for how one of the seven characters could have killed Ridley."

CHAPTER 29

Eve's bent glasses slipped down her nose as she pulled a cell phone out of a slim fanny pack she was wearing under her flannel shirt. She held up a photograph of the walls of Nathaniel Gallo's locked workshop.

I needed to figure out what to do with Eve. As long as she was talking, she wasn't running. And I had no doubt that if we pushed her too hard, she would flee. She was both grieving and on a mission. Eve was a minor, but an accomplished one.

"He had the whole board game worked out in that locked room of his." Eve pointed at a photo of a wall with photos of the suspects next to colorful illustrations of the characters in his game. "Ridley's childhood friend Amber is this pink fish with long eyelashes, Miss Fisher. Her other old friend Emilio, who joined the army after high school, is the sand-colored Colonel Carp. Her brother, who was getting a Master of Fine Art and became a professor, is this purple pufferfish, Professor Blowfish. Light blue Doctor Dover is Ridley's friend Joona. She went by June in high school because people couldn't remember her Korean name. That's messed up, right?"

"Totally messed up," Veronica agreed. I was glad she'd stopped scowling at Eve.

"Green Sir Seaweed, who goes with the flow, was Ridley's dad, Mr. Price. He died not long after she did, but he's still a suspect. And charcoal gray Ms. Mackerel is the suspicious fish who hides in the seaweed and judges the others—Ridley's mom, Mrs. Price."

"Looks like Nathaniel didn't like Mrs. Price," Brixton commented. "My mom didn't either."

"There are two more characters," I said.

"Right," Eve said. "I haven't gotten to Nathaniel himself. The character that's kinda like the Wizard of Oz. He's pulling the strings. But he's also honest about his past. Mr. Octopus, a rainbow-tentacled thief with many arms. Nathaniel's parents went to jail for theft before he was born. That's why Ridley's parents didn't like him. Or at least that's what he thinks."

"That's seven." Veronica pointed at Eve's phone but didn't try to take it from her. "Is there more on the wall we can't see in that photo? I've played the game. I remember there being an eighth character."

"You're right." Eve tucked the phone away. "The eighth character is the missing crimson fish."

"Ridley herself," Veronica whispered.

"I've looked up everything about the game since I found that room at his house two nights ago," Eve said. "Nathaniel's name isn't listed anywhere on the game. Most people don't know he created it, so nobody spotted the parallels. Ridley was already out of the news by the time the game came out, so nobody was looking."

I thought about what Max had told me about the investigation. The detective had indeed made the connection and been on the right track, but hadn't quite reached the right conclusion about why Nathaniel had created the game.

"Why didn't he talk about his motivation for the game publicly?" I wondered aloud. "If the purpose of the game was to find Ridley's killer, wouldn't he want people to weigh in?"

"That's the weird thing," Eve said. "I think he kinda did. He didn't want weirdos giving false leads. But he did know the gaming world, and how people talk about game characters. So even though I think he created the game as a way to work through his ideas about these people without seeing their faces all the time, I wonder if he also thought people might see connections between the characters that he didn't see. Because a lot of the clues are related to activities the real-life people were involved in."

"Like a satellite view of the crime," Veronica said.

"Exactly." Eve gripped Veronica's hand.

"Um, okay." Brixton looked confused.

"The setup of the game isn't exactly what happened," I pointed out. I pulled a notepad and archival ink pen from the desk and began to scribble.

"You're right," Eve agreed. "But it's close. The Crimson Fish is missing, which is what happened that day. Even though there was blood…" Eve closed her eyes and breathed deeply.

"I'm sorry," Veronica whispered. "You don't have to tell us more."

Eve smiled at her. "Thanks. It's weird. I never knew Ridley, and of course I can't remember my first month on earth, but I know how much she loved me. I want to find out what happened to her."

"I'm in," said Veronica.

"Me too," Brixton added a bit too loudly.

"Hold on." In spite of my curiosity, I had to be the voice of reason. "We're helping by finding Eve a safe place to stay and giving the police this missing information."

"But Ms. Faust," Veronica said, "we can give them even better information if we think through Crimson Fish like Nathaniel Gallo did. Since Eve has information nobody else does—"

"I know." I held up the notebook I'd been scribbling in. I had drawn a table with each suspect in Ridley's death and their corresponding Crimson Fish board character.

THE ALCHEMIST OF RIDDLE AND RUIN

SUSPECTS	PARALLEL GAME CHARACTERS	ROLE
Ridley "Riddle" Price	Crimson Fish	Victim
Nathaniel Gallo (boyfriend)	Mr. Octopus	Thief
Amber Cook (old friend)	Miss Fisher	Friendly flirt
Emilio Acosta (old friend)	Colonel Carp	Army man
Roman Price (Ridley's brother)	Professor Blowfish	Professor
Joona Kim (new friend)	Dr. Dover	Observant friend
John Price (Ridley's dad)	Sir Seaweed	Goes with the flow
Tess Price (Ridley's mom)	Ms. Mackerel	Suspicious of everyone

Eve nodded appreciatively. "That's much easier to follow than the stuff on Nathaniel's wall."

"I know far less than he does. We can start simple."

"You've all played?" Eve asked.

We all nodded, but Brixton was also frowning. "I don't remember the game being a murder mystery. I played it when I was younger, and I thought the fish was missing, not dead."

"That's one of the genius elements of the game," I said. "I remember this from when I played it with young kids. It can be a fun game with little ones, with the colorful characters and the idea that a red fish is hiding. But for adults, crimson takes another association, and when the winner 'finds' the fish, it never says explicitly whether the fish is dead or was just hiding."

"Whoa," Veronica murmured.

"Until this week," said Eve, "I never knew how many layers of the game existed. Since you've all played, you know there are 21 theories about what happened to the missing fish. Three versions for each of the seven characters—just like all the people on Nathaniel's wall. All the people who were there that day. In each game, the players figure out where the fish is really hidden and who's the guilty fish who lured them there somehow."

"But it's not a role-playing game," I pointed out. "It's a board game with only a set number of possible explanations. One of the seven characters is guilty, so the fish is taken with a different ruse to a different location. It's a bunch of potential combinations—like Colonel Carp giving a treasure map to the fish so she'd explore the underwater cave, or Professor Blowfish giving the fish a pile of entertaining books so the fish would stay too long hidden behind a school of fish."

"But people have made up a lot more stories beyond the board." Eve took the notepad table from my hand. "Fan fiction. I looked into it the last two days. There are so many fictional stories with these cartoon characters that people post online."

"Crowdsourcing the answer to the crime without anyone realizing they were doing it," Veronica said. "It's really clever."

"If that's what he meant to do," I said. "Eve, you haven't talked to him, right?"

"I'm not ready to do that. I don't want Nathaniel to know I'm Ridley's daughter. That I'm *his* daught—No! I can't." She flung the notebook back into my hands and began pacing. "Not yet. I just can't!"

"It's all right," I said. "We'll figure this out. Let's first make sure the couple you're supposed to be staying with knows you're safe."

"I've been texting them. They know I'm fine. Like I already told you, they think I'm staying with extended family."

"But they don't know where you are right now."

Eve didn't answer me right away. "I *want* your help," she said slowly. "But I don't *need* it." Color rose in her cheeks. I knew if I pushed too hard, we'd lose her. But I didn't want her out there on her own. One of the people at that party sixteen years ago was a killer.

"Does anyone else know what you're doing? Any friends?"

She looked at the floor and shook her head. Without the contact lenses and fake posturing, she looked so much like the grieving and confused sixteen-year-old she was.

"Let me help you," I said.

"Let *us* help," Brixton added.

"Yeah," Veronica added, her voice every bit as enthusiastic as Brixton's.

Eve looked up and smiled at us. "Really? You'll all help me?" Her smile fell away as the attic door creaked.

"It's nothing." I hurried to the door. "Old house. This door moves on its own when people are in here moving the floorboards."

Dorian grimaced at me from the slit in the door. I should have known he'd be lurking about. I was glad he at least had the sense to hide.

"Yup," I said. "Just the creaking of the old house." I faced the teenagers' expectant faces looking up at me from the midst of the historical objects I'd collected over the centuries, long before they were antiques. Some things change over time, but many more stay the same. Like the desire for justice and closure.

"I'll help," I said. "But only if we do it safely. Eve, we're finding you a safe place to stay—no objections. Veronica, your dad works from home, right? Good. You and Brixton can do some armchair detecting from your living room." The Chen-Mendoza household was much stricter, so I knew Veronica's dad would keep an eye on them.

"But—" Brixton began.

"My condition for not going to the police this second is that you do what I say to stay safe. Someone shot an arrow, remember? Since it wasn't Eve—"

"It wasn't," she insisted.

"I know," I assured her. "But that's worse. We don't know who to worry about. We do this my way or not at all."

Eve adjusted her glasses. "You said what Veronica and Brix would be doing. What does that mean for me?"

"Our friend Blue, the woman who runs Blue Sky Teas—the café you haunted yesterday morning—has an extra room and loves visitors. I'm sure she'd love to have you. You'll also love her yard of wildflowers, so you'll be able to occupy yourself there this afternoon." Blue understood far better than most the need for a woman to get away from a bad situation in secrecy.

"What about you, Zoe?" Veronica asked.

I was startled not by the question, but by the fact that Veronica had finally used my given name. She'd always called me Ms. Faust, in spite of my insistence that it was fine to call me Zoe.

"After we get all of you safe, I know where to start."

CHAPTER 30

"I'm not giving interviews." Nathaniel Gallo cracked his front door open only two inches. The security chain cut across his nose, but even with the obstruction, his resemblance to Eve was striking. His thick head of chestnut hair with glints of copper would have been his most eye-catching feature if not for his oversize eyes and perfectly round glasses that made him rather resemble one of the characters in his board game.

Though I already knew he was Eve's father, standing here in front of him gave me pause. This wasn't a game. Someone had killed the young woman he loved and altered the course of so many lives.

"I was originally planning on making something up so you'd talk with me," I said, "but I'm no good at lying. I'm a good friend of Heather Taylor. She and I saw what she believed to be the ghost of Ridley Price this week. Heather hasn't been able to sleep since. I'm here to help her find out what's really going on."

Before dropping Eve at Blue's, I had taken her to meet Heather. After quite some time spent on hugs and Heather telling Eve all about Ridley, Heather had made the correct statement that there was no way Nathaniel Gallo could look at Eve and not know exactly who she was. I was glad Eve wasn't ready to meet him. I wanted to be the one to talk with him first.

"Sorry, I can't help." Nathaniel pushed the door closed.

"Is it true you created Crimson Fish to crowdsource finding answers?" I called through the door.

The door swung open. Fully, this time. His eyes bulged nearly as large as the crimson fish on his board game's cover. After the impulsive gesture, he hesitated. "I'm not sure if you want to come inside the house of someone accused of murder, or if I should come outside."

"You've been searching for her killer for sixteen years. I know you didn't kill her. I'd like to see your research."

With his hand gripping the door frame, he hesitated once more. "How do you know what I've been doing?"

"I know about the room." No need to tell him about Eve. He was a man with a guilty conscience, so I'd let him think whatever he wanted to. His mind would fill in whatever made sense to him. Not that the daughter he never knew he had was pretending to be her mother and had broken into his house.

He pinched the bridge of his nose with his hand that wasn't in a cast. "Nancy Drew...I wondered if using my bathroom was a ruse, but I didn't know she'd gotten into—"

"What? You saw a girl get into your house?"

"Of course. I let her in. She and her friend came to talk to me yesterday. Isn't that who you—?"

"Yes, of course," I blurted out. "It's just been a stressful couple of days." Brixton and Veronica hadn't told me just how much they'd already been investigating. I hadn't yet insisted they limit their activities to armchair detecting, so I couldn't be angry with them. Only with Dorian. I was certain he was the instigator.

"I understand about the stressful couple of days." Nathaniel held up his cast. "What's your name?"

"Zoe Faust." I handed him a business card from Elixir. Brixton and Veronica thought I was old-fashioned to have physical cards, but they regularly came in handy. I used a local letterpress business to print short runs of them, and I was going to need a new order soon.

He ran his fingers over the embossed letters on the thick, textured paper, and half a smile appeared on his lips. "You want to come inside, Zoe Faust? Or would you feel more comfortable staying outside with a supposed murderer?"

"I don't believe you killed her." It was a risk. A big one. I knew that. If murderers were obvious from their appearance, they'd be a lot easier to catch.

"Because of the game?"

"Because you didn't make a publicity stunt about making the game. It's not easy to find out you're the creator."

He tucked my card into his pocket before nodding and ushering me through the door.

Inside the house, Nathaniel Gallo appeared to be having a pity party, as Brixton and Veronica would say. A half-empty box of pizza sat open on a messy coffee table next to the sludgy remnants of a cup of coffee and an empty can of soda on its side. The brown corduroy couch sagged in only one spot, as if only one person used it. Dozens of boardgames were crammed into a particleboard bookcase, with more stacked haphazardly on the carpet. In a brief glance I saw Risk, Wit's End, several Sherlock Holmes-inspired games, and multiple versions of Clue, including the British version, Cluedo, and several editions based on television shows and movies.

Nathaniel led me through the sad living room and into the hallway. Framed photos of Ridley filled the wall at the end of a hallway, above a bouquet of fresh daisies in a glass vase resting on a wrought iron end table with ornate legs of curlicues. It wasn't quite the shrine Veronica had described, but Nathaniel hadn't gotten over his first love.

"You're not old enough to be Veronica's mom," he said as he unlocked a door next to the flowers. "You employ teenage detectives?"

"Of course not. I live in the neighborhood where you, Ridley, and Heather grew up. That's how I met Heather."

"So Heather was the one who sent her son to see me yesterday?"

"You remember what it was like to be that age. They came here on their own." Or, I suspected, at Dorian's prompting. "Heather didn't know he came here either. She knows I'm here, though. It's too painful for her to get involved, but she's desperate for answers. I know you are too."

Nathaniel pushed open the door and flipped on a light. The locked room Veronica had noticed and Eve had gotten inside.

Eve's photos hadn't done it justice. Corkboards covered two walls, a giant whiteboard blocked the only window in the room, and built-in bookshelves lined the wall next to the door. A rickety table was barely visible beneath a stack of books and loose papers. On the corner of the table, a printer sat on top of an ornate sandalwood box. Every inch of the room was filled with fleeting scraps of information that might tell him what had become of Ridley. But that box…. It struck me as the most personal of all the items.

The whiteboard had a table similar to the one I'd drawn, but with additional columns that listed additional notes about each of the people who'd been there the night Ridley was killed. And illustrations. Unlike Heather's realistic sketches, cartoon figures adorned Nathaniel's room. The whimsical figures were almost enough to brighten the room. I gravitated toward the largest illustration, one with a giant cartoon octopus. Behind the central octopus, a second octopi's suction-cupped arms were wrapped around a classic car, and two others were attempting to tug the car free. Nathaniel wasn't only the game's creator. He was the illustrator. The cartoon faces on the octopi showed just as much personality as Heather's life-like sketches, just in a different medium. Nathaniel followed my gaze to the family of octopi.

"Mr. Octopus," he said. "That's me. Me and my family of thieves."

"All the characters are based on characteristics of the real-life people they parallel?" I knew this to be the case from Heather, but I wanted to hear his answer.

"You're wondering about me?" He attempted a smile. "I liked the dual purpose of the octopus. With his eight arms, the octopus can pull the strings of the other characters, like I was doing creating the game. But the octopus also has many sticky fingers, like my dad—the octopus holding onto that classic car. He was good at stealing cars. Really good." Nathaniel shrugged. "He stopped before I was born. Or so my mom thought. He was in prison during my kindergarten graduation and my older brother's elementary school graduation, so that's what got to him. He's been a model citizen ever since. He's even one of those people who gives talks at high schools so kids won't follow his example. Until Ridley died, I thought *that* was the worst thing about high school."

"I'm sorry." I really was. He had been the same age I was when my life fell apart. But at least I had my brother and then the Flamels to help me. It didn't look like Nathaniel had anyone.

My eyes fell to a word circled in red. "Diaries," I read aloud.

"Her diaries were stolen. All of them. I wish I had them, just to have that piece of her—or maybe I don't."

"She had secrets she was holding over people?"

"She wasn't like that." His expression darkened. "She wouldn't blackmail anyone. I just meant it would be something to remember her by."

"I didn't mean blackmail. She was young. It would have been a puzzle to her, right?"

He shrugged. "I've gone over this so many times, I can't see straight anymore. I didn't know who to trust. Everyone besides her killer thought I did it, and I knew one of them was a murderer. The police believe in my guilt as well. And my relationships of any kind, whenever they started to get serious, ended when my obsession came to light. I learned to stop telling people…"

"But that also means you locked part of yourself away."

Nathaniel looked up at me and studied my face. "You've lost someone."

"More than one. I'd like to say it gets better, and it really does in so many ways. But it's never *fine*. It's never the way it was. And that's okay. Because it means you truly loved."

For a moment, it looked like he was about to either laugh or cry. He shook himself. "Sorry. Can I get you a coffee? Glass of water?"

"Tea, if it's not too much trouble."

"Afraid I've run out of black tea. I've only got herbals."

"That's perfect."

I should have requested coffee. Not that I could drink it. Even a few sips of coffee would have sent me climbing up the walls. But since I didn't smell any brewed coffee, it would have taken him longer to make—giving me more time to explore. At least boiling water for tea would take slightly longer than pouring a glass of water.

As soon as Nathaniel slipped out of the room, I went straight to the printer. Everything in this room was open—except for the sandalwood box with the printer on top. After glancing over my shoulder, I lifted the printer off the box. It wasn't locked, as I'd feared it might be. I lifted the lid, and my senses went haywire.

Bundles of dried flowers filled the box. Red tulips. Wild roses. Yarrow. The scent of the roses was most prominent. I hurriedly closed the lid and put the printer back. I hoped it was only my sensitivity to scents that made the fragrances so strong. I didn't want Nathaniel to realize I'd been snooping. If he didn't smell—

"What are you doing?"

CHAPTER 31

Nathaniel rushed to the table with the sandalwood box, sloshing tea onto the carpeted floor as he did so.

"Sorry if the scent of my hand cream is strong." I held up a small tin I kept in my purse. "I garden, and I use some flower essences, like roses—"

"No, it's fine. It just reminded me of something from Ridley." He stole a glance at the box I'd put back, then frowned at the mug of chamomile and lavender tea. "Half a cup of tea? Afraid the carpet got the rest."

I accepted the warm, half-empty mug. "I didn't mean to distress you."

"It's fine. You're here to talk about Ridley. I'm just not used to talking to other people about her. But since you're friends with Heather, and you use Miguel's letterpress shop—"

"That's when you decided to trust me? When I showed you my business card?"

He shrugged. "I don't get out much, so most of my social interactions are with the local businesses I frequent. My ten-year-old nephew says I'm a hot mess."

I couldn't stop myself from laughing. Nathaniel Gallo was definitely a hot mess.

He joined in, and with that, the ice was officially broken. I was glad for it, since the tea was atrocious and I wasn't going to drink more than necessary to be polite. How did someone get it so wrong when using a pre-packaged tea bag?

"You're a talented artist," I said.

"I know the game isn't real, but it helps me focus. I didn't make the game to get help from other people, not at first. But when I put their stories into the game, I did wonder if anyone would see connections I missed. I was there that day and I have no idea how I missed something! I loved her. I didn't care that she'd broken up with me. I knew we were too young to not go off and see more of the world first. But I always thought we'd end up together later… Only there was no later."

"Besides the octopus—you—and the crimson fish—Ridley—these are the other six people who were there that day?"

He nodded. "Colonel Carp: Emilio Acosta, who always tried to steal Ridley from me. He was in the army for a decade and now works private security.

"Miss Fisher: Amber Cook. She and Emilio were childhood friends of Ridley, before I met the rest of them. She was jealous of Emilio's interest in Ridley as they got older, but I didn't take that too seriously because she was a flirt, so she was just jealous whenever anyone got more attention than her.

"Professor Blowfish: Ridley's brother Roman Price. He was in an MFA program when Ridley died, and became a lit professor.

"Sir Seaweed: Ridley's easygoing chemistry professor dad, John Price. He was there that day but died not long after she did. He died of a broken heart, so I doubt he killed her. Unless I'm wrong and it was guilt.

"Ms. Mackerel: Ridley's widowed mom, Tess Price. She was so judgey. She was a serious scientist, and none of us were good enough for her daughter. So the Mackerel fish is the snooty-looking one, hiding in the seaweed to watch the others.

"Doctor Dover: Joona Park, the girl who saw everything in high school. All the reviews say that's the fish with the least amount of character. Because I didn't ever get to know her well. Ridley was the one she was close to.

"That's the short version. For the longer version, you'd need to be here all night, which I doubt you'd appreciate. I appreciate you trying to help Heather, but I've been working on this for so long already. Nobody has figured out what happened."

"But something changed."

"I was thinking about why she came back. Her diaries were never found. Maybe that's why she came back as a ghost."

I stopped myself from blurting out Eve's secret. It wasn't mine to tell. "I don't believe it was a ghost," I said instead. "I believe someone was disguising themselves as Ridley—"

"Roman?"

"Her brother?" *That* answer, I wasn't expecting. I should have, though, from Heather's sketch of him. Here in Nathaniel's wall of real photos, though, Roman Price couldn't be confused for his sister.

"Roman looked a lot like her. People often mixed them up when they were little kids, before he had a growth spirt. He *hated* that."

"You really think it could have been him you saw?" I knew the answer was something else, but this was still an interesting development. Could their similarities have been why she was killed? Mistaken identity? No, they couldn't have looked *that much* alike. Heather said he was over six feet tall.

He hesitated. "No. Not after all these years. If he could have turned back time by 20 years, maybe. If he could have disguised his height. But not now. You're right. It had to have been a woman who got a mask made—technology can do that now." Nathaniel's face fell. "Part of me hoped it was her. That's why I must have believed it. Because I wanted to."

"She ran you off the road."

"Not on purpose." He winced. "I mean, if it was Ridley's ghost, she'd never do that on purpose. But if it's a person in a mask?" He shrugged. "You're right. That makes a lot more sense. They all think I did it. But I keep wondering *why now*? I should have gone."

"Wait. I thought Heather was the only one who didn't go to the party."

He shook his head. "I'm talking about this morning. I got a note yesterday. Or at least I thought I might have."

"Asking you to meet at the cemetery?"

Nathaniel's body jerked, causing his broken arm to knock into the table. He winced. "How did you—?"

"Heather got a note."

"She went? Was it Ridley?"

I considered the question. "I went with Heather. It wasn't Ridley. It was a trick."

"I didn't know if I'd imagined the note. It was so windy yesterday. Do you remember? Someone left a bouquet of flowers at my door. A note on faux-aged paper was tied to it with twine. I read it before it blew away in a strong gust of wind. I searched for it, but never found it, so I convinced myself I'd imagined it. I'd barely slept at all. But that means *someone* wanted us all there."

I was considering what I could tell him when we were interrupted by a knock at the door.

"I'll be right back." Nathaniel scratched the edge of his cast as he slunk out of the room.

I turned to the bookshelf, which I hadn't yet explored. Below dozens of thrillers, a shelf dedicated to puzzles, codes, and mazes. I spotted Roman Price's first book of poetry, *Hansel*, amongst the books on puzzles. The dog-eared thrillers weren't so different. The titles I recognized featured codes, many of them with the word *even* in the title. He wasn't lying about loving riddles like Ridley.

I tapped my fingers on the top of each of the books as I moved my hand across the shelves, searching for any that were hollowed out. When I reached the last book, I had a paper cut to show for it, but no secret hiding spots. Nathaniel Gallo was looking more and more like who he appeared to be. A guy grieving after the woman he loved was stolen from him. He should have moved on, but I was no one to judge. It had taken me far too long to learn to live again after Ambrose died.

"Zoe?" Nathaniel's voice called.

I found my way back to the living room and found Nathaniel wasn't alone. Two police officers stood in the living room.

"She's the only other person here," Nathaniel said. "Now will you tell me what this is about?" He spoke the words in the resigned voice of a man who had been questioned by the police many times.

I was wary too. It wasn't a solo officer standing before us, but two of them, both on high alert.

Instead of answering him, one of the officers turned to me. She took down my name and asked, "How long have you been here with Mr. Gallo?"

"Around an hour. What's going on?"

"You sure it was that long?"

I retrieved my cell phone from my bag. "A bit longer," I confirmed. "Why—"

"They suspect me of something," Nathaniel said. "I'm used to it. But I'm still curious what I'm suspected of this time."

The two officers exchanged a look. "Thirty minutes ago, there was a break-in at Tess Price's house."

CHAPTER 32

Dorian steepled his index fingers together, his claws tapping as he did so.

"Nathaniel Gallo has created a false alibi," he said to Brixton. "By using our Zoe, no less! She has unwittingly provided his alibi. A time shift, perhaps. Yes. This is a brilliant theory. The burglary could have taken place at another time."

Brixton raised a skeptical eyebrow. "But Tess Price heard the crash at her house when Nathaniel was at his house talking to Zoe."

The pair were sitting together in the attic, waiting for Veronica to arrive with her family's box containing Crimson Fish. Zoe had informed them of the latest twist in the investigation, and Dorian did not like the direction this case was heading. He was not ready to concede that Nathaniel Gallo was not the prime suspect.

Zoe had the gall to suggest Eve could have been the perpetrator! Yet Blue had confirmed that Eve had been with her at Blue Sky Teas not only during the break-in, but ever since the girl had been introduced to her that morning.

"The sound of a crash," stated Dorian, "does not confirm the time of the break-in. Perhaps Nathaniel left an ice cube underneath the edge of a Ming vase and when it melted, the priceless vase crashed to the floor, creating noise and alerting the inhabitants that there was a break-in."

"Um, okay. I don't think they had any priceless vases. Zoe said nothing was missing. Mrs. Price saw some guy running away as well. Right after the crash."

Dorian scowled. "We do not know for certain that it was the same man. Tess Price only saw a figure outside. This person could have simply been a jogger looking for a short-cut between the houses." Even to Dorian himself, this theory did not ring true. Yet he did not trust *monsieur* Gallo. It must have been a trick! How was it done?

"But we agreed Nathaniel Gallo is innocent," Brixton insisted. "He didn't kill Ridley. Otherwise, he wouldn't have been searching for a killer all these years."

"I," Dorian said primly, "was not able to participate in the conversation with Eve, once Zoe returned home. I was only able to observe, not question or give my opinion."

"That's why you're making up ridiculously complicated solutions to prove you're Poirot? Why don't we call Eve? She left us her cell phone number."

Dorian considered the question. Zoe had insisted it was not safe for Eve to lodge with them. Dorian agreed with this assessment, because he did not wish to hide in the shadows within the walls of his own home. Nor was it appropriate for Eve to stay at Brixton's house, even though Heather welcomed her with open arms. Eve would have had to sleep in a cot in the living room, plus Zoe had noticed the way Brixton looked at Eve. They did not want this distraction.

Instead, Blue Sky, the owner of Blue Sky Teas and the woman for whom Dorian worked (though Blue had never seen Dorian's true visage), took in Eve. Blue had not always had the name "Blue Sky." It was her own choice of name after she had fled an old life. Therefore, Zoe knew Blue would understand Eve's plight and take her in with no judgment. Plus, Blue's home possessed a comfortable spare bedroom, and a yard filled with wildflowers that were sure to please the young woman who had grown up on a farm.

While Dorian was considering the question of whether or not to call Eve, Brixton had already dialed the number. It only took one touch of his index finger to his phone screen to do so. Dorian sighed. Occasionally he wished his own fingers could be more like Zoe and Brixton's, so he could use modern devices. Though when he spotted the zombie-like gazes the devices inspired, he decided he was better off.

"It went to voicemail." Brixton slipped the phone back into his pocket.

"You did not leave a message."

The boy rolled his eyes. "Why would I leave a message?"

"Who are you not leaving a message for?" Veronica came through the door carrying a colorful box in her arms. The largest character on the top of the box was a purple octopus, whose playful tentacles wrapped around to the sides of the box. The other characters peeked out from behind the octopus's curled arms, each with a cartoon expression indicating their personalities. The only character besides the octopus that was not partially obscured was a red fish. When he looked more closely at the fish, Dorian noticed the lines on its face were more than they seemed. A question mark encircled one eye of the fish. At the very top, the words *Crimson Fish* were written in a font far too modern for Dorian's taste. Yet the image Dorian was searching for was not on the cover of the box.

"Sweet." Brixton took the Crimson Fish box from Veronica's arms and lifted off the lid.

As he was doing so, Dorian snatched the folded board.

"Hey." Brixton attempted to grab it, but Dorian scampered out of reach.

"I will return the board momentarily." Dorian unfolded the painted cardboard and scanned the ocean images. "Aha! I have found it. Proof that Nathaniel Gallo is the killer."

CHAPTER 33

I silenced my buzzing cell phone. It was Dorian calling, but I couldn't take the call where I was currently standing.

"As much as I hate to admit it," said Tess Price, "she's the only one of them I can trust." She tilted her head toward the only other person in her living room with us. Heather.

In the wake of the backhanded compliment, Heather shrunk away from Tess. "She called me over here because the burglar ransacked Ridley's old room. Tess asked if I could go through her room and see what they might have been after."

"I know kids don't always tell their parents everything." Tess sighed. "I know she might have confided in one of her friends, so I wouldn't even know what to look for. I told the police nothing had been taken, because that's what it looked like to me. After all, the person who—the person who hurt Ridley already stole all her diaries. So *what were they looking for?*" Tess's body drooped.

"Like a riddle she left behind," I said. "Something only her friends might notice."

"Exactly." Tess perked up. "Heather is the only one of Ridley's close friends who wasn't there at the party that night, so I know she wasn't involved in what happened. But I also know how close they were... Heather, please put aside your fears—"

"That's why I called Zoe." Heather stood even further away from Tess than she had a moment ago, but a smile from me made her smile as well. "She's my moral support."

"Heather thinks we're being haunted." Tess spat out the words. "It's not my daughter's ghost. Someone is playing a terrible joke."

That answered one question. Heather hadn't let it slip that we knew who the ghost really was. Heather knew there was no haunting. Why was she lying to Tess Price?

Five minutes later, I learned the answer.

Stepping into the bedroom behind me, Heather closed the door and leaned against it. "I thought she was trying to frame me."

"That's why you lied to Tess and wanted me here?"

Heather nodded. "Look at this room. She needs someone to blame. I don't know if she really believes I'm innocent, or if she's going to call the police and say the burglar is back."

"Well, she can't do that now. Let's see if you can figure out what they were after."

Ransacked was the right word to describe it. The twin-size bed with bright orange bedding was off kilter and the bedspread littered with the remnants of posters ripped from the walls. The sole bookshelf sat empty, its books strewn haphazardly across the floor, along with knickknacks ranging from a menagerie of plastic animals to smooth rocks like the ones from the flower garden. Glass littered the carpet next to the window.

"Who are you calling?" Heather asked me.

"Listening to a voicemail."

Dorian's message was enigmatic for no reason that I could discern. "I have proof, *mon amie*. Proof that Nathaniel Gallo is the villain we seek. Return home *tout de suite*."

"You're frowning," said Heather. "Something important?"

"It can wait."

"Why did Ridley's mom think I'd know what to look for? Riddle pushed me away that semester." Heather lowered her voice to a whisper. "I know now it was because of Eve. Her precious baby girl. But I really didn't know anything back then. Whatever was going on with her, she didn't confide in me."

"She loved literature, like her brother." I picked up one of the books that lay askew on the floor. *Frankenstein*. "Were they close?"

"He was so much older than us, you know? Six years felt like such a big age difference back then. She looked up to him, but I don't think he was a confidante."

I ran my fingers over the cracked spine of the well-loved book. Mary Shelley had written *Frankenstein* when she was only eighteen years old. A young age that Ridley hadn't lived to see. Inside, Ridley had underlined passages and made notes in the margins. Nothing that looked like a riddle. Simply the private musings of a teenager reading the powerful novel for the first time. I set the book carefully aside, thinking Eve might like to see it.

I picked up one of the books that hadn't fared as well. *D'aulaires Book of Greek Myths*. A page of the Pandora story was torn but hadn't been ripped out. It must have been a casualty of the ransacking. I looked back at the posters that had been ripped from the walls. One of them was of a grunge band that was already far past their prime and popularity when Ridley was a teenager. This wasn't a woman who'd cared about what her peers thought was popular.

But I was getting sidetracked from a more important observation. This was a hasty search of *both* books and posters....

"What was the thief searching for," I mused, "that could have been either inside a book or behind a poster?"

Heather tugged at the ends of her hair. "I don't know. Her diaries were all already stolen."

"Were they?"

Heather scrunched her face in frustration. She was clearly uncomfortable in this room. "I just said that."

"What if the killer thinks—or *knows*—that they didn't get all the diaries?"

"Or all of the pages from a diary." Heather fell to her knees amongst the books. "A piece of paper. That could have been hidden behind a poster or inside a book. But how do we know they didn't find it?"

"We don't. But Tess heard a crash and investigated. It was probably the sound of breaking glass, but it might have been something else the thief crashed into. They might not have had time to finish their search."

While Heather searched the books for any loose pages, I went to the broken window. We were on the second floor, overlooking the backyard. A crab apple tree's hearty branches stretched within feet of the window. So that's how the intruder had gotten into the high window. But then they had to break the glass upon finding it locked. The glass was inside the room, as you'd expect for someone breaking in from the outside.

The crab apple tree's spring blossoms were gone, and tiny, tart crabapples dotted the twenty-five-foot tree. I stepped out the open window and onto the closest branch of the crabapple tree. It swayed but held. Stepping closer to the rough bark of the trunk, I spotted the clean marks of a saw next to what had once been another branch. A thick one. This wasn't a recent break, but something done many years ago.

"Zoe!" Heather stood in the window.

The branch swayed under my weight. The branch beside me wasn't quite as sturdy. It had snapped under the weight of the burglar. A broken branch lay on the ground below me, along with a displacement of dirt where it had bounced on the loose earth of the flowerbed directly beneath me.

"Zoe," Heather said again. "That branch doesn't look very stable."

She was right. But I had to get a better look. The tree branch swayed underfoot as I crouched down. Maybe I'd better head back to the window. There was a better way to look. I gripped the window frame.

Seeing the room from the vantage point of the window, something else was clear. Though the room had indeed been plundered, there was nothing besides the glass to shatter. The noise Tess Price had heard was the window breaking. Which didn't make sense. The burglar wouldn't have had time to do this much damage once Tess heard the glass break.

I had to get a closer look at the dirt.

I hurried past Heather, flung open the bedroom door, and ran down the stairs.

"Did the police examine the flowerbed below the window?" I asked Tess.

"They looked. No footprints." Her lip curled into a disdainful sneer. "At least none they noticed. Not that I'd expect them to do an exhaustive search of the tread marks of different shoes for a burglary where nothing was stolen. They had the audacity to tell me I live in a neighborhood where there are frequently nonviolent thefts. When Nathaniel had an alibi, they dismissed this as random."

"Even though it was only Ridley's room?" Heather asked.

"That's the only reason they looked into it as much as they did."

"Could I look at the area outside the window?" I asked.

Tess narrowed her eyes. "Why?"

"Because I don't think there were any footprints."

Tess stared at me. "I should have known Heather's friends would be as flakey and nonsensical as she was," she grumbled, but at least she muttered the words as she led the way to the backyard.

I knelt in the flowerbed of tulips. As I'd noticed from above, the dirt was loose rather than compacted here. The branch that had fallen from above had crushed a handful of tulips and rolled in the dirt. Its marks were obvious.

Tess stood at the base of the tree, outside of the bed of flowers. "Enough damage has been done here already."

I looked past her to the higher branches of the tree, where I'd noticed the old saw mark. "When was one of the larger tree branches cut down?"

"My husband John cut that branch down after we realized Ridley was sneaking out at night through her window. The tree was barely big enough to hold the weight of a person, but she was fearless like that."

Heather wiped a tear from her cheek.

The branch that had fallen wasn't too big either. This wasn't a massive tree. The branch in the flowerbed couldn't have been heavier than a person. If someone had walked through this flowerbed or fallen onto it, there would be evidence of their presence. Yet there wasn't.

The tree and the window were a misdirect. The person who'd

ransacked Ridley's old room had stepped outside onto a branch to smash the window glass.

The burglar had come from inside the house. Had Tess Price ransacked her daughter's room? But why? She could have easily searched in private without drawing attention to it, unless she really did need someone else like Heather to look for something she'd missed. Or had she simply torn it apart because she wanted the police to look into Nathaniel more seriously? She told the police that the person she saw running away was a man, but she didn't go as far as saying she recognized Nathaniel. Did she think he wouldn't have an alibi?

CHAPTER 34

"A cartoon drawing of a villainous gargoyle?" I stared at Dorian. "That's why you called me? *That's* your reasoning for thinking Nathaniel killed his girlfriend?"

Dorian blinked at me. "Veronica and Brixton agreed with my sound theory."

"Really?" I glanced at the board game Dorian had convinced Veronica to leave behind. I was home after leaving Tess Price's house and dropping Heather off.

Dorian mumbled a French curse word I hadn't heard in at least a century. "I did not say they agreed with me that Nathaniel Gallo was the killer. Merely that they agreed with my astute reasoning that an innocent man would not have such a twisted imagination. He is hiding something."

I lifted the board game to get a closer look at the gargoyle cartoon figure in question. It was actually two water-spout gargoyles flanking the underwater cave. One gargoyle's lips were pursed in the shape of an "o" as bubbles instead of water flowed from his mouth. That was a clever spin on the purpose of a gargoyle. The other was sticking out his tongue at a little yellow fish who wore a look of surprise on his face.

"They're tricksters," I commented.

"Tricksters?" Dorian huffed. "The figure on the right is scaring this poor fish half to death. What kind of message is that to send small children?"

"That gargoyles are playful?"

"His teeth, Zoe. They are shaped like fangs. This board game encourages children to fear benevolent gargoyles."

"What about his research? He's been working for years to find Ridley's killer."

"A double bluff. If *les flics* were to have arrested him, he could simply show them his room of research."

"It's way more involved than a bluff needs to be."

"The product of a twisted mind."

I sighed. This was an argument I wasn't going to win.

"What have you learned at the home of Eve's murdered mother?"

I told Dorian what I'd discovered about the broken branch and indentations in the flowerbed. "Tess ransacked the room," I concluded, "but I don't understand her motive."

"I believe I have the answer," he said with a giddy smile on his lips.

"You do?"

"I have already discovered the pivotal clue." He scampered to my laptop and opened the screen. Pointing at a photograph of Ridley and her parents in a news article from sixteen years ago, he declared, "Ridley had brown eyes, yet her parents have blue eyes. Therefore, she was not their biological child at all!"

I looked more closely at the photograph. "You're suggesting Tess Price wrecked the room and called the police with a fake story to divert suspicion away from herself as the killer?"

"*Oui.*"

"There are two huge problems with that," I said. "First, even if Ridley was adopted, that's no reason for Tess to love her any less."

"You are correct. Yet we do not know her true parentage. There could be a secret worth killing over. I once read a novel in which a child was the illegitimate heir to the throne, discovered through her eye color—"

"Dorian. It's bad science. That's the second reason your theory is wrong."

"*Pardon?*"

"There's a low probability that blue-eyed parents would have a brown-eyed child, but it's not impossible. That's old science that's been debunked."

"*C'est vrai?*" Dorian's wings slumped. "How is a gargoyle to keep up with modern scientific discoveries?"

"You've read nearly everything else at the library. I'm sure they have a big science section."

Dorian narrowed his liquid black eyes at me. "If a certain alchemist had not had her library card revoked, this would not be a problem."

Even though it had been his scribbles in the library books, I was never going to live down not convincing the library staff of the importance of his "corrections" to cookbooks.

"Regardless of the accuracy of that particular theory," said Dorian, "you are the one who informed me that only Tess Price could have ransacked the room."

"It's what makes the most sense, but it's not necessarily true. Ridley might have given a key to her boyfriend. Tess's son most likely has a key to the house. Plus, the French doors of the living room that open into the back garden don't look very secure. There are any number of ways someone could have gotten into the house. The most important question is that breaking glass. It sounded only when the burglar left, not when they broke inside. Yet Tess swears she saw a man running away through the backyard."

"You admit, then," said Dorian, "that Tess herself is likely the culprit."

"I said it could be *any* of them."

"*Ça n'fait rien.* I forgive you, Zoe. I am a generous gargoyle. I am willing to accept that I *might* be mistaken in my theories of Nathaniel Gallo and Tess Price. We have become distracted by the wrong thing. Tell me more about your search of Ridley's room."

Dorian's wacky theories had served more of a purpose than he realized. There was so much we hadn't considered about what had happened before Ridley was killed, which in itself was important.

"Your face has grown pale," Dorian commented with concern. "Do you need sustenance? Ah! You have not had time for lunch. We must remedy this."

"In a minute. I need to think this through first. We made a big oversight. We didn't stop to think about the fact that Ridley's secret was *Eve*."

"You believe that the secret is in the missing pages of her diary?"

I shook my head. "That doesn't work, though. Everyone knew Ridley had spent the summer at the farm. If someone knew about the child, they would know where to find her. But nobody ever went after Aggie and Eve."

"Even a cold-blooded killer might not harm a child."

"Maybe, but it still doesn't fit. Aggie raised Eve because she thought the baby was in danger from someone at the party. That's why she didn't want the family to know." I gasped as a new idea struck me.

"Yes?" Dorian flapped his wings impatiently.

"That's what Aggie told Eve. But we only have her word for that. It might not be true. The killer could have blackmailed Aggie into silence."

I hated to think that a fellow plant-whisperer could have been involved in covering up a murder. Her homestead was so serene that I couldn't picture it. But people were complex. There was too much we didn't yet know.

"Blackmail." Dorian drummed his claws together.

We both jumped as a loud knock sounded at the front door.

"Have I summoned a blackmailer?" Dorian said cautiously.

The knock sounded again. I hurried down the stairs, where I found our friendly neighborhood postal worker. She needed me to sign for a small package. I grinned as I did so. I knew exactly what it was. I thanked her, locked the door, and headed back up the stairs.

"This is for you." I handed Dorian the flat package.

Dorian frowned, but his black eyes grew wide as he opened the package. "An original photograph of my first home."

Old postcards of Notre Dame Cathedral's gargoyles are relatively easy to find, but this was a photograph taken when the architects, restorers, stonemasons, and other workers had installed the first phase of the gallery of gargoyles in the late 1850s. Dorian's stone form, before he was alive, had been meant to join the other gargoyles, but he was too small. He had been replaced with a larger carving, but these were the gargoyles that had been his original intended family. They were all carved with intent for the cathedral, which was tied to Dorian's life force. And unlike the faux-aged modern reproductions meant to look vintage, this photograph had been held in the hands of the people working on the cathedral's restoration, before it was open to the public.

"This is a most kind gift, indeed." Dorian grinned at me and clutched the 150-year-old photograph to his chest.

"I thought you might be missing home—this is the point at which I remember feeling most homesick when I first left home—so I got in touch with several antique dealers to let them know I'd be interested in something like this."

Dorian wriggled his horns. "But it must have cost much money… Yet you are a terrible businesswoman. And are even more terrible at making gold."

I couldn't help laughing. There's something to be said for friends who state things like they are. "I'm also patient. You know how many treasures are in our attic."

"*My* attic," Dorian mumbled.

"I had an antique box the dealer was interested in, so we traded."

Dorian bowed his head. "You are a good friend indeed. I will treasure this always." He narrowed his eyes. "Yet you have also distracted me yet again! We have dealt with dastardly blackmailers before. We will triumph once more. We have much more to discuss. But first, we must eat."

CHAPTER 35

I stepped into my backyard garden while Dorian cooked lunch. It was still ailing from the strong winds that had shaken the less hearty plants, but I reminded myself that even the gentlest herbs were surprisingly strong—in more ways than one.

I picked boxwood basil, dark opal basil, and heirloom tomatoes for the light pasta lunch Dorian was making. The boxwood basil was perfect for a pesto, and the dark opal basil and Lucky Cross tomatoes would be perfect drizzled with garlic-infused olive oil. I knew Dorian would never make a pesto out of a purple-colored basil, because the color of the blended sauce wouldn't look as vibrant on the plate. To my gourmet roommate, the presentation of a meal was nearly as important as the flavor itself. I had far simpler tastes and had eaten much more simply before meeting Dorian.

Before coming inside, I checked on the rest of the plants and called the Flamels to let them know we had been wrong in thinking that Ridley Price was an alchemist.

When I stepped inside, Dorian was whisking a quickly thickening white sauce.

"Purple basil?" He frowned at the basket brimming with the tomatoes and basil.

"Green basil is hidden underneath," I assured him.

"*Bon.*" He whisked more rapidly. "I will make use of both. This cashew sauce will momentarily transform into a cheesy mozzarella to accompany the tomatoes and that purple basil."

While Dorian finished cooking, I retrieved the notebook where I'd drawn a table of Crimson Fish characters, this time adding more details we now knew about each of them.

SUSPECTS	PARALLEL GAME CHARACTERS	ROLE
Ridley "Riddle" Price (victim)	Crimson Fish	Victim — *Parallel to the game, not clear at first if she was dead. Dead in real life, found after many years. Had a secret baby – who knew the secret?*
Nathaniel Gallo (boyfriend)	Mr. Octopus	Thief — *Main suspect, but I'm his alibi for a recent crime and he spent years trying to find killer. A misdirect, or truly innocent?*
Amber Cook (long-time friend)	Miss Fisher	Friendly flirt — *Underestimated because of outward impression?*
Emilio Acosta (long-time friend)	Colonel Carp	Army man — *Tough exterior, but only a first impression.*
Roman Price (older brother)	Professor Blowfish	Professor — *Teaches poetry in an English Literature department at a local university. Writes beautiful poetry. Features that resemble his dead sister, but he wasn't the one impersonating her.*
Joona Kim (new friend)	Dr. Dover	Observant friend — *Wild card. No information.*
John Price (Ridley's dad, deceased)	Sir Seaweed	Goes with the flow — *Science teacher, died shortly after Ridley.*
Tess Price (Ridley's mom)	Ms. Mackerel	Suspicious of everyone — *Scientist who works as a flavorist. Prickly but appears to love her family. Tends Ridley's Riddle Garden and maintains her daughter's room as it was.*

Dorian pried the notebook out of my hands and placed a plate in front of me that smelled heavenly. The sweet aroma of basil, the spicy scent of garlic, and the subtler fragrances of pistachios and pepper. I ate more quickly than I should have, but I was famished from having skipped breakfast.

"I will do the dishes while you retrieve Crimson Fish from the attic." Dorian scooped my empty plate from the dining table.

"You want to play the game right now?" Maybe he was more homesick than I thought and wished to have company.

"The game is itself a clue," Dorian reminded me in a more arrogant voice than was strictly necessary. "Nathaniel Gallo's devious mind created this multilayered game not merely as a diversion from the doldrums of everyday life for those who might be feeling lonely or homesick—" He cleared his throat. "No. This game is a riddle! We must undertake further examination to see what we may learn."

"I've talked to him," I reminded Dorian. "And I've seen that creepy room of his. I don't think he's hiding anything else about the game itself. He was working through what he knew and seeing if ideas other people might have about the game could give him clues about what really happened."

Dorian flapped his wings. "*Creepy*. You were the one who used this word. Not I. You have made my point."

I agreed to play a game of Crimson Fish. "Maybe it'll help me think of more that I can add to the list of suspects."

I spread out the board on the dining table.

Visually, the board was divided similarly to the famous board game Clue, except under water. The house where the crimson fish lives was at the center of the board. Around it, the seaweed swamp, an underwater garden, a cave with an empty treasure chest (with the two gargoyles guarding the entrance), a sunken ship, a schoolhouse for little fish, and a rocky beach.

Instead of squares, bubbles formed the steps where players could advance to spots where they could read an additional clue. The seven suspects were each represented by a plastic fish in a different color, the dice were sea-foam green, and a dozen small notepads bore the illustration of a crimson fish at the top.

The most important piece of the game were the clues. Twenty-one packets of clues and solutions. Each packet was to be opened only when a new game was started, divided among the players, and the sealed packet containing the solution to be set aside until all the clues were completed and each player could take a guess. That's why it was possible to play it as a solo game as well, because you could be all of the characters without knowing the solution.

This wasn't just a game of chance or memorization. The clues didn't tell you exactly who was where when, but rather provided plenty of red herrings and word play. Which, as we played, I realized were quite similar to riddles. To help decipher the clues, a spiral-bound dictionary was also included to help the players. The dictionary was far from comprehensive, and seemed to me more like a thesaurus, giving both definitions and synonyms for words underlined in the clues.

Dorian read the latest clue:

> *Teacher believes the crimson fish*
> *Was led <u>amiss</u>*
> *By the gold sparkle of the miss*
> *Or was it only near the seaweed dish?*

"I do not like this game." Dorian tossed his cards of clues aside. "This is both a poor clue and poor grammar."

"Because we're supposed to look up *amiss* in the thesaurus." I reached for the booklet. "One of the synonyms for *amiss* is *afield*. There's 'a field' as part of the schoolhouse, for the fish to play bubble ball—which is also next to the seaweed patch. So this clue suggests the crimson fish was led *afield* to 'a field' that also fits with the rest of the clue that it has to be either near the cave or the seaweed."

"This is hardly a fair clue," Dorian grumbled.

"The game *is* called Crimson Fish instead of red herring," I reminded him. "All the meanings are hidden. This one is saying Professor Blowfish says the crimson fish was led to the schoolhouse field. The main red herring of the clue is to choose between the cave with treasure and the patch of seaweed, but the real clue is found when we look in the mini dictionary."

"A grammatically questionable dictionary," Dorian grumbled once more.

I scribbled down the answer to the clue on my notepad. "We also have to keep in mind the professor might be lying, so we have to see what the other clues say. Now that I'm playing again, I remember why it's such a diverting game."

Dorian looked up from writing his own notes. "The complexity of clues indicates why Nathaniel Gallo believed this might bring additional ideas to light about not only who killed Ridley, but how. This clue could mean many things."

In theory, it was a game you could only play twenty-one times. But with how complex the clues and solutions were, only someone with a photographic memory would remember which iteration they were playing. I had no idea if I'd played this particular packet of clues years ago or not.

"I could not play many games such as this for so many years," said Dorian in a softer voice. "My father taught me *écarté*, as it was one of the few card games that worked well for only two people." He chuckled. "I was quite adept."

Though I didn't have to hide my appearance from others like Dorian did, a deck of cards was the only game I had space for in the Airstream trailer I lived out of for decades, when I moved from place to place in the United States. I could never stay too long, because people would see I wasn't aging.

"I've played a lot of solitaire," I said.

"Jigsaw puzzles," Dorian said through closed eyes, as if remembering. "One of the men I cooked for had amassed a collection of jigsaw puzzles—which were quite expensive at that time, when they were being made out of wood. He could no longer assemble the pictures, after losing his sight, so he presented them to me as a gift. I completed many of his puzzles."

"I had no idea you were a fan of jigsaw puzzles. We could get some—"

"Never!" Dorian's eyes flew open. "I would say these puzzles are the work of the Devil himself, if I were inclined to literary fancy. Jigsaw puzzles did not used to come with pretty pictures on the boxes."

"I know. That was considered cheating."

"One had no idea what one was putting together. How was this seen as enjoyable? My employer had also mixed the pieces of two puzzles into one box." He shuddered. "It was enough to drive a perfectly reasonable gargoyle mad."

I tried to suppress a laugh, but it was impossible. "Did you finish the puzzles?"

"After many nights of arduous work. The great Dorian Robert-Houdin will not let a challenge stand in the way of completing a project." He wriggled his horns. "It is your turn to roll the dice to see what next clue you will read."

"Water flows left," I read. *"Water flows with heft..."*

"This is the entire clue?"

"No." The card dropped from my fingers. "Dorian, these clues aren't just clues."

"I am aware. As we have discussed already, they are riddles."

"And poems. Not good ones, but the structure and rhyme could be considered poetry."

Dorian shrugged his wings. "Perhaps *monsieur* Gallo is a frustrated poet. He appears to be frustrated by many things in his life ever since Ridley was murdered. I still maintain his frustration might be due to guilt and a twisted mind. He—what are you looking at?"

I pulled up the photo on my phone that I'd taken of Ridley's invitation to her party and showed it to Dorian.

A springtime daisy means you'll keep a secret,
whether for a moment or a lifetime of regret.
Tear off the petals, deep in thought:
will this be the beginning or will it not?

"This poem is much better," Dorian agreed.

"Exactly," I said. "Out of context, it reads like a poem."

"Out of context?"

"This is from the invitation Ridley gave guests for the party where she was killed. Ridley called it a riddle." I flipped to the photo of the front of the card. *"Join me for my welcome-home party and see the riddle solved."*

"A riddle that is also a poem," Dorian mused. "Why are you standing up? We have not yet finished the game."

"It'll wait. There's someone I need to ask about Ridley's riddles."

CHAPTER 36

I drove to Heather's house rather than walking, opting for speed rather than fresh air.

The party invitation riddle made sense now that we knew about Eve. The imagery was about a new life: Ridley's baby, Eve. But it wasn't exactly a riddle. It was far more like a poem to express emotion.

> *A springtime daisy means you'll keep a secret,*
> *whether for a moment or a lifetime of regret.*
> *Tear off the petals, deep in thought:*
> *will this be the beginning or will it not?*

I wanted to ask Heather if Ridley had given her other similar riddle-poems. Something that might be hidden in plain sight.

As I knocked, the wooden front door swung open under the weight of my fist.

"Heather?"

The living room was empty, but it didn't feel that way. The sketches of the people who were suspects in Ridley Price's murder were still tacked to the wall, with one glaring omission: Ridley herself. *The sketch of Ridley was gone.*

"Heather?" I called again.

No answer.

My skin prickled as I heard a faint thumping. It was barely detectable, but I was certain I heard it.

I hurried to the kitchen. It, too, was empty. So were the two bedrooms and the bathroom. That left only….I flung open the door to the garage.

"Zoe!" Heather set down her paintbrush and reached for her phone to turn off the music—music with deep bass that I'd heard thumping. "I was just about to take a break. Want a glass of iced tea?"

"You know your front door is open?"

"Brix doesn't always remember his keys, and I can't hear the door when I'm in the garage. We got it sound-proofed so Brix can practice guitar, and he and Abel can play music together, without bothering the neighbors."

"He can call you if he's locked out. I'm going to lock your front door. There's a murderer somewhere out there."

Heather's paint-covered hand flew to her mouth. "But you don't really think they'd—"

"I think you should keep your doors and windows locked."

By the time I returned to the garage after making sure the doors and windows were locked, Heather was back to being her usual cheerful, if flighty, self. It was simultaneously one of her best and worst qualities. She was adding a dot of white gouache to the portrait, to capture a reflection in Ridley's eye. It was the type of detail that as an observer, I wouldn't have noticed, but now that she'd added it, the painting came to life so much more. All from that simple dot.

"How's Eve doing?" she asked without looking up.

"I haven't checked on her since getting her set up with Blue. I came by because I have a question for you. I wondered—"

Whack.

We both jumped, but a second later Heather laughed. "That's why I keep the door to the garage closed even when the music isn't too loud. It's off-kilter—probably from an earthquake years ago—and never stays open. Abel and Brix are always losing the doorstop." She laughed again. "I think it's really so they can have guy time. Which is fine with me. I'm glad Brix has a better role model than me. Oh, don't look at me like that, Zoe. I know I'm a good person, but also that I'm not someone whose footsteps I want my son to follow." She wriggled the toes of her bare feet. Her toenails were painted yellow, and the big toes also had little purple flowers.

"I'm glad he's got both of you."

"And he's learned so much from you about plants. But that's not why you came by. You said you had a question for me?"

"I do. I wondered if Ridley's riddles were all like the one from her party invitation."

"Maybe... why?" Heather swished the tip of her paintbrush in a mason jar of cloudy water, dried it on a damp rag, then spun around in her swiveling stool.

"It's not really a proper riddle. It's more like a poem that hints at the truth. I'm wondering if she could have revealed more about the person who ended up killing her in other ways. It could help us narrow things down."

"Roman might have ideas. I think he helped her make some of her riddles sound more like poetry. She wasn't into writing like he was, but his poetry inspired her. Oh! That's what this portrait needs. Some lines of text in the background smoke."

It would have been a good idea if Roman hadn't been one of the main suspects.

"I'll let myself out," I said, but she didn't hear me.

She'd already picked up another brush and was engrossed in her portrait of Ridley once more.

The front door of Heather's rental house had a deadbolt I couldn't lock from the outside, so I let myself out through the back door. As I stepped through the side gate, a face I wasn't expecting came into view.

It was of the people at the cemetery that morning. One of the seven suspects, who happened to be the one who'd joined the army and could very easily have been trained in archery, who had mysteriously disappeared at the cemetery that morning, was now at Heather's house. Emilio Acosta.

CHAPTER 37

Emilio stepped into a small blue car parked directly across the street from Heather's house. As soon as he pulled away from the curb, I hurried to my truck and followed.

I doubted Emilio would recognize me or my truck—and I'd even been parked a couple of houses away to avoid flowers from nearby trees falling onto my windshield—but I hung back as far as I could without losing him. Luckily, the roads weren't deserted or overly crowded, so I was able to keep pace with him without being seen.

Fifteen minutes later, he pulled into a university parking lot. Wait... Wasn't this the university where Roman Price taught?

I parked one row over from Emilio, facing his car. He didn't get out of the car immediately. I couldn't see him clearly, but he might have been on the phone.

I should make my own phone call as well.

"Are you, perchance, calling from a food market?" Dorian asked as soon as he picked up the phone. "I have several more items to request."

"I'm calling from a parking lot, where I followed Emilio Acosta."

"Army man, the yellow fish suspect in Crimson Fish?"

"That's him. He's just arrived at the university where Roman Price works."

"Aha! The two men are in league. You wish me to come rescue you?"

I cringed at the thought, but also smiled. In spite of his many eccentricities, he was a loyal and brave friend. "I don't think that's necessary yet, but something weird is going on, so I needed someone to know where I was. Emilio was at Heather's house earlier."

"Why does he wish to see Ridley's brother?" Dorian asked.

"No idea. Hang on. He's getting out of his car. I need to follow."

"*Attendez!*"

"I can't *wait*." I fumbled with the door handle. "I don't want to lose him."

"Do not disconnect our call. Keep your phone where I can hear you. In this way I may call for assistance if the suspect turns dangerous."

It wasn't a bad idea. I hurried to keep up with Emilio. The summer session must have started, because the parking lot was half full, and many other people were milling about. "One question," I added before slipping the phone back into my bag. "Is this what you did when you sent Brixton and Veronica to Nathaniel Gallo's house? You didn't tell me you asked them to do that, or you knew I'd have talked you out of it."

"It was the girl's idea!"

"Dorian—"

"I speak the truth. Yet this is not the time for such a discussion. *Vite!* Do not lose the rascal."

I tucked the phone into my bag and hurried after Emilio.

I followed him inside a four-story building, but as soon as I got into the entryway, he'd vanished. Had he really come inside, or had I missed him?

"Can I help?" a friendly young woman asked.

"I don't know if I'm in the right place. I'm looking for Professor Price."

She pointed at a directory on the wall. "I don't know him, but that old-fashioned thing will tell you if he's in this building. Or if he's not, check his website and it'll tell you where his office is."

I thanked her and went to the directory she'd pointed to.

Professor Price was listed as having an office on the fourth floor. Emilio must have disappeared into the elevator.

I found Roman's office. The door was closed, and through it, I could hear them speaking.

"It's shaken me up," a voice I didn't recognize was saying. That must have been Emilio. "It's made me decide I need to act now, before it's too late."

"I'll support you," Roman said. "I know it won't be easy, but I'll back you."

Were the two men working together? Roman had seemed surprised when Heather mentioned Emilio and Amber were at the cemetery, but that reaction could have been feigned.

"But first," Roman added, "we need to figure out—"

"I know. You coming later?"

"I'm meeting a student in half an hour, but that won't last long. I'll be at her grave by three. Did you reach Joona?"

"Yeah, it'll be the four of us."

Were *all of them* working together? And why were they going back to the cemetery?

"See ya there," Emilio said.

I ran down the hallway before I was exposed.

CHAPTER 38

"All of the suspects are returning to Ridley Price's grave?" Dorian asked.

"That's what it sounds like." Zoe's face was inscrutable. She was confused, yes. Yet there was something more.

"This is curious. Curious indeed."

"There's a very real possibility they're working together. I should go to the police."

Aha! This was the cause of her consternation.

"I will call Veronica," Dorian assured her. "This will ensure she and Brixton will remain safely under the care of her father."

Yet Zoe glared at him. Glared! This was entirely uncalled for. He was being such a responsible gargoyle.

"You lured both Brixton and Veronica into interviewing a murder suspect," the unreasonable alchemist stated. It was as if she had slapped him. The only worse words she could have spoken would have been if she had addressed him in French and cried out, *Je t'accuse!* Yet this was effectively what she had done.

"I did no such thing." Dorian flapped his wings at the injustice of the accusation. He stopped mid-swoop. The flapping of one's wings in the limited space of the attic might be construed as a tantrum. This would do little to improve his argument. Instead, he straightened his wings.

"I apologize for my momentary outburst," he continued. "We will call Veronica together. This assures you will believe me."

She assented. "Good. She's the sensible one."

Zoe insisted they call Veronica's land line. She wished to make sure Brixton had not been a bad influence on her and taken her elsewhere, and also to speak with Veronica's father, *monsieur* Mendoza, or her mother, *madame* Chen-Mendoza.

It was her father who was working from his home office this afternoon, and the responsible young Veronica had already told him that one of Brixton's mother's old friends had been killed many years ago and that something strange was afoot. (The girl did not use the word "afoot," yet Dorian was proud of the rest of her explanation to her father, for conveying facts without overly worrying the man.)

Dorian contained his curiosity while Zoe was speaking with *monsieur* Mendoza, but once Veronica's father handed the telephone receiver back to his daughter, Dorian inquired whether she had sighted any of the suspects.

"We've been here all afternoon." Veronica went on to assure them both that it had been a low-key afternoon, which Zoe translated to mean that it was quiet and nothing either exciting or bad had transpired.

"We believe the suspects will all be meeting at the cemetery," Dorian said in a hushed voice, "as it appears they may be in league. Therefore, you must take care. Lock your doors. Zoe and I will assure they are brought to justice."

"We'll be safe," Veronica said. "Coming, Dad!"

"*Bon*," Dorian declared once they hung up the phone.

"We'll ensure they're brought to justice?" Zoe asked.

"*Oui*. This is our plan, is it not?"

"My plan is to bring flowers to leave on Ridley's grave. I'll hide in the trees if I can get close enough to hear them. But if anyone sees me, I have a perfectly innocent reason to be at the cemetery."

"This is an unwise plan."

"I'll have my phone in my hand to call 9-1-1 at the touch of a button."

"You need more immediate backup."

"If I call Max now, and he drives like the devil, maybe he could be back—"

"There is no time. Nor is there time to explain our theory to anyone who is not yet involved. That leaves only Heather, who cannot be trusted."

"Of course Heather can be trusted." Zoe frowned at him.

"Trusted to be a good person, yes. Yet I fear she would hug them to death."

"Or bind their hands with daisy chains." Zoe laughed, yet it was the nervous laugh of someone pushed to the brink.

"I fear you are giddy from lack of food, *mon amie*."

"We just ate."

"There is always an occasion for a delectable snack. I noticed the garlic scapes in your back garden are ready for harvesting."

Zoe swore. "I forgot about them. I need to snip them before they flower, otherwise the garlic plants will put more energy into their flowers than into the bulbs in the earth I want to harvest this fall."

"*Bon*. You harvest the greens from the tops of the garlic, and I will sauté them as a topping for sourdough toast. This will give us sustenance for our journey."

"You'll wear your cape and hide in the trees?"

"But of course." Dorian grinned. He had won the argument. He would accompany Zoe to the graveyard and catch Ridley Price's killers.

∽

Dorian's wing slammed into the side of truck. This was a most distasteful way to travel. Zoe was not a poor driver, yet lying under a tarp in the rear of a pickup truck was not a comfortable form of travel.

"Sorry," Zoe whispered when they finally came to a stop and she stepped out of the comfortable front seat. "There was a pothole I couldn't avoid."

"No matter."

"There's nobody around right now, so you should head for the trees. You remember where her grave is?"

He assured her he did. He had a marvelous sense of direction.

A few minutes later, Dorian was comfortably ensconced on a solid branch of a cedar that towered over the nearby trees. He appreciated the smooth bark and the view it afforded him. From his perch, he saw both Zoe—who was behind the base of a fir tree with a bouquet of flowers—and Ridley's nearby grave.

Three figures stood at the grave. He recognized them from the online photographs, though they had aged many years. A tall man who resembled Ridley, and two women who did not.

"We all know he did it," the dark-haired woman stated calmly. "Why are we here?"

"You really didn't see her?" Ridley's brother asked.

The woman shrugged. "Maybe her ghost couldn't get across the state line to Washington."

"That's not funny, Joona." The blonde woman who had not yet spoken rubbed her hands over her arms. It was not the slightest bit cold. She was nervous to be in the cemetery.

"None of this is funny," Joona snapped. "It's the middle of the day. I should have been at work and then picking up my kids from school. Instead, I had to drive down from Seattle to have a forced reunion to talk about Nathaniel Gallows getting away with murder and going off the rails. My husband is probably going to let them get pizza for dinner."

"This is a little bit more important than your kids eating junk food for one meal." Ridley's brother's voice was calm on the surface, yet even from a distance Dorian could sense the man was far from calm.

"Pizza isn't necessarily junk food," the other woman said. Amber, Dorian recalled her name. The flirtatious fish in Nathaniel's game. Another old friend of Ridley's. "Kids are getting different food groups—"

"Would you two stop talking about pizza! He shot an arrow at me. He's unstable."

From Zoe's account of the arrow, Dorian did not believe the shot was intended for Roman Price. It had been closest to Heather Taylor. Yet it did not surprise him that a man whose sister had been murdered would be frightened.

"Just so I'm clear," Joona said, "do you really think you saw Ridley's ghost, or that Nathaniel has lost it and is going around with an archer's bow?"

"Seeing her could have pushed him over the edge and then—" Roman began.

"Isn't Emilio the one who knew how to use a bow and arrow?" asked Joona.

"It wasn't Emilio," Amber insisted.

Three people arguing... Did not Zoe theorize that they were working *together*? And that there would be four? Where was Emilio?

Zut alors!

A fourth person was approaching, but not from the main path. He would certainly see Zoe.

CHAPTER 39

I caught sight of Emilio in time to step forward with my flowers and approach the grave.

"Oh!" I hoped I wasn't overacting as I stopped a few yards away from them. "I didn't mean to interrupt. There were no flowers on her grave this morning, so I thought I'd bring these."

"You were here this morning," Amber said.

"She's a friend of Heather's," Roman said. "Zola."

"Zoe," I corrected.

"You've been in touch with Heather?" Emilio stepped into the half-circle. "I wanted to invite her here this afternoon, but I didn't have her contact info. Wasted a bunch of time tracking her down through her posts on social, but she wasn't at home. You didn't tell me you'd seen her, Roman."

"I didn't have a chance to tell you anything. You interrupted my office hours today. *This* is when we agreed we were all going to talk."

"What are we even talking about?" Joona shouted. "It has to be a joke. I don't know what you all saw, but it can't have been Ridley. Nathaniel never got over killing her, so now he's hired someone to impersonate her—but didn't pay her enough money to drive further than locally—and is messing with all of you. Trying to make you as miserable as he is."

Emilio frowned. "He was never convicted. We don't really know—"

"Who else would it be?" Roman spoke through a clenched jaw. "Nobody else had a reason to hurt her. But she'd just broken up with Nathaniel."

"You're all ridiculous." Joona rolled her eyes before turning to me. "I'm Joona. It appears you already know the others."

"I came here with Heather at dawn," I said. "We ran into Roman and his mom. We saw Emilio and Amber briefly, but I didn't get a proper introduction."

"I was scared," Amber whispered.

"She didn't want to stay," Emilio added.

Amber glanced at Emilio. Was she questioning his account of what happened this morning? "Emi agreed to leave with me."

Emi? It was clearly an affectionate nickname. From what I'd seen of them today, perhaps Heather was mistaken that they'd gotten divorced.

"So everyone was here except me," Joona mused. "All of you and Heather."

"And my sister's ghost," Roman snapped. "Don't forget that part."

"Yeah." Emilio shook his head. "We got notes from someone claiming to be Ridley. Same as the rest of you, it seems. I made sure we got here early."

"From his tactical army training," Amber cut in.

Emilio nodded. "Nathaniel must've hired an actress. A ghost wouldn't have been getting out of an ancient Subaru."

That was the make of Eve's car. I'd seen it when I dropped her at Blue's.

"I'd be more relieved," Roman said, "if Nathaniel hadn't also fired an arrow at me *and* broken into my mom's house."

"*What?*" Joona looked shaken for the first time. "When did that happen?"

"Back up," Emilio said. "We're talking in circles and going back and forth in time. Zoe, you're the impartial one. Talk us through what you know."

Joona pulled a mauve cloth from her hulking purse. She flicked her wrists and it unraveled into a picnic blanket. "I've got two little kids. I'm prepared for anything. Anyone need a granola bar?"

"You expect us to sit on her grave?" Amber gaped at Joona.

"We're here to visit her, aren't we?" Joona smoothed the blanket onto a patch of grass several feet away from Ridley's gravestone.

"Cemeteries are traditional spots for picnics," I added. "This is a good spot to remember Ridley."

The *memento mori* reminder that we, too, would die, was close at hand in cemeteries. This wasn't a bad thing, but a reminder to live our lives well and to the fullest for our time on earth, and cemeteries also allowed people to spend time with their departed loved ones. During some periods of time, the Latin phrase evoked imagery such as skulls or an hourglass. The Grim Reaper was en vogue for a time, but so were flowers and more serene images of death.

I'd lived through the Victorian era, when far more death surrounded people than it does now. Picnicking in cemeteries was normal then. I joined Joona on the blanket.

Amber was the last to sit, but the only one who accepted Joona's offer of a chocolate chip granola bar.

"We're wasting time." Roman's gaze flicked to Amber, the only one eating.

"What?" she said. "I didn't eat lunch and I'm hungry. I never said the rest of you couldn't keep talking."

I surveyed the group around me, hoping Dorian hadn't sought help once I'd been spotted. I didn't get the sense they were working together. One of them was most likely a killer, but I was safe as long as I was in the larger group.

They'd all aged in the last sixteen years, of course, yet they were so clearly recognizable from Heather's sketches—and even from Nathaniel's cartoon illustrations in Crimson Fish.

Roman, so tall and thin he was almost awkward. Professor Blowfish from the board game was shown inflated and round, but with thin and delicate facial features.

Emilio's dark curls of his youth had been cut short and his cocky smile softened, but the hint of both shone through. He sat with a straight back that somehow resembled Colonel Carp.

Amber's flirtatious expression was directed at Emilio, especially when she thought he wasn't looking. It was as visible two feet in front of me as it was in the pout in Heather's sketch and the coyly batted eyelashes of Miss Fisher. I didn't expect to see it in real life, but her eyelashes were even longer and more curled than those of her cartoon character.

Joona was the least recognizable from either her board game fish counterpart or the sketch on Heather's wall. I got the sense that Heather and Nathaniel hadn't known her well enough to capture her personality. I couldn't even remember which fish was meant to represent her. Dr. Dover? But here in the cemetery, she was the most self-assured of all of them. The long black hair of her youth was now cut in a stylish bob that suited her. I imagined her short hair would be much easier to manage with two young kids.

Nathaniel had put so much effort into the game. Why would he have done that if he was guilty? Was he really a disturbed man? Was Dorian right that he'd somehow faked the timing of the burglary?

"I agree with Emilio." Joona adjusted the small pillow she'd pulled from the depths of her bag. "Let's hear from the woman who has no skin in the game. What's the story, Zoe?"

"Zoe?" Emilio repeated. "You okay there?"

"I'll tell you what I know," I said, "but I need you to listen with an open mind."

"Of course," Roman agreed with an added click of his tongue in frustration. The others also murmured their agreement.

"Why are you all so convinced Nathaniel Gallo is guilty?" I asked. "Why would he create *Crimson Fish* if he's guilty?"

They all stared at me like I was mad.

Amber was the first to speak. "What are you talking about?" Her lips formed a pout once she was done speaking, looking even more like Miss Fisher.

"What does that game have to do with Nathaniel Gallows?" Emilio didn't gape, but his jaw tightened.

Joona rummaged through her bag and pulled out a box roughly twice the size of a deck of cards. "Crimson Fish mini-mysteries travel edition," she said. "Our Nathaniel created this?"

Damn. "You didn't know?" When Max had told me the police had used the game to investigate, I assumed it was public knowledge. But it was simply good police work. I should have realized as much when online searches didn't draw the connection. Instead, the game's cult following enjoyed making up different scenarios, just as Nathaniel had hoped.

"This is ridiculous," Roman sputtered.

Joona laughed as she spread out the cards featuring character illustrations. "You sound just like I'd expect Professor Blowfish to sound, Roman. And Colonel Carp? So Nathaniel created this after Emilio finished high school and joined the army. Am I Dr. Dover? I never did finish my PhD, but I've always had a soft spot for that fish."

"This is so embarrassing," Amber muttered. "I'm a scientist, for God's sake!"

"You make fluorescent-colored potato chips," Roman snapped.

"That's not fair," Joona stuck up for her.

"You're right," Roman added. "Most of her products probably don't even contain any real potatoes."

"Why do I care what an adjunct professor who hasn't had a decent book in more than a decade thinks?" Amber glared at him. "And to think I felt bad for you when I saw a dozen copies of your latest book of poetry selling for 99 cents at Powell's Books."

"Hang on." Roman snatched the card of Professor Blowfish. "How do you know this?"

"It's public record." I hoped it was. "Nathaniel didn't want any public credit for the game, because he created it to see if people who played it would draw connections between the characters and the scenarios he created. Each of the clues is somehow related to ideas about what could have caused the crimson fish to be killed."

"Since nobody ever figured out her secret." Joona picked up one of the clue cards. "That's why the clues were always so poetic. It was so personal to him."

"So you're like a private detective?" Emilio asked. "That's how you found this?"

"Or," said Joona, "she's working with Nathaniel. Zoe could be the one who's his accomplice. Her story could be a red herring."

CHAPTER 40

Mon Dieu! The suspects were turning on Zoe!

Dorian grasped the branch, preparing to swing down to fetch help, when the next speaker changed his course of action.

"Zoe isn't Nathaniel's accomplice," Roman Price said. "Don't you think I looked her up after someone shot an arrow at me? She runs an antique shop and only moved here a couple of years ago."

"Too bad," said Joona. "It was a nice idea that it's not one of us."

Dorian held his breath. Zoe could use this opportunity, but she must also tread carefully. They had not wished her to speak with the group, but since she had been seen, he hoped she would take advantage of the opportunity. If she were in physical danger, he would risk his life to attack, no matter what the implications for his own wellbeing.

"Heather and I were having tea yesterday morning at Blue Sky Teas," Zoe stated. Her voice was cautious. She was being careful in her words. "It's in the neighborhood where we both live. We saw a teenage girl behaving oddly, and Heather thought she looked like Ridley Price, which frightened her. That's when she told me about what happened sixteen years ago."

"She didn't give you a note?" Emilio asked.

Joona glared at him. "Let her tell her story."

"The girl pretending to be Ridley left behind a note for Heather," Zoe said. "It was on charred paper, and it looked like a falling leaf, so we didn't notice it then. Our friend Blue found it when she swept up later. I understand why you all could have been spooked into thinking she was a ghost. The... actress played her role very well. But she's flesh and blood."

"You got close enough to touch her?" Emilio asked. "Make sure she was real?"

"No," Zoe admitted. "But do we really need to debate the ghost idea? You said you saw her getting out of a car."

"Wish I'd written down the license plate." Emilio ran a hand over his face. "Go on."

"Heather and I saw the same girl again at the cemetery this morning, where the note told Heather to meet her. I went with Heather for moral support. You all must remember Heather didn't go to the party where Ridley was killed. She's felt guilty all these years, because she was mad that her friend had abandoned her. So I was there for moral support, to find out why someone was impersonating Ridley. But we didn't get to talk to her. Before we could get close, someone fired an arrow that landed in a tree near me and Heather, and not too far from Roman and his mom Tess either."

"So she was aiming at Heather," Emilio said. "Not Roman?"

"It wasn't her," Zoe said. "I saw her, and she wasn't holding a bow."

"Because it was Nathaniel," Roman said. "And it doesn't matter who he was aiming at. Emilio, you and Amber didn't see any of this? You said you were here."

Amber crumpled the granola bar wrapper tightly. "I couldn't face Ridley's grave. Besides Emi, she was my closest friend when I was young. I just couldn't—" Her voice broke.

Emilio made a move to reach for her hand, but pulled back before he reached it. Neither of them wore a wedding ring, but perhaps this traumatic experience was getting them back together.

"I understand," Zoe said. "I've lost people close to me. That's why I wanted to be here for Heather."

This was quite true. Zoe had lived through many tragedies before Dorian had met her. He knew of the pain she experienced when her brother died, the death of her first love, Ambrose, and then losing Nicolas and Perenelle Flamel for many years. It was no wonder she had been only the shell of a woman when they had first met. She had barely cared about food! Yes, she had prepared healthy food for herself, but she had not explored the full flavor complexities that a true chef could add to the plants she grew. Dorian had showed her the error of her ways, elevating the healing herbs and vegetables to legendary proportions. He was convinced that if he could work at a full restaurant, he would have a Michelin star by now. But this was of little importance compared to the drama unfolding below him. He shifted his position on the branch to get a better view.

"Why isn't Heather here with you?" Emilio nodded toward the flowers at Zoe's knee.

"I didn't tell her I was coming. I got the sense she feels like Amber. That it's all too much. When Ridley's old room was ransacked this afternoon—that's the break-in Roman mentioned—Tess Price asked Heather to look through what was left behind, to see if she could spot what had been stolen. She couldn't."

"Why *Heather*?" Amber's expression was cold for the first time.

"Can't you guess?" Roman asked. "Heather was the only one of Ridley's friends who wasn't there the day my sister died. Like all of us, my mother thinks Nathaniel is guilty. But she knows it could also have been one of the three of you."

Emilio swore.

"She never said...." Amber blinked back tears.

"You're in touch with her?" Zoe asked.

Amber nodded. "I was always interested in her work in chemistry. She advised me about programs and applying for school, and that was after Ridley... *No*. Tess doesn't believe I could have killed Ridley. She can't think that."

"It's okay, babe," Emilio whispered. "It's—"

"It's most certainly *not* okay," Joona cut in. "Did the police arrest Nathaniel after the break-in? Or are the rest of us in danger?"

"He had an alibi." Zoe did not add that she herself was his alibi.

Emilio swore creatively. Dorian made a mental note of one of the words he had never before heard.

"The girl," Emilio said. "Of course. The actress Nathaniel hired to play the ghost. She's his accomplice. I can't think straight."

"Chocolate covered coffee beans?" Joona held out a snack pack, pulled from the depth of her gargantuan purse. "They do wonders for mental clarity."

"I gave up coffee years ago. Makes me too jittery. But I could use some poetry to focus." He removed his phone from his pocket.

"Are you seriously scrolling for poetry?" Joona asked.

"It's because of times like this that the world needs more poetry."

Amber beamed at him. "You're thinking of applying after all?"

Emilio's cheeks reddened as the group watched him. "This week was yet another reminder that life's short. Yeah, a little while after our breakfast, I went to see Roman to ask him about the English Lit grad program he teaches in."

"That's wonderful." Amber squeezed his arm.

"Are you two serious?" Joona shook her head at them before turning her attention to Zoe. "They've been married and divorced twice already." She counted on her fingers. "They get married every seven years or so. At twenty, twenty-seven, and we're thirty-three now, so they've got one more year to plan their next wedding."

"I really will support your application," Roman said to Emilio, ignoring the woman with the bottomless bag, "but can we *please* get back to the matter at hand?"

That was the subject of which Roman and Emilio had been speaking when Zoe overheard only part of their conversation. She had jumped to the wrong conclusion. Emilio wished to apply to a graduate program of poetry, and he had mentioned earlier that he had located Heather to invite her to this meeting. All was explained. And yet… this also meant there was no way to know which of them was lying!

"Clearly Nathaniel has an accomplice," Roman continued. "But why act now? Is he really just that unstable—?"

Roman broke off at the sound of tree branches snapping. Dorian had been so focused on the group below him that he had not paid attention to his surroundings. Had a large bird of prey landed nearby?

No. It was far worse. A larger crack sounded, followed by a shriek and a thud.

Joona was the first to stand. Her movements were composed, but her eyes widened with the confusion that was visible on everyone's face. "I think," she said calmly, "we've found Nathaniel's accomplices."

Amber screamed. Her banshee wail pierced the serene setting of the cemetery far more than the crash from moments ago. Birds took flight from the trees. Dorian hoped the suspects would not look upward toward the birds and see him instead.

He need not have feared. Their attention was transfixed on one of the two young women who had fallen from a nearby tree.

"Ridley?" Roman rose but stumbled backward.

Amber clasped her hands around Emilio's arm.

"Get a hold of yourselves," Joona snapped. "It's not Ridley's ghost. Can't you all see? She looks a bit like Ridley. But also Nathaniel. She's Ridley and Nathaniel's kid."

Eve stood up. The girl was dressed once more like Ridley, except she was wearing her spectacles. She was not alone. By her side was Veronica, who Dorian had previously thought of as sensible.

While the suspects were stunned into inaction, the two young women ran. *Mon Dieu.* The killer of Ridley Price now knew about Eve.

CHAPTER 41

"I did not expect Veronica would escape from her father's care and bring Eve to the cemetery." Dorian blinked his black eyes at me as he wriggled his horns. "This was most unexpected for Veronica."

"I believe you, Dorian. I didn't see it coming either."

The last two hours had been a hectic mess, and Dorian and I were now back in the attic—with a fresh platter of food, of course. Not that I'd had the stomach to touch any of it.

Veronica and Eve had run away and turned off their phones. Veronica's parents were horrified and said Eve had kidnapped their daughter. Blue was anguished that she hadn't taken Eve's keys, but she hadn't wanted Eve to feel trapped—a situation Blue knew all too well.

The police had put out an alert for the car and license plate registered to Aggie Messenger, but it hadn't been spotted. Max was on the road back to Portland from Astoria and had already yelled at me on the phone. He was right to be mad. It was my fault. I thought I had more control than I did.

I remembered how lost I was at Eve's age, let down by all the adults in my life. They had turned me in to the authorities for the crime of witchcraft. I'd already felt like an outcast, but that betrayal hurt me more than I thought possible. That's why I'd

THE ALCHEMIST OF RIDDLE AND RUIN

acted with my heart in this case, instead of my head. And I was wrong.

"It is not your fault," Dorian insisted. "Do not be dejected. Perhaps if you finish creating a perfect gift for Max, he will forgive you."

"I don't need a perfect gift for him to forgive me."

"It could not hurt. Neither could tasting a bite of my cucumber, mint, and strawberry salad…"

"I'm not worried about forgiveness. I'm worried that Veronica and Eve are unaccounted for, and very soon a killer will be on the loose."

Dorian served a small bowl and handed it to me. I took a bite of the cucumber salad. It was heavenly.

We weren't as frantic as we otherwise would have been if the suspects hadn't agreed to stay together and talk with the authorities. Even Nathaniel Gallo and Tess Price came into the police station as soon as they heard about Eve's existence. Tess broke down when she learned she had a granddaughter, and Nathaniel was speechless. As for the rest of them? I could have sworn that everyone was surprised about Eve. But I had to be wrong about one of them.

Eve wasn't in immediate danger, as long as everyone was giving statements. But the police couldn't hold them too much longer. It was already early evening.

I abandoned the bowl and let my gaze fall to the shelves of antiques. My organizational system made little sense to others but perfect sense to me. Because I was the one who'd tried many methods before settling on what worked best for my particular collection. I had thought that because I was an outsider who hadn't experienced Ridley's death in the same way as Heather that I'd be an objective observer who could see more clearly. But what if I was wrong? What if I was missing something key that only that group of friends knew?

"We must be missing a key piece of information," I said.

"Feeding your mind would help." Dorian pointed at my abandoned bowl. "Perhaps you are ready for a proper dinner?"

"How does Eve's existence fit into the puzzle?"

"I forgive you for failing to answer my question about sustenance." Dorian drummed his clawed fingertips together. "I understand, because I, too, have been using my little gray cells to analyze our current facts, and I agree this is an angle we have not yet considered. How does Eve fit?"

"Eve came to Portland to get answers. She was manipulating people and took Nathaniel's key to break into his house. But someone else fired an arrow and searched Ridley's old room. *Why?*"

"Perhaps now that all the suspects know about Eve, there will be no more danger. The secret is exposed."

I thought about Ridley's flower garden riddle and all the other riddles she'd created. "How do we know Eve is the secret the killer was trying to protect?"

Dorian gasped. *"Mon Dieu.* What else could the secret be?"

"Something the killer still thinks is out there to cover up. Why else fire an arrow and search Ridley's room? Tess was probably the person to ransack her daughter's room, but we still don't know why."

"Those are two different crimes," Dorian pointed out. "Two culprits?"

"Both with unclear motivations. I don't know if the arrow was meant to hurt anyone. It was one shot and went wide. It was either a warning or a distraction."

"Both attributes which could be said of Nathaniel Gallo."

"If a riddle had been stuck to the arrow, I'd agree."

Dorian threw his hands into the air before scampering to his typewriter.

"You have an idea?" I asked.

"Not yet. But my little gray cells often work well when tapping at the keyboard. I am making a list of all possibilities."

"I can't think. I'll be outside in the garden. I've got my cell phone turned on, so call me if you think of anything."

I hated feeling so helpless. On my back porch, I took off my ankle-high boots. I stepped barefoot into my garden and closed my eyes, letting the earth curl around my toes. The dirt was soft and friendly. It made sense, unlike any of the confusing people. There were too many suspects. Too many pieces of information that didn't seem to fit together. It was like one of the riddles Ridley liked to create.

But regardless of the mess elsewhere in the world, here in my garden I felt alive. And truly at home.

I savored the feeling, letting my hands brush the leaves of my familiar plants as my eyes remained closed. My nettles were confined to one corner, so my fingertips were safe to explore. The thorn of a blackberry bush brushed against my palm. The jolt made me smile. A reminder of the complex berry growing on the thick stem. Both sweet and tart.

My eyes flew open as my side gate creaked open. A moment later, Heather appeared.

"It's just like it was all those years ago," she cried. "Ridley missing and presumed dead. Now her daughter is missing!"

"Eve left on her own. She's not in danger." Not yet, at least. "Why aren't you at the police station?"

"Why would I be? They let us all go."

I swore. Now Eve *would* be in danger.

"You want me to be stuck at the police station?" She frowned. Tears streaked her face, but she hadn't bothered to wipe them away.

"I want Eve and Veronica to be safe from Ridley's killer. A killer who's still after something."

Her hands flew to her mouth. "But they didn't say—I mean, do you really think one of them wants to hurt Eve and Veronica? But we told them everything we knew...I can't believe it's Veronica who snuck out, not Brix. Her parents are going to ground her until she and Brix are out of high school. What's he going to do without her?"

"What did the police question you about?" I asked. "About this week, or sixteen years ago?" They'd only asked me about this week, because I wasn't there sixteen years ago, but I hoped they'd take the connection seriously.

"Both. I even gave them Ridley's poem again."

"Ridley's poem?"

"I meant the party invitation riddle. I don't know why I called it a poem."

"Because it *is* a poem..."

Ridley's party invitation was important... It was a riddle. A poem. *A clue.* It told us something I could almost see, but not quite.

CHAPTER 42

Tires screeched to a halt in my driveway. Heather had left a few minutes ago to be with Brixton while they waited for news about Veronica. Why was she back already?

But instead of the sound of the side gate, a fist knocked on the front door.

I ran through the side gate to the front of the house, where I found a disheveled Max Liu standing at my door.

"Zoe." He spoke my name as a loving murmur and swept me into his arms. After a distracting few moments intertwined with Max, I smoothed my hair and blouse. I left my fingers looped through his but stepped back to assess him.

"I thought you were mad at me."

"Furious. But I still love you. And we need to work together to find Veronica and Eve. I can be mad at you later."

"You're not a detective anymore, Max. It's not your job to—"

"To help the people I care about? That'll always be important to me. I've known Veronica since she was little. If something happens to her, I'll never forgive myself for being so wrapped up in opening my shop that I didn't come back to help as soon as you told me what was going on."

I kissed him again. This time hard and fast. "That's one of the many reasons I love you. But I don't think she's in danger. And I think I know where they went."

"Then let's go find them."

I looked down at my bare feet, dirty but happy from the earth. "Let me grab my shoes and keys."

"We'll take my car—it's the only one with a backseat. If we find them, we'll need it."

I brushed the dirt off my feet on the back porch, grabbed my shoes and bag, and climbed the stairs to the attic to tell Dorian that Max and I were off to find Veronica and Eve.

"You know where they are? Zoe, you did not confide in me."

"I only thought of it a couple of minutes ago. In my garden. Think about it. If you felt attacked and didn't know where to run, where would you retreat to?"

Dorian spread his arms and wings at the expanse of the attic that he had transformed into a cozy space, with antiques on one side and what was effectively his studio apartment on the other.

"*Snug as a bug in a rug,*" said Dorian. "Is that the expression? I am sheltered, safe, and comfortable here."

"Exactly," I said. "Home."

He smiled as he tilted his head toward the skylight. "With an escape route, if one is needed." He folded his wings back to his side. "But the local authorities already searched her home, did they not?"

"I visited her little homestead. Even though it's small, the area is rural and you can't see any other houses from hers. I doubt the local police broke down the door to check. Remember, nobody thinks they're presently in physical danger. Just runaways."

"Yet there is a murderer who now knows she exists—and all the suspects have now been released from questioning."

Max and I were on the road five minutes later. Through his contacts, he confirmed that the local authorities had not only stopped by Eve's house but also checked with her closest neighbors, the elderly couple who Eve planned to live with while she finished high school.

"You think they could be involved?" I asked.

He shook his head and maneuvered around a slow-moving car.

"Not in what happened to Ridley. But they love Eve enough to take her in for the last two years of high school. They could be lying about whether she's with them, to protect her. If we don't find Eve and Veronica at Messenger Farm, we'll try them next."

When Veronica saw that it was me and Max, I was hoping it would be different than seeing strangers in uniform.

A little over an hour later, we turned onto the unpaved driveway.

"Stop here," I said.

"Anyone in the house can already see us from here," Max pointed out, but he did so while stopping. "We should have parked in the road if you wanted to approach without them seeing us."

"I don't." I rolled down my window. "They're here."

"Please don't tell me you've been holding back about your powers of X-Ray vision." Max gave a nervous laugh. He was still learning the full extent of what I could—and couldn't—do as an alchemist.

"You already know my one superpower," I insisted.

"The power to extract magic from plants."

"It's not—"

"I know." He squeezed my hand. "I shouldn't have said anything. This isn't the time. I'm sorry."

I accepted the apology by squeezing his hand back. "I can smell the chemical compounds released when plants are harvested. Something we all can do."

"But you're more sensitive to it than most people."

"The last time I was here, nobody had harvested anything here in quite some time. But someone did so today. That's why I asked you to stop here. They took a cutting from right here. Recently."

Max reached for his door handle when he saw me reach for mine. I put my hand on his arm to stop him. "You should wait in the car."

"If Eve is watching from inside, she's already seen me."

"A stranger is still less threatening inside a car than standing on her porch."

"If Veronica is with her, she'll tell her who I am."

"We don't know if Veronica is with her."

"Fine, fine. I'll go around back, then."

"Max. I know you want to help. But I don't want her to feel trapped. She's not dangerous."

"She ran Nathaniel Gallo off the road."

"Accidentally."

Max hesitated, then let go of the door handle. "Don't go inside without me, okay?"

I nodded my agreement and stepped out of the jeep.

Unlike the first time I'd been here, the curtains were now pulled back. Nobody was visible in the windows, but that was smart of her. She must have opened the curtains so people looking for her would see she wasn't inside. Then nobody would force the door and do a more thorough search.

My knock was met with no answer. "I know you're in there," I called.

Again, there was no answer.

I took a step back from the front door after knocking once more. "You were smart enough to park your car somewhere else, but I can smell the freshly cut nettles and bee balm."

I waited another few seconds. "And you're steeping spearmint and roses inside the house."

The door flew open. Her feet were bare, and her jeans were rolled up nearly to her knees. For a second, Eve glared at me, but then the fight went out of her. "I was careless using the roses. Rose petals are too fragrant. But freshly cut nettle? That was a guess. Wasn't it?"

I shrugged. "Not really. I know plants."

"My car is in a friend's barn a few miles away—turned out it wasn't an easy walk, because I wanted to stay off the main road." She pointed at her bare feet, which were also dripping wet. "That's why I made a foot bath with the mint and rose petals."

Without thinking, I stooped to examine her sore feet. "No abrasions, but a nasty blister is going to form here. That's a good foot bath combination for hot and tired feet, and I have a salve back home that's perfect for—"

"Who *are you*, Zoe Faust?"

I stood back up. "If you invite us inside, you can find out."

Eve gripped the edge of the door. "I'm not going back."

"Is Veronica with you? I at least need to take her home. But you don't have to go back to Blue's house—"

"Please tell Blue I'm sorry. I bet she took it personally, but it wasn't her fault. I loved her house and her wildflower garden. I'm just… When Veronica told me the whole group of them was meeting at Ridley's grave, I knew I had to hear what they said. Veronica insisted on going with me. She said she'd helped you and Dorian solve mysteries before, so she thought she could help. It was her idea to hide in the tree. But then when the branch broke and we fell… I freaked." A smile ticked up on her lips. "Veronica and I had both seen this classic movie, *Thelma and Louise*, so when I said I couldn't face them yet, Veronica said we should be like them and go on the run."

"Where's Veronica, Eve?"

"Hi, Ms. Faust." Veronica appeared behind Eve. She held an oversize mug of nettle tea in her hands and bore a few scratches on her arms, but otherwise looked unharmed.

"I thought you were calling me Zoe now?"

Veronica shrugged. "Too much effort to be someone I'm not."

"Are your feet hurt, too?"

She smiled and lifted a hiking boot. "I dressed appropriately for our adventure." Her face fell. "But it's not an adventure anymore. The local police were knocking and peeking inside. I didn't turn my phone back on, but when I do, there are going to be a gazillion messages from my parents. I only wanted to help Eve. It's not fair what happened."

"I'm here with a friend," I said. "Let us take you both—"

"I'm not coming," Eve said. "I'm not ready to meet Nathaniel and Tess. Please tell Blue that's why I can't come back to Portland to stay with her."

"I will. But you can't stay here alone. There's someone who's already killed once before, who's still out there getting desperate."

Veronica clenched the mug more tightly. "It's Amber. Eve and I heard enough before we were caught. It's totally Amber. She was totally jealous of Ridley. She wanted Emilio to herself."

Eve nodded slowly. "I thought so, too. But I'm pretty sure we just think that because she's like the boujee girls we go to school with. Did you see her eyelashes? Those can't have been real. And her hair? Who gets a glow-up to meet people at a cemetery? She was faking being scared to get with Emilio." She turned from Veronica to me. "Speaking of hot guys, ask your friend to park behind the shed, then you can both come inside."

Veronica reddened. "That's just Max."

"Your husband?" Eve asked me.

"Boyfriend," Veronica answered. "Unless a lot's happened in the few hours we've had our phones off. I don't think I've been away from my phone for this long in... *ever*." She gave me a sardonic smile that I didn't know she had in her.

"You didn't miss any change in relationship status this afternoon," I assured her. "Only a disagreement. Max took issue with my decision to leave an underage runaway with a friend instead of calling the police."

"Yikes." Veronica frowned. "Sorry he got mad at you, Ms. Faust."

My phone buzzed. It was a text message from Max.

Emilio Acosta is being held for Ridley's murder.

CHAPTER 43

Max set two mugs of matcha on the small tree-ring table in front of me. We didn't have a window, but we'd snagged the last free table at Blue Sky Teas.

"Back in a sec." He left the mugs and ducked under the leaves of a drooping branch of the weeping fig tree.

I breathed in the earthy scent of the tea, still processing everything that had happened last night. After the news of Emilio's arrest, Eve had gone to stay with the couple who lived next door to Messenger Farm, and Veronica went back home to her parents.

I took a cautious sip. Normally the caffeine from the powdered tea leaves would have been too much for me. But I hadn't gone to sleep until after midnight, and I'd still woken up at dawn. I hadn't wanted to disturb Max, so I'd crept out of bed and into his kitchen to make tea, but he'd slipped into the kitchen behind me and lured me back to bed. By the time we got up, Blue Sky Teas was already open, so we walked the few blocks from Max's house to the café.

Max returned with two small mason jars, one filled with what looked like chia pudding, the other a chilled oatmeal, both topped with flaked nuts and summer berries. "Take your pick. Since it's a warm day, I thought these looked good."

I took the chia pudding, which smelled like cinnamon and vanilla and was filled with blueberries and topped with blackberries. Max happily scooped up a spoonful of the oatmeal.

"I suppose it should feel befitting to end this mystery at the same place where it began." I stirred the pudding but didn't take a bite. "But it doesn't."

"I know it feels rather anticlimactic. Not all cases end dramatically."

"I know…but Emilio's arrest feels almost too easy."

"After sixteen years?" Max raised an eyebrow. "That's hardly easy. But yes, he was sloppier than in the past. Posting a photo of her poetry was a mistake. He's the one who stole her diaries."

A combination of two clues had led the police to Emilio as Ridley's killer. First was his own mistake. After our group discussion at the cemetery, he'd posted a photo of one of Ridley's old poems on social media—in her own handwriting. One of Ridley's old friends saw the post and wondered how Emilio got the poem. Had he been the one to steal her diaries?

Second was the burglary at Tess Price's house. Emilio knew that Tess kept a spare key in a fake rock, and even though Tess had moved the location of the rock, a person who knew of it could have used it to get inside. But that only narrowed it down to a few people. And a phone tip came in from someone who claimed to have seen a 'suspicious' man who fit Emilio's description running away from a house in Tess's neighborhood at the time of the burglary.

That was enough for them to search Emilio's apartment, where they found pages of poetry from Ridley's diaries.

"But the poems were single sheets of paper," I said. "Not full diaries."

"Pages that had been ripped out of the diaries, which he'd hidden inside other books. He was smart enough not to keep the diaries. They got Ridley's killer, Zoe."

"Why did he kill her?" I stirred the blackberries but didn't feel like I could eat. Having Max to myself had momentarily distracted me from what was going on around us. But now I had to face that fact that something felt very wrong about Emilio's arrest.

"Unrequited love," said Max. "It's a tragedy, but now at least her daughter can have closure. Nathaniel is eager to meet her. I'm glad I was wrong about him. Now Eve will be able to have a loving father in her life."

"Maybe."

Max took another spoonful of his oatmeal, a blissful smile appearing on his face. "Your friend Dorian is a genius in the kitchen. I'm glad I'll finally get to meet him in person this week."

"Wait, *what?*" My spoon clattered to the floor.

"I'll get you another one." Max grabbed the fallen spoon and returned a few seconds later with a clean one. "We're still on for summer solstice dinner to celebrate the opening of The Alchemy of Tea, right?"

"We are, but I didn't know Dorian was coming."

"He said he had a gift for me. Sweet guy. I'm glad he's gotten over his shyness about his looks. I'm glad he knows he can trust me. I know how close you two are, so I'm excited to meet him. Now eat up. You promised you'd help me unpack boxes in the storefront today."

"I will. I need to take a couple of items to the post office first." It was true. A couple of antiques had sold on the Elixir website, so I needed to pack and mail them. But what I really wanted to do was talk to Dorian.

CHAPTER 44

"You can really help me?"

"*Oui*," Dorian answered. "I, too, feel the investigation has ended prematurely. Would Emilio be so careless? *Non!* He has been framed."

"I've gotta go, Dorian," Eve whispered into the telephone. "Breakfast is ready for me downstairs."

"Never fear. Dorian Robert-Houdin is on the case."

"Thanks, Poirot."

Dorian chuckled as the girl hung up. He appreciated having his superior deductive skills recognized. His little gray cells had been hard at work on the puzzle, yet he had not quite reached the solution.

He wondered if he had been thinking *too* hard. He had thrown himself into cooking in the Blue Sky Teas kitchen before dawn this morning, yet this did not allow his mind the rest it needed. He had experimented with two new summer recipes for the scorching summer day it was predicted to be. (Zoe would correct him that it would not officially be summer until later in the week, when the solstice occurred, but this was pedantic reasoning.)

Dorian's time cooking in the night had been more challenging than he had anticipated. Therefore, his brain cells were occupied by perfecting his new recipes. He had begun work slightly after midnight, to have time to test various flavor combinations. The results were exquisite. He only mourned the fact that each of the four dozen jars of chia pudding and cold oats looked *magnifique*—therefore he could not justify bringing any home with him to share with Zoe.

He glanced at the antique clock. Zoe had not returned home last night, yet he knew she needed to package two items from Elixir for the post before she assisted Max in putting the finishing touches on The Alchemy of Tea.

In the meantime, he would distract his mind with perfecting the most perfect tea-related gift imaginable for Max. With a ticking clock before the day The Alchemy of Tea opened, Dorian had much to do.

After feasting on a second breakfast, Dorian descended the basement steps.

He began work on the preparation. Why could he not see what to do? If he had been in France, this would not have been a problem...

Ah! Of course. That was his answer. He had neglected the first lesson of alchemy. Inward intent. He had been so focused on the transformation itself that he had neglected to ground himself here in his new home.

He scampered up to the attic, bringing two photographs and one item from the kitchen down to the basement with him. It would not do to abandon all memories of his first home. Yet he also needed to fully embrace his new life here.

He set a stiff whisk on his wooden worktable. In its spokes, he placed two photographs. The first was the 150-year-old photograph Zoe had given to him. The second was a photo of Zoe and Brixton laughing in the back garden, taken by Heather. With the central elements that defined his life—cooking, France, and his friends—he returned to the preparation of Max's gift.

When Zoe stepped into the basement one hour later, he beamed up at her.

"I have done it, Zoe! I have the perfect gift for Max's new venture."

"That's wonderful." Zoe grinned at Dorian, though he did not think the smile reached her eyes.

"What is amiss?"

"I don't think Emilio is guilty."

"His innocence is the commonly accepted theory."

Zoe frowned at him. "It is?"

"*Oui.* I was discussing this with Eve earlier this morning."

"You're in touch with Eve?"

Dorian detected a hint of judgement in her voice, but he chose to ignore it. "In anticipation of meeting her father tonight, she is quite concerned that the wrong culprit has been apprehended. Not because she believes Nathaniel to be guilty, mind you. But because she will be returning to Portland with a murderer at large."

"I wish I could get them all back together. Before we were interrupted at the cemetery by Eve and Veronica falling out of the tree, I felt like I was so close to putting everything together."

The phone rang from the floor above.

"I'll be right back." Zoe hurried up the stairs.

After many minutes had passed, Dorian did not wish to wait any longer. Zoe was hanging up the telephone when he reached the top of the stairs.

"Emilio was framed," she said. "They released him an hour ago."

CHAPTER 45

My knocking on the glass door went unanswered. A generic sign informing would-be customers "Sorry, we're closed" hung crookedly behind the glass. A larger "Summer Solstice Grand Opening!" sign, printed in bright orange with the "o" replaced by a yellow image of the sun, was affixed inside the large window next to the door. No lights were on inside the store that would soon celebrate its grand opening as The Alchemy of Tea.

I knocked once more. This time, banging hard enough that I hoped I wouldn't crack the glass. Where was Max? He was supposed to be here.

Emilio had been released when the tip was found to be from an anonymous caller who gave dubious details. Emilio claimed Ridley had given him the pages from her diary when they were both teenagers experimenting with writing bad poetry, and Amber backed up his story. There wasn't enough information to charge him.

No matter whether Emilio was the killer or not, a murderer was at large. Dorian had already left a message for Eve that she shouldn't come to Portland to meet Nathaniel and Tess yet. But I didn't like that the supposedly neat resolution was unraveling before our eyes.

I knew, rationally, that there was nothing more I could do. Everyone involved was on alert to be careful, and the authorities were investigating. But with Emilio released by the police, would the real killer become even more desperate? *What would they do?*

As I stepped back, my gaze fell upon the hand-painted wooden sign hung above the door of The Alchemy of Tea. Max had commissioned a stencil of the interlocking letters, then painted the wood himself during one of the many periods of waiting for permits to come through, using paint Perenelle had mixed from the pigment garden plants I'd been growing in my yard. Woad, madder, and yarrow created vibrant dyes, if you knew how to coax them from the plants. I knew how to nurture the plants that most people thought of as weeds, and Perenelle knew how to tease vivid colors from them.

As beautiful as the sign was, I didn't have time to appreciate Perenelle and Max's handiwork. I hurried around the corner to the back alley, where I'd find the back door of the shop. I rattled the handle, but it, too, was locked. My knocking was again met with no reply. Max must have been running last-minute errands.

I sent him a text message, then went to see Nicolas and Perenelle. They'd always had wise words. I needed their counsel now.

"Our door is open!" Nicolas called out upon hearing my knock.

"You shouldn't leave your doors unlocked." I bolted the door behind me.

Perenelle was nowhere to be seen, but Nicolas was in the living room, which was now piled even higher with books. His glasses sat on top of his head, half hidden beneath his untamable hair. Only his head and shoulders were visible. The rest of his body was hidden behind a stack of books on astrophysics and organic chemistry.

"So much knowledge," he murmured, emerging from the teetering stack of books. "There is *so much* knowledge shared in the modern age. How does one consume it all?"

"It's impossible. But truly, Nicolas, it's not safe to leave your doors unlocked."

"My dear, you're distressed. Has something else happened? You told me they were holding the man responsible for killing Ridley Price, so what could be wrong? I'm saddened she did not turn out to be an alchemist. I had hoped that she faked her own death."

"Where's Perenelle?" I picked up a book that weighed as much as the largest copper pot in my kitchen, which was in danger of toppling an entire stack of books.

Nicolas took the book from my hands. "I haven't finished this one yet. The author thinks the use of obscure words and longwinded paragraphs are a sign of his intelligence."

"Perenelle?" I asked once more.

"Ah, yes. She was so pleased with the colors she mixed for Max's shop signage that she took the leftover bottles to the cemetery with her easel and a canvas. She saw photographs of the headstone for Ridley Price. She wished to paint the angel above the poor girl's grave."

Oh no.... Nicolas and Perenelle weren't mixed up in the murder of Ridley Price, so I hadn't thought to warn them. But if Perenelle was at the cemetery....

"My dear." Nicolas dropped the hefty book and rushed to my side. "What have I said?"

"Emilio was released. It looks like he was framed."

Nicolas cursed and shook his head. "There will always be those who wish to harm others, and they will do even more harm to cover up their crimes."

"Nicolas, it's even worse than that. Don't you see? The real killer is out there."

"Human nature never changes. Oh! Oh dear.... You mean that my wife is at Ridley Price's grave, a place intimately tied to the person who's killed before—"

"A person who's getting desperate."

∼

Nicolas and I found Perenelle at Ridley's gravesite, as expected.

She stood under the shade of the trees, wielding a paintbrush in her right hand while the gentle wind stirred both tree branches and the locks of her auburn hair. In her composition, the edges of the canvas were dotted with leaves and branches, as if the viewer was stepping through a lush forest to reach the subject of the painting. The angel. Perenelle's version of the peaceful stone angel was rendered entirely with blues and grays extracted from woad leaves. I felt the woad's energy as I came up beside her.

"It's beautiful," I said, momentarily forgetting why we were there.

At the sound of my voice, Perenelle gave a start. Her shoulders tensed, and her head turned toward me, but her steady hand never faltered. "I didn't see you there."

"Which is exactly why we've come to fetch you." Nicolas plucked the paintbrush from her fingers.

I explained the situation to her as we bundled her supplies and headed back to my truck. I kept an eye out, but among the few people we passed, I didn't spot anyone we knew.

Back at my truck, we secured her easel and canvas in back, careful not to smear the wet canvas, and the three of us squeezed into the front seats.

"This is most uncomfortable." Perenelle's limbs were intertwined with those of her husband as they got situated in the bucket seat.

I put the truck in gear, jostling Nicolas's elbow as I did so.

"I know you wish to keep your loved ones safe," Nicolas said through a mouthful of Perenelle's voluminous hair. "You can relax now. You have done everything you can do."

"Have I?" I glanced in my rearview mirror. He was right. I was worrying too much.

"In spite of the horrors of what this miscreant has done, there will always be people like you. Good people who wish to set things right."

"You're missing the point, my dear." Perenelle gripped the dashboard as I turned a corner. "Zoe feels helpless not only in solving this crime, but in her current role as backyard gardener and proprietor of Elixir."

I stole a glance at Perenelle before turning my attention back to the road. "I used to help so many more people when I used my alchemical skills as an herbalist. The world had different challenges in the past, but when I was on my own and moving around, I could help people. I feel like it's selfish of me to put down roots." I came to a stop in front of the Flamels' house.

"That's what you're most upset about?" Nicolas's mischievous eyes twinkled. No matter how many years he lived, or how much hardship he faced, I hoped he'd never lose that playful spirit. "I see it now. You feel that you're betraying yourself because you're focused inward right now. But Zoe, there are billions of people on earth. Although you are wise and generous of heart, you should not feel such a burden. You saved me and Perenelle. That was truly something nobody else could have done. Your friends here love you. You bring them so much joy, and they to you. I don't know how long it will be before people become suspicious about how you don't age, but that time is not yet upon us. Do not worry about problems before they arise. We shall figure that out when the challenge presents itself. As we've always done. Seasons change. This is your time to be here doing what you do so well. Being Zoe Faust."

I leaned over and gave him a big kiss on the cheek. There was a reason the wise old alchemist was an amazing mentor. He was right, of course. I was right where I needed to be. Where I *wanted* to be. It felt right. *Almost.*

Nicolas grinned at me as he shifted in the seat. "Now, would you mind helping my wife off my lap so we may extricate ourselves from this steel monstrosity?"

I helped them out of the truck and through the front door of the house. Which, I was disappointed to note, Nicolas hadn't locked.

"My husband is a wise man," Perenelle said, "yet he continues to miss the point here, does he not? He's right that it's enough to enjoy your life here for as long as you can, and to bring joy to those of us in your orbit. Yet at the same time, you must do what you can to assist your new friend Eve. Do not do it out of a sense of obligation. Do it because you're unhappy *not* to do so."

Perenelle and Nicolas were the perfect complements to each other. I'd been on my own for so long, without a family, that I'd forgotten what it was like to be able to lean on people. To know that they were both wise and had only the best in mind for me. Between them, I knew exactly what I needed to do.

Nicolas beamed at Perenelle. "How did I end up with the most perfect woman on earth? Could one of you please help me find my spectacles?"

I handed him his glasses from where he'd left them on the top of his head, gave them both a big hug, and set off to catch a killer before the killer caught up with Eve.

I headed home to figure out my next steps. I needed to clear my head with a brief walk in my garden, where I could also pick some berries to fuel whatever came next. Dorian would no doubt have some ludicrous ideas for how to trap a killer, but I appreciated that he was a creative thinker. He'd often had the gem of a great idea buried in an otherwise asinine plan.

But when I pulled into my driveway, someone else was waiting for me. Max. Leaning against my silver Airstream trailer, dressed in a white shirt and black jeans, he looked as if he'd stepped out of an old black and white photograph. I wished I could step into the photograph with him and take him by the hand into my trailer that had been my sanctuary for decades. But the look on his face told me he was even more worried than I was.

The heavy door of my old truck squeaked when I pushed it open. "I tried to find you at The Alchemy of Tea."

Max was already at my side before I'd finished my sentence or closed the door behind me. He took my hand and steered me back into my truck. "Let's go."

"Where are we going?"

"I was running an errand for the shop and missed your texts, but I needed to find you as soon I heard this: Nathaniel Gallo's house is burning down."

CHAPTER 46

The air smelled of cedar, smoke, and brimstone.

Nathaniel Gallo's house was on the outskirts of town, so thankfully it wasn't close to any other houses, and his had been the only one lost. By the time we reached the site of the fire, all that was left of it was a few charred beams and smoldering ashes.

The police had cordoned off the area close to the house, but the smoking rubble was visible from beyond their barrier.

I pulled over and turned off the engine, wondering if this was my fault. "Because of me, the suspects know about Crimson Fish now. Did someone search his house and want to destroy something they found?"

"You can't think like that." Max put a hand on mine. "No good would happen if people were afraid that making things better might come at the cost of some mistakes. Nobody was hurt. That's the important thing."

"You're sure?" I pried my eyes from the wreckage to look at Max.

"That's what I heard. But let's go check for sure."

We got out of the car and walked as close as we could. I didn't see anyone I recognized, but Max walked over to one of the police officers he knew. Other curious people were gathering, so I went back to the truck to wait for Max.

"No casualties," he told me five minutes later. "But things are a mess in there. It's still considered toxic, but some kid was in there playing."

"A kid? Not Eve—?"

"No. A little kid in a superhero cape. They're looking for the child now. Worried the child might be burned but didn't want to ask for help because they're afraid of getting in trouble. It's still blazingly hot over there."

I gripped the steering wheel and looked out at the rubble. I didn't want Max to read my expression. I knew exactly who had been there. And it wasn't a kid playing superhero.

"Zoe, are you okay? Do you want to come with me to help search for the child?" Max was already stepping out of the truck again.

"I don't think it was a kid, Max."

He shook his head. "It wasn't one of the suspects. It was clearly a little kid. I'm going to help them search the surrounding area. You don't look good, Zoe. I think the bad air is affecting you. You don't need to stay."

"I really don't think—"

Max leaned back inside the truck just long enough to give me a kiss, then was off.

"Dorian," I whispered to myself. What was the gargoyle looking for in the rubble of the house? He knew better than to go out in broad daylight. The cape kept him partly hidden, but not entirely. I wasn't worried about Dorian being burned. His skin was better adapted to high heat, so physically he'd be fine. The biggest danger was being seen—or caught.

I called the number of the land line of my house, but Dorian didn't pick up. I hoped he'd gotten away before this search picked up in earnest.

I tried calling once more, but again, nobody answered.

My phone buzzed in my hand. It was a text message from Blue. *Can you get over to my café?*

What's up? I texted back.

They're here.

I stared at my phone screen. I knew I was tired and anxious, but was I really that dense? What was Blue trying to tell me?

Who? I asked.

The people who may have killed Eve's mom.

CHAPTER 47

I stepped through the orange door of Blue Sky Teas, underneath the plaque that read "'There is no trouble so great or grave that cannot be diminished by a nice cup of tea.' —Bernard-Paul Heroux." Somehow, I didn't believe Heroux today. The faces that looked up at me seemed to agree.

Five tired-looking, soot-covered people were seated around tree-ring tables at Blue Sky Teas, along with three others. Tess and Roman sat together at a table in the front window. The residue of ashes clung to Tess's hair and coated Roman's white dress shirt that was rolled to his elbows. Emilio and Amber were seated under the weeping fig tree, where Amber was scrubbing at a dark smudge on the back of her hand with a linen napkin. Dirt was visible under Emilio's fingernails, and a smear of soot that remained on his face resembled camouflage paint.

Nathaniel—the most soot-covered of all—sat alone, apart from the others. He hadn't even tried to wipe away the grime. I couldn't stop myself from worrying that he'd breathed in smoke before escaping the house fire, or that dangerous sediment from the fire might be trapped underneath his dirt-covered cast, but I told myself to focus.

Joona and Heather were there as well, but neither was touched by soot and both were standing. Joona stood against the wall near the counter, with her massive purse at her hip, tapping on her cell phone. Heather hovered near Nathaniel's table, poised between joining him and running for the door.

Blue stood in front of the counter with her arms crossed and her forehead creased with worry. Blue Sky Teas closed daily in the mid-afternoon, and had already closed for the day, so there were no other customers.

"Is everyone okay?" I asked. "The fire—"

"I was at Tess's house when it broke out." Nathaniel looked at the tree rings of the table as he spoke softly. The lenses of his glasses were so thick with grime that I wondered if he was even aware of where he was. "We were told Emilio... We were told there was evidence, so we knew it wasn't any of us, so we all got together...."

"Except for me." Joona looked up from her phone. "I was back in Seattle. I thought this was over, so I went home last night."

"We were talking about Eve," Nathaniel said, "when I got the call about my house. Arson. The killer wanted to cover up any clues they thought I could have discovered without knowing their significance."

"Or you could have been drawing attention away from yourself," said Joona.

Amber laughed nervously.

"What?" Joona said. "That's exactly what you're all thinking. All of you except for whoever killed Riddle."

"We all went to Nathaniel's house after he got the call," Tess whispered. She didn't look like she'd sustained any external injuries, but from the soot on her face, I wondered how much smoke she'd breathed in. Had she been looking for something in the ashes? "All his photos of my Ridley... Gone. They're all gone. Then the police wanted to question each of us afterward."

"That's why I had to drive back down," Joona added.

"You could have given me a heads-up that you'd invited them over here after they left the police station," Blue said to me, but she didn't seem angry. Instead, she stole a glance at each of their cups, as if checking to see if any of them needed their tea refreshed.

"I didn't invite anyone," I said. "Why are they all here?"

Only now did Blue look concerned. She ran a hand through her gray curls and she looked back at the group, though this time with suspicion. "Aren't you the one who called them all and asked them to meet here?"

"Wait, what?" I stared at Blue. "Who told you that?" I had told Dorian I *wished* I could get everyone together, because I was so close to figuring out what was going on. He wouldn't have... would he? I took a deep breath. *Of course* he would.

Emilio stood, tucking in his already neatly tucked shirt as he did so. "You're kidding, right? You said you had important news, so we all needed to meet you here."

"I didn't call any of you," I said slowly.

"Yeah, I know it wasn't *you* yourself." Emilio glared at me. "Your assistant. Guy with a French accent."

I didn't know if I was relieved or upset that my hunch was confirmed and this was indeed Dorian's doing.

"Hang on." Roman's chair squealed on the floor as he stood quickly. "The guy who called us knew everything you did. That's why we thought he was really calling on your behalf—Oh, god. The killer. The killer brought us all here together." He sniffed the air.

"I don't smell gas," Joona said calmly. "Nobody's blowing us up. We've been pranked. That's all."

"I know who it was." Heather tugged nervously at the fabric of her sundress. "He's not an assistant. He's Zoe and Blue's friend, Dorian. The French chef who bakes here at Blue's. When he called me, he asked me to bring the riddle—"

"A French chef?" Roman gaped at her. "I don't care who it was, but he has a terrible sense of humor. Come on everyone." He stepped toward me and the front door of the café.

I stepped in front of the door to stop him. "I just need a couple of minutes. Please, everyone. I think I know why you were invited here."

"You said it wasn't you—" Emilio began.

"I want to see this over," Amber cut in. The back of her hand was raw where she'd been scrubbing away the grime from the fire. "I want to know what really happened, so we can go on with our lives properly." Under her thick eyelashes, she peeked at Emilio.

"Heather," I said. "Did you bring the riddle like Dorian asked?"

She plucked the invitation from sixteen years ago from an oversize pocket and read the outside of the folded card: *"Join me for my welcome-home party and see the riddle solved."* She opened the card, where the pressed chrysanthemum was affixed above the four lines she now read:

> *A springtime daisy means you'll keep a secret,*
> *whether for a moment or a lifetime of regret.*
> *Tear off the petals, deep in thought:*
> *will this be the beginning or will it not?*

In the silence that filled the teashop after the last word Heather read, I knew I was right. The killer was in Blue Sky Teas with us. *Why hadn't I seen it sooner?*

I quickly looked up one date on my phone. It told me my theory was right.

"This is morbid." Joona was the one to break the silence. For the first time since I'd met her, she looked shaken. "Riddle was talking about her baby. She'd just given birth when she wrote that. The lines are talking about the new beginning of springtime, but her party was at the end of summer. Her new baby is the answer to the riddle. We already know that. Why do we have to relive it?"

"Ridley called that a riddle," I said. "But if we look more carefully at it, it's a poem. The police are currently analyzing the poetry from the pages of Ridley's diary that Emilio had."

It was a lie, but one that was only untrue because they didn't yet have the next bit of information. I was sure once I told them my theory, they'd analyze the poems and find I was right.

Ridley's poetry was the reason for her death.

CHAPTER 48

"This isn't just morbid," Roman said. "It's ridiculous." He snatched the invitation from Heather's hand and pushed me aside to get at the door.

Roman was close to a foot taller than me. I wouldn't have been able to stop him from where I stood, so I didn't try. Instead, I dropped to my knees and yanked his lower leg as he took a final step toward the door.

Roman Price fell backward and knocked into the weeping fig tree.

"She's deranged," he shouted.

"She also saw something I should have seen sixteen years ago." Emilio was already using his belt to tie Roman's hands behind his back. "I should have seen it in her poems," he muttered as he cinched the belt tightly around Roman's wrists.

"What are you doing, Emi?" Amber cried.

"Ridley was always the poet," I said. "Not Roman."

"That's not true," Heather said. "Roman was getting his MFA in poetry when Ridley and the rest of us were in high school."

"You were all about the same age as her," I said, "so you saw a confident young woman who was smart and seemed to have her life figured out. But Ridley was also a self-conscious teenager in many ways. She showed her poetry only to her friend who also loved poetry. Emilio. That's why he had some of the pages from her diaries. She had given them to him. She was sharing her poetry with him, because she didn't think he would judge her."

"Emi always loved poetry," Amber said. "It took him forever to even tell me about it. It didn't fit with his image."

"There were other clues that pointed to Ridley being a poet," I said. "Her riddles themselves were poetry. She didn't call them that, but they were. Ridley's poems were far better than she realized. The only person who *did* know how good they were was the only other person she showed her poetry to. Her brother."

"What are you saying?" Tess's eyes were wild. "My Roman is a wonderful poet. He has books of critically acclaimed poetry. Emilio, let go of my boy. He—"

"It's over, Mother," Roman said. "I've known this day would come. When someone analyzed my poems against hers. How did you know?" He looked up at me. "Are you a poet?"

"I know human nature. I know you didn't mean to kill your sister. The date of your first publication was right after Ridley died. Journals take time to come out. That means you had already stolen one of her poems."

"I never meant to do it!" he cried. "Any of it."

Tess stifled a sob, and both Amber and Heather went to her side. Emilio, apparently satisfied by his binding, stepped away from Roman with a disgusted look on his face.

"It wasn't my fault," Roman said. "I didn't know my professor would submit that first poem for publication. I only shared it in class. I was tired of my own work not being respected. I was *missing a certain spark*, they all said. What did they know? But Ridley always loved my work. She looked up to me. She showed me some of her own attempts at poetry, making me promise I wouldn't tell anyone else she was playing with poetry, which she knew was my thing. She loved gardening and games."

"What kind of man steals from his baby sister?" Emilio spat out the words.

"I didn't mean to do it! Like I said, I only shared one of her poems with my class. I thought I'd get feedback for her. But then my professor thought it was good enough to be published. It's his fault. The journal was coming out that fall, so I was trying to figure out how to tell Ridley about the mistake. I thought it would be better to tell her in person. But when Ridley was about to come home at the end of the summer, she gave us all that riddle about new beginnings. I thought she had somehow found out. I thought she was about to expose me."

"She wasn't like that." Nathaniel, who'd been silent until now, stood so quickly that his chair toppled and crashed to the floor. "How could you even *think* she'd do something like that?"

Roman shrank away from him. "She'd changed so much that year. It was like I barely knew her anymore."

Nathaniel flew at him, but Emilio and Blue pulled him back.

"How did you do it? How?" Nathaniel's voice broke. "I tried to figure it out. We were all there. How did you kill her and get her body out of that house?"

"She was never at the party," Roman whispered.

"Of course she was," Joona said. "We all saw her." Her matter-of-fact voice had an effect on Roman. He met her gaze when he spoke.

"No. I told her I wanted to talk with her before the party. I was staying at a friend's apartment while I was home in Portland for the summer. She met me there. I hadn't planned to hurt her. But when I saw how smug she was about her riddle…I snapped. I don't even know what I did, but when I came to my senses, it was too late. My hands were around her neck and there was no life left in her. I didn't know what to do. People had always said I looked so much like her, except for my height."

Amber gasped. "We saw her figure only for a second, and at the top of the stairs."

"She—I mean you," Joona said, "only said a few words, that you'd be down in a few minutes."

"And I only saw the back of her head." Emilio swore. "A wig?"

Roman nodded. "I found a cheap wig that looked like her hair, and I made a cut on Ridley's hand to collect some blood to plant at the house. Everybody knew that Ridley was at the party and that's where she was killed. Her body was never found there, since she was never there in the first place. That gave me time to bury her later."

Tess let out a wailing sob.

"I'm sorry," Roman whispered. "None of this was supposed to happen. None of it."

"Your most famous book of poetry," I said, "with *Hansel* as the lead story. That was Ridley's?"

Roman nodded. "Mostly. But it was originally *Gretel*. Gretel was the original name of that poem. I changed it just enough to make it mine."

"Like hell you did," Emilio said. "It was still Ridley's."

"That's why I felt like I was a hair's breadth away from being caught. Don't you see? I never got to enjoy any of my success. All of her work went into that first collection. It got me my professorial appointment. But I couldn't live up to it. My failure to reproduce the caliber of my previous work was attributed to the fact that I was grieving after the death of my beloved sister. It was true! I never wanted it to come to this."

"That poor baby," Joona said.

"I never knew that Eve existed," Roman sputtered. "I'm not a monster! I would have done things differently if I'd known. I would have—"

He broke off as Nathaniel punched him. Hard. As Nathaniel cradled his hand with his broken arm, Tess went to check on his hand.

"I was wondering how long it would take for somebody to do that." Eve raised her head above the counter where she'd been hiding.

"Eve?" Nathaniel took a hesitant step toward her, as did Tess.

She smiled. "Thanks, Dad and Gran."

CHAPTER 49

Dorian had been watching the proceedings from his hiding spot in the kitchen of Blue Sky Teas, which had a door that did not fit snugly and afforded a narrow line of sight into the café. He was pleased that Zoe had been correct to suggest this meeting. It was the right thing to do to gather the suspects once more. It was his initiative that had actually brought them all together, of course. He sighed. He would never get the credit he was due for his first-rate sleuthing.

No matter. He was a humble gargoyle who did not require accolades. He was content knowing that he had always suspected Roman. This was not revisionist history. Dorian had truly believed Roman Price was a bad seed. The rogue had misremembered Zoe's name. That was not the type of thing a nice person would do.

After Nathaniel Gallo punched the murderous Roman Price, one of Ridley's old friends had called the police. In the time it took them to arrive, they also coaxed the rest of the story from Roman. The brute knew that all was lost, so he at least wished to tell his story. Joona and Zoe had both had the forethought to record the confession. Dorian himself would have done this as well, had he been able to use a cell phone.

The remainder of the story they extracted from Roman was exactly as Dorian had expected. When Eve pretended to be Ridley this week, Roman was terrified. He became more and more desperate. When both he and his mother received letters from the "ghost," he expected others would as well. Therefore, he needed to make sure they would be scared off before the "ghost" did whatever she had in mind, by faking the attack with an arrow. He arrived early and stuck the arrow in the tree next to her grave, then when he saw "Ridley" appear in the cemetery, he used his phone to play the sound of an arrow whisking through the air.

When Roman felt things were closing in, he wanted to make sure there was no more of Ridley's poetry hidden in her untouched room. He had a key to the house, so he used it when he thought his mother would be gone for the afternoon. He climbed onto the tree branch outside the window to break the glass from the outside, barely making it back inside before the branch snapped and fell. He then waited in the backyard, disguised in an oversize thrift store coat, until his mother returned home, at which point he threw two of the stones from Ridley's flower garden into the remaining glass of the broken window, so his mother would hear it and see a male figure running away.

As Roman had expected, his mother guessed it was Nathaniel, who she had always assumed guilty. After Nathaniel was found to have an alibi and Emilio posted a photograph of Ridley's old poetry online, Roman falsified the anonymous tip about Emilio being in the neighborhood acting suspiciously at the time of the burglary. Roman had nothing against either of the two men, yet he would rather one of them go to prison instead of himself.

Roman's last attempt at covering up his crime was the fire. After Roman learned of Eve's existence and Nathaniel's Crimson Fish game, he put in place his last desperate move to cover up any inadvertent clues that might point to him. After Nathaniel left his home, Roman set a small fire that would take time to get going, then he went to meet the others as planned.

Ah, the fire. Dorian had not been able to resist searching through the remains of the fire to see if there were truly clues hidden at the home of Nathaniel Gallo. Dorian was in a unique position to search through a hot environment. He did not find anything of use, and retreated before the authorities went in search of a child that had been seen.

As Roman was completing his story, four police officers burst through the door of Blue Sky Teas.

"Book him," said the burly officer who yanked Roman to his feet and whisked him away.

Well, that was not *exactly* what transpired when the police arrived. If Dorian were being truly honest, that is not what transpired at all. There was, in truth, much more confusion as the officers came upon the soot-covered tea party, and none of the Portland PD police officers at the scene could be considered remotely "burly."

Dorian wriggled his horns as he watched the scene unfold. The confounded officers did not know who to arrest! Was it Emilio Acosta, who had tied up the sad-looking soul underneath the tree? Or perhaps it was Nathaniel Gallo, who they knew to be the main suspect in this strange case? Or had the citizen's arrest of the man tied with a belt identified the true killer? And why had these people not washed themselves after being at the site of a fire?

Dorian covered his mouth with his clawed hand so nobody would hear his chuckle at his joke to himself. He knew it was a risk to remain at the café, yet he also knew he could turn to stone, to hide in plain sight as a statue, if required. Then the authorities would merely see a stone gargoyle in the kitchen. "A good luck charm," perhaps they would think. Many kitchens contained figures of patron saints.

The risk was worth it, for after a few minutes of confusion and much shouting, Blue was now fixing tea for Eve, Nathaniel, and Tess.

The others had left immediately for the police station to give their statements, and the newly connected family members promised to follow shortly. They wished to have at least few minutes of peace to become acquainted before reliving the tragic events of sixteen years before.

"This isn't how I imagined this reunion would go," Eve said, holding a cold compress to Nathaniel's bruised hand, "but I'm so happy to meet you both."

Dorian felt such an affinity for the young woman who thought of him as Poirot. He was pleased that even though she did not have a fairy tale happy ending, she did indeed have two people who would love and care for her.

CHAPTER 50

"Gretel," I read aloud with a smile. The notification popped up on my phone as I was harvesting strawberries in my backyard. Roman's plagiarized book of poetry, *Hansel*, was going to be republished with his sister's original, unaltered poems, as *Gretel* by Ridley Price.

The news in the days following Roman's arrest was even better than I had imagined.

Eve had invited Nathaniel to live with her in her inherited farmhouse, since he now had no place to live after his house had burned down. That way, she could also stay in her childhood home while finishing high school there. Eve told Tess she was invited over to brunch every Sunday. And the Flamels and I were invited to visit any time to help out with the plants in the permaculture garden. I hesitated to think of it as mentoring, as it sounded like Aggie Messenger had been every bit as skilled as I was, just from a different perspective.

Heather had completed her full painted portrait of Ridley, which Tess adored and purchased on the spot for a generous price. And Perenelle gave Nathaniel the painting she'd made of the scribe angel watching over Ridley's grave.

Even Veronica hadn't fared as badly as I'd feared. Her parents decided she might have rebelled because they were stricter than necessary. That didn't let her completely off the hook. Her parents thought it would be a good idea for her to spend her summer doing community service instead of having unstructured time with her friends.

It was now the day before the summer solstice. I breathed in the sweet scents of the summer garden. Tonight, Max was hosting a small dinner party at his house down the street from mine, and tomorrow was the grand opening of The Alchemy of Tea.

When my basket was filled past the brim with fresh berries, I carried it inside to Dorian and told him the news about Ridley's book of poetry.

"This is old news, Zoe." Dorian wriggled his horns. "Brixton has already informed me that his mother has been commissioned to illustrate the book cover."

"That's perfect."

"She is not as accomplished as *mademoiselle* Flamel, yet I agree this is the best choice." Dorian took the basket of strawberries from my hands and scampered to the counter, where he used his stepping stool to work comfortably on the kitchen countertops.

"I'm going to have a cup of tea with Max at Blue Sky Teas," I said. Max was relieved that the Ridley Price case was finally solved after all these years, so he was able to happily throw himself into the finishing touches on The Alchemy of Tea—and to take a short break with me this morning.

"*Bon.* And I will be creating a most delectable dessert with this bountiful basket of strawberries. Or perhaps something savory. Perhaps…"

I left Dorian scribbling in his recipe journal and slipped out the door.

Max was already at the café when I arrived, and he wasn't alone. He was sitting at a cozy table with Amber and Emilio, who I'd heard were getting back together.

"You really think I can start over with a new career at thirty-three?" Emilio was asking Max as I sat down.

"I'm starting a new venture and I'm a decade older than you," Max answered.

"Our friend Blue, who runs this place, started over in her fifties," I added as I joined them. "She's never been happier."

"She's the one who told me I should talk to Max," Emilio said.

"We came in this morning to apologize for the mess we made of the place earlier this week," Amber said. "Before we knew it, she had us sitting with Max."

"I still don't know if I have it in me to go back to school so late." Emilio spun his empty cup on the tree ring table.

"Think about it like this," said Max. "How do you want to spend your day when you wake up tomorrow? And the day after that? That's what you should be doing. Because who knows how much time any of us have? I know I want to spend however much time I have doing what I love—and with the people I love." Max was looking at Emilio when he spoke, but I felt as if he was speaking to me now as well. He squeezed my hand and confirmed my suspicion.

"Thanks," Emilio said as he and Amber stood up. "I appreciate it."

They walked to the door holding hands, and Emilio held open the door for two people. Max chuckled as I held my breath.

"Remember," said Max, "there never was a ghost."

I gave him a playful kick under the table. "I'm not worried about Emilio letting a ghost into Blue's. I still can't quite believe I get to have a peaceful day."

"Morning," Max corrected. "You agreed to help me with the finishing touches of The Alchemy of Tea this afternoon, before I go home to get ready for the dinner party."

"Helping you with the shop *is* peaceful. I love what you've created."

"I hope I have room for all the gifts friends and family are giving me as good luck charms for the new shop. Don't get me wrong—I'm fortunate to have so many thoughtful people in my life."

"Don't worry." I laughed. "Both my and Dorian's gifts are small."

Dorian had confided in me about the gift he'd created: a magical stone. He used his own stone energy to imbue a stone from the rubble of Notre Dame (which he had pilfered when we returned to

Paris after the fire) with eternal warmth. This gift was especially relevant to Max's new shop, because Max wanted to have a teapot with sample tea, yet if people were only trying a few sips, the tea would grow cold. This way, the teapot could stay warm in a safe way, and help Max's shop flourish. Dorian had asked me to give Max his gift that night at the small dinner party he wasn't attending.

"I don't want to spoil the surprise," I said, "So I won't tell you what our gifts are right now, but I'll bring both of them this evening."

Max frowned. "You will?"

"Is something wrong?"

"Only that Dorian told me he'd be bringing me his gift himself."

I nearly choked on my tea. "Dorian is coming to your dinner party?"

Max grinned. "He finally trusts me enough not to judge him by his appearance. I'm honored. I can't wait to see you both tonight."

This was certainly going to be interesting.

THE END

The Accidental Alchemist Mysteries will continue in 2023! Never miss a new release in the Accidental Alchemist series when you sign up for Gigi's newsletter. Scan the code below, or go to www.gigipandian.com.

Scan to subscribe to Gigi's newsletter!

Keep reading for a preview of Under Lock & Skeleton Key, *from Gigi's latest series, the Secret Staircase Mysteries.*

RECIPES

CHOCOLATE STRAWBERRY OVERNIGHT OATMEAL

A chilled oatmeal that's perfect for a hearty start to a warm day.

Ingredients:

- 1/2 cup rolled oats
- 3/4 cup almond milk (or other milk of choice)
- 1/4 cup plant-based plain yogurt (or other plain yogurt of choice)
- 1 tsp chia seeds
- 1 Tbsp cacao powder
- 1/4 cup fresh strawberries, chopped
- 1/2 Tbsp maple syrup
- 1 Tbsp sunflower seeds
- Dash salt
- Cinnamon

Directions:

Mix all the ingredients together in a 2-cup mason jar or bowl. Cover and place in the fridge overnight, or for at least 4 hours. When you're ready to eat it, top with cinnamon and additional fruit, if desired. Enjoy!

Variations:

Don't like strawberries? Substitute any summer berry, or 1 Tbsp dried fruit of choice.

Want a more decadent treat? Instead of sunflower seeds, add 1 Tbsp nut butter.

Want to turn this into a dessert? Mix in an additional Tbsp maple syrup, and when you're ready to serve it, divide the mixture into two martini glasses and sprinkle with chocolate chips.

VANILLA BLUEBERRY CHIA PUDDING

A hearty breakfast pudding that's a perfect combination of delicious, healthy, and filling.

Ingredients:

- 3 Tbsp chia seeds
- 3/4 cup almond milk (or other milk of choice)
- 1/4 cup plant-based plain yogurt (or other plain yogurt of choice)
- 1/2 cup fresh blueberries
- 1/2 tsp vanilla extract
- 1/2 Tbsp maple syrup, or adjust up or down to preferred sweetness

Directions:

Mix all the ingredients together in a 2-cup mason jar or bowl. Cover and place in the fridge overnight. The chia seeds will plump a lot, so the patience of waiting overnight results in a creamy pudding. Yum!

SUMMER FRUIT POPSICLES

An easy warm-weather treat—no popsicle molds required.

Ingredients:

- 1 cup fresh summer fruit, diced (e.g. strawberries, peaches, raspberries)
- 1 cup coconut milk (full fat, not "light")
- 2 Tbsp maple syrup

Directions:

Mix ingredients together in a bowl. Divide into popsicle molds, if you have them. Don't have popsicle molds? Simply use ice-cube trays and toothpicks. To keep the toothpicks from falling over before the mixture sets, place foil over the filled cubes, then poke toothpicks through the foil. Chill for at least 4 hours before eating.

AUTHOR'S NOTE

The Alchemist of Riddle and Ruin is being published 11 years after I wrote a first draft of the book that became *The Accidental Alchemist*. That novel changed my life. I was going through chemotherapy treatments when I wrote that first draft, so I found myself writing about the Elixir of Life—and also a whimsical gargoyle who I never thought anyone besides me would get a kick out of. I was writing as therapy to get myself through a brutal year, but it turned into something far greater. This summer I'm celebrating an exciting anniversary: I'm 10 years cancer-free.

I have so much fun writing each of the books in the Accidental Alchemist Mystery Series, and I have ideas for so many more. But at the same time, I have to pry myself away from my research to begin writing. Books and videos lead me to courses and workshops, and depending on the subject, also often my own trial and error. For this book, I went down a rabbit hole of gardening, tea, and board games.

The history and principles discussed in the book are rooted in fact, but then fantasy takes over.

On my website, you'll find blog posts (at www.gigipandian.com/AoRR) where I share more about the research I've drawn upon. As for what's next? I've already got a list of books and workshops for the *next* Accidental Alchemist novel.

AN ALMANAC OF FLOWERS: A POEM

BY SUE PARMAN (AKA GIGI'S MOM)

Beware the riddles of the human tongue,
the misdirections of a lonely heart gone numb;
but trust the surge of nature and its fragrant hours,
and learn to read the language of the flowers.

January
Snowdrops for sympathy. A single bloom
in a graveyard is a harbinger of doom
but scattered in a landscape of snow they grieve
for the loss of Paradise by Adam and Eve.

February
In the coldest month the violets roam wild,
and with silent velvet slippers climb the side
of sleepers' dreams and guarded tenements
where dwell the modest, faithful innocents.

March
March blows cold. Avert your gaze
from drooping daffodils that symbolize the grave.
A sign of wealth, an aphrodisiac,
an antidote for baldness and a cure for plaque.

April
A springtime daisy means you'll keep a secret,
whether for a moment or a lifetime of regret.
Tear off the petals, deep in thought:
will this be the beginning or will it not?

May
Use hawthorn stakes to banish evil, cure
a broken heart or court the Fay of Celtic lore.
Beware of change; the slide of spring to summer
opens you up to hope, and then to her.

June
Choose the colors of your roses carefully:
red for romance, yellow for jealousy.
Throw petals in the path of brides and kings
as candles melt with joy and new life sings.

July
The mules that angels ride were shaped
from water lilies floating on a crimson lake
of blood and Buddhist resurrection:
from dirt and darkness, let the flowers open.

August
Poppies cascade from the hands of Demeter,
goddess of nostalgia and agriculture.
Sweet life! It's time to wake from sleep and choose
between the poppy and the rose.

September
September radiates a quiet story
with a touch of aster and a burst of morning glory:
plants of sweet affection heaven-sent
to ward off rain and serpents.

October
As days grow short, we age, grow old
and follow the neon light of marigold
into the dark. The dead wait there,
and plait the golden flowers in their raven hair.

November
A single petal of a red chrysanthemum
placed in a glass of wine ensures protection
against aging, gray hair, and loneliness.
It tastes like Happiness.

December
Holly is beautiful and sharp
and semi-toxic to the human heart.
Reserve it for the time your love begins to roam.
Draw blood and whisper, "Love, stay home."

BOOKS BY GIGI PANDIAN

The Accidental Alchemist Mysteries

The Accidental Alchemist (Book 1)
The Masquerading Magician (Book 2)
The Elusive Elixir (Book 3)
The Alchemist's Illusion (Book 4)
The Lost Gargoyle of Paris (Book 4.5, a novella)
The Alchemist of Fire and Fortune (Book 5)
The Alchemist of Riddle and Ruin (Book 6)

Jaya Jones Treasure Hunt Mysteries

Artifact (Book 1)
Pirate Vishnu (Book 2)
Quicksand (Book 3)
Michelangelo's Ghost (Book 4)
The Ninja's Illusion (Book 5)
The Glass Thief (Book 6)
The Cambodian Curse & Other Stories (Locked Room Mystery Short Story Collection)

The Secret Staircase Mysteries

Under Lock & Skeleton Key (Book 1)
The Raven Thief (Book 2) - coming in March 2023

Available now from Minotaur Books: *Under Lock & Skeleton Key*, the first book in the new Secret Staircase Mysteries.

An impossible crime. A family legacy. The intrigue of hidden rooms and secret staircases.

Multiple award-winning author Gigi Pandian introduces her newest heroine in this heartfelt series debut. *Under Lock & Skeleton Key* layers stunning architecture with mouthwatering food in an ode to classic locked-room mysteries that will leave readers enchanted.

Praise for *Under Lock & Skeleton Key*

"**Wildly entertaining.**" —*The New York Times Book Review*

"An enchanting new series... **a must-read.**" —Deanna Raybourn

"Pandian is **this generation's queen of the locked-room mystery!** A whimsical confection." —Naomi Hirahara

"**Excellent... a fresh and magical locked-room mystery** filled with fascinating and likable characters, incredible settings, and Tempest's grandfather's home-cooked Indian meals." —*Library Journal*

"**Pandian is in top form** in this thoroughly enjoyable series launch... Lovers of traditional mysteries with quirky characters will be well rewarded." —*Publishers Weekly* (starred review)

"**An absolute sparkling gem of a book!**" —Jenn McKinlay

NEW SERIES: THE SECRET STAIRCASE MYSTERIES

UNDER LOCK & SKELETON KEY: CHAPTER 1

Tempest Raj tested the smooth, hardwood floor once more. Following the floorboards from the beaten-up steamer trunk with three false bottoms to the window letting in moonlight, she didn't hear a squeak anywhere. Good.

In the dim light, she walked the length of the room once more in her ruby red ballet flats that were wearing thin over her left pinkie toe. She glanced at the antique clock on the wall. Seven minutes past midnight. There was no way she'd get to sleep for hours.

Satisfied that the floor wouldn't make a sound, she stretched her shoulders, then arched into a backbend kick-over. As soon as her feet touched down, she pushed off into a pirouette. Then another. Spinning, she felt almost free.

Almost.

When she came to an abrupt halt a full minute later, she was breathing harder than she should have been, and she hadn't vanished. Of course she hadn't. This wasn't a stage. There was no trap door underneath her. No audience. She was no longer The Tempest. She was simply Tempest Raj, back at home in her childhood bedroom. And apparently, she was already getting out of shape.

She took a bow for an audience of no one, then kicked off her shoes and flopped onto the bed. Unlike the solid floorboards, the box springs protested with a dreadful screech. The twin-size mattress poking her hip was oh-so-different from the luxurious California king she'd had in Las Vegas up until two weeks ago—when she'd had to sell nearly everything she owned and get out of Dodge.

She was trying to adjust. Really, she was. The schedule of a stage magician meant she never made it to bed until the "wee hours of the morning," as Grannie Mor would say. But she needed sleep. Tomorrow was a big day. No, that wasn't quite true. It *might* be a big day. She knew she shouldn't get her hopes up. The proposal he mentioned might mean a number of things. She'd narrowed it down to the two most likely possibilities, one of which she was desperately hoping for. It was her way out of this mess. As for the other possibility? She'd decide what she thought after she saw him.

NEW SERIES: THE SECRET STAIRCASE MYSTERIES

She shifted and tried to get away from the most offensive mattress spring. Looking up at the glow-in-the-dark stars from her childhood that still dotted the ceiling, Tempest wondered yet again how she'd gotten here. Everyone believed the stage accident that had wrecked her career and nearly killed her was due to her own negligence. The public, her manager, the venue, and even her supposed friends were quick to accept the worst about her, assuming it was true that she'd replaced the vetted illusions for something far more dangerous. *Tempestuous Tempest, who knew she couldn't top her previous show, but went too far trying to, putting her own life and those of many others in danger...* Her actions preparing for the new, unsafe stunt had supposedly been witnessed. But there was someone who could easily impersonate Tempest. Her former stage double, Cassidy Sparrow.

When Cassidy dyed her naturally mahogany hair black, she looked eerily similar to Tempest. Cassidy wasn't quite Tempest's doppelgänger, but with her strong and curvy five-foot-ten frame, large brown eyes, and wild black hair that reached halfway down her back, she came close.

Cassidy had purposefully wrecked Tempest's career. *Sabotage.* The threat of lawsuits still hung over Tempest's head like a guillotine.

There was no other explanation for what had happened that terrible night. No, that wasn't quite true. There was one other possible explanation, but Tempest couldn't let herself believe it. There was no way it could be true. The first glimmer of such a terrible possibility appeared five years ago, when she first began to wonder if—no. She pushed all thought of it from her mind.

At least one person besides her family believed in her innocence. That's why she was hopeful about seeing him tomorrow. This could be the first step in getting her life back on track.

She closed her eyes, but they popped back open. The constellations on the ceiling didn't mirror reality, but if you looked carefully, you could see that the pinpricks of light formed a constellation in the shape of a skeleton key. A symbol that connected her and her mom, guiding the way home.

Tracing the familiar path of the stars must have been like counting sheep, because the next thing she knew, far too much light was

NEW SERIES: THE SECRET STAIRCASE MYSTERIES

streaming in through the window. She squeezed a pillow over her eyes—then flung it away as she realized it wasn't the light that had awakened her. She'd distinctly heard a jarring sound. Strange noises were to be expected in Vegas. Not in Hidden Creek.

Was someone shouting?

Definitely shouting. The raised voices came from the direction of the tree house in the backyard where her grandparents lived.

It wasn't exactly fair to call the structure a tree house. Not for the past fifteen years, at least. What had started as a small child's playroom for a ten-year-old Tempest had, like the rest of the house, grown into something much bigger than its original intention. The original tree house deck still wrapped around the massive trunk of the oak tree that had lent its support for years, and a second deck now surrounded its twin, but in between the trees, the rest of the structure was a proper two-story house that served as an in-law unit for Ashok Raj and Morag Ferguson-Raj.

Tempest leapt out of bed, still disoriented. It wasn't even seven o'clock in the morning. She hadn't been awake at this time of day for years. Crossing the section of floorboards assembled in the shape of a skeleton key and opening the antique steamer trunk serving as her dresser, she slipped on a pair of jeans and was pulling a T-shirt over her head when she heard her grandfather's distinctive voice give another shout. She shoved her phone in her back pocket and hurried down the secret staircase that separated her room from the rest of the house.

This was the same house Tempest's parents had moved into shortly before Tempest was born. At the time it was a modest 960-square-foot bungalow. The most unique feature of the original house was the land that went with it. Nestled into the hillside next to the hidden creek that gave the town its name, the half-acre of land had never been used for a larger dwelling because it was situated on such a steep slope—until Emma and Darius moved in. They had experimented over the years on their own house until it was over 4,500 square feet of magical, hidden hideaways across four separate structures.

As her dad loved to say: *What happens when a carpenter and a stage*

NEW SERIES: THE SECRET STAIRCASE MYSTERIES

magician fall in love? They form a Secret Staircase Construction business to bring magic to people through their homes.

The idea was quite romantic. Tempest's parents specialized in building ingeniously hidden rooms for people who fancied a bookshelf that slid open when you reached for *The Adventures of Sherlock Holmes* or *Nancy Drew and the Hidden Staircase*; or a secret reading nook that only appeared when you said the words "open sesame"; or perhaps a door in a grandfather clock that led to a secret garden. Tempest's house—named Fiddler's Folly for her mom's favorite instrument, and a tongue-in-cheek reference to the architectural term for decorative buildings different inside than their outward appearance—had all three features. And many more, including the tree house in back. Tempest loved every inch of it. What she didn't love was the fact that at twenty-six, she'd been forced to move back.

Worse yet, if she didn't receive the job offer she hoped for today, she'd be forced to accept her dad's idea that she come work for Secret Staircase Construction. She'd been named one of the "Top 25 Under 25" young entertainers in a prominent entertainment magazine three years ago, and that success meant she could not only live lavishly but also send money home. It was humiliating enough to be back in her childhood bedroom, but to work as her dad's assistant when she knew he didn't need one? She hoped it didn't come to that.

Tempest rounded the gnarled trunk of the first oak tree and spotted her grandparents. Grandpa Ash and Grannie Mor were the only two people in sight, and they were scowling. Tempest grimaced as she stepped on a sharp root. She hadn't taken time to put on shoes.

"You two finally decided to murder each other after fifty-five years?" Tempest asked, rubbing the ball of her foot

"Fifty-six years, dear," her grandmother corrected. Grannie Mor's glamorous white hair was perfectly coiffed as usual, an argyle scarf of bright azure and white curled effortlessly around her neck. She always looked as if she'd stepped out of a 1940s Hollywood movie. Except as soon as she opened her mouth to speak, you knew she'd been born and raised in Scotland.

"Where did he go?" Grandpa Ash asked. A plaid newsboy cap covered his bald brown head. Tempest hadn't seen that particular hat before. Her grandfather's hat collection was as extensive as her grandmother's stockpile of scarves.

"Someone else is here?" Tempest whipped her head around.

Grannie Mor hooked her arm through Tempest's elbow. "That rabbit of yours is the devil himself."

Tempest sighed. Now she really wished she'd taken time to put her shoes on. "What did Abra do now?"

Abracadabra was Tempest's five-year-old, fifteen-pound, lop-eared rabbit. He'd already been a big bunny before Grandpa Ash began feeding him under the table. Tempest could have sworn Abra had gained at least a pound since they'd been back. The mischievous, tubby bunny should have been in his hutch in Secret Fort, the unfinished stone tower that made up the most recent Fiddler's Folly structure on the hillside.

"He ran that way." Grannie Mor pointed up the hill. "Whiskers must have attempted to invade his territory."

Abracadabra's favorite pastime, besides eating, was chasing cats. He was used to having free rein during the day, because he always came home. But that was back in Vegas. In his new surroundings, Tempest was keeping him in his hutch unless he was supervised, but clearly Abra was having none of that. The massive gray lop was smarter than your average rabbit. Or at least Tempest thought so. Maybe all rabbits were this intelligent but she'd never had the opportunity to find out. In a life-long attempt to eschew magician stereotypes, she'd never owned a rabbit before receiving Abra as a gift. She hadn't planned on keeping him, but it was love at first bite. The curmudgeonly bunny was a superb judge of character and had bitten the awful woman who was dating Tempest's friend Sanjay. Who could give up such an intelligent creature after that?

"Abracadabra!" Tempest called. "Come on, Abra."

"He'll show up in his own good time." Morag led the way back to the tree house. "Your grandfather was fixing breakfast when he spotted Abra on the loose. He insisted we check on the rascal. I hope his affection for that rabbit hasn't burnt our kitchen down."

"That rabbit is going to get into trouble one of these days," Ash

NEW SERIES: THE SECRET STAIRCASE MYSTERIES

called after them before shaking his head and following them back to the house.

Tempest agreed. She reluctantly went with her grandmother, telling herself that Abra had as many lives as a cat.

They followed the downward slope of the hill to the bright red front door of the tree house. No ordinary key unlocked this door. The door handle was smooth, with no opening for a key. It was the grinning gargoyle door knocker that held the secret to letting you into the house. The person standing on the threshold needed to place a three-inch brass skeleton key sideways in the gargoyle's mouth, as if he were clenching it in his pointy teeth, then twist. As the gargoyle's teeth bit down on the key, the door unlocked.

The door wasn't locked just now. Even if it had been, it wasn't especially secure. This was never meant to be a permanent house. Much like the rest of the dwelling, the front door lock was one of Tempest's parents' many experiments to create whimsical keys for indoor secret rooms. When her grandparents moved in five years ago, they never got around to installing a proper lock. It wasn't like much crime ever happened in Hidden Creek. The only crime of interest that had happened in the town's long history was the one that involved Tempest's own family.

Tempest glanced at the eight silver charms dangling from the bracelet she wore all the time. The thick bracelet, made up of chunky charms related to her mom Emma's love of magic, was the last thing her mom had given her before she vanished live onstage five years ago. The vanishing act wasn't part of the show, and Emma Raj hadn't been seen since. That was the first time Tempest began to wonder if the legendary Raj family curse was real.

Learn more about *Under Lock & Skeleton Key,* **at www.gigipandian.com. Available now at bookstores everywhere!**

ABOUT THE AUTHOR

Gigi Pandian is a *USA Today* bestselling and award-winning mystery author, breast cancer survivor, and accidental almost-vegan. The child of cultural anthropologists from New Mexico and the southern tip of India, she spent her childhood traveling around the world on their research trips. She now lives in the San Francisco Bay Area with her husband and a gargoyle who watches over the backyard vegetable garden. A cancer diagnosis in her thirties taught her that life's too short to waste a single moment, so she's having fun writing quirky novels and cooking recipes from around the world. Her debut novel, *Artifact*, was awarded the Malice Domestic Grant, and she's won Anthony, Agatha, Lefty, and Derringer awards, and was a finalist for the Edgar Award. Her books include the Accidental Alchemist Mysteries, the Jaya Jones Treasure Hunt Mysteries, and the Secret Staircase Mysteries. Read more and sign up for Gigi's email newsletter at www.gigipandian.com.

- bookbub.com/profile/gigi-pandian
- facebook.com/GigiPandian
- instagram.com/GigiPandian

CPSIA information can be obtained
at www.ICGtesting.com
Printed in the USA
BVHW030129290822
645604BV00027B/1294

9 781938 213205